Going the Distance

Going the Distance

Erin Mahoney

This book is a work of fiction. Names, characters, places, and incidents are the product of the author's imagination or are used fictitiously. Any resemblance to actual events, locales, or persons, living or dead, is coincidental.

ISBN : 978-1-329-05905-4

For my Mom
The most selfless person I know.
Your support never goes unnoticed.

Chapter 1

"It's today, it's today!" Samantha, my roommate, came singing into our bedroom.

"I know. You've been counting down for months. I know it's today," I replied as I slowly got out of bed. I glanced at the clock. It was already noon.

We went to school at The University of California. It was January. This was our final year, and our last semester.

"I just can't believe it's finally here!" She chirped as she dried off her wet hair with a towel. "I mean, it seems like just yesterday we bought the tickets."

"This concert better be amazing," I said as I walked over to my dresser. "I mean, I didn't even want to go in the first place, but since you're dragging me…"

"Chloe, you will not regret this! Big Time Elevation is one of the best up and coming bands right now. And plus, they are super cute."

She had been obsessing about this band ever since she caught a glimpse of them on television one day. They had their own show on a kids network, but she was convinced it wasn't just for kids. When they announced a huge United States tour last November she told me I had to go with her. She was convinced I would love them in person so she got us both VIP passes that included front row. I had never listened to their music or watched the television show but I figured I would give her the benefit of the doubt and at least give them a chance.

Sam and I had been roommates ever since freshman year. She was a tall brunette. I was a short blonde. Our appearances couldn't look more different. She was very bubbly and friendly while I was more shy and quiet. We bonded instantly.

"So, I'm thinking of wearing this. Do you think this screams *Look at me!* or *I'm desperate*?" She asked as she held up a red, strapless mini dress.

"I think it screams *I'm the color of a fire truck.* Don't you have anything less bright, you're practically blinding me."

She shrugged as she put it back and kept looking through the closet. "You know, you can borrow anything of mine."

"What's wrong with my clothes?" I asked as I flicked a piece of lint off my pajamas. "And technically, it's too early to start picking on Chloe."

She liked to point out what I could do with my makeup and show me how to piece together the perfect outfit. I knew that she was only trying to help but I liked the way I looked.

She rolled her eyes, "You just don't have any concert-y clothes. I have the perfect outfit for you!"

This went on for another hour before I finally agreed to a black one-shoulder top and she agreed to let me choose my own pants. Except, once I got over to my dresser, I realized all of my jeans were too big. I had just started eating healthy and exercising over winter break and I lost two pant sizes.

"Ah, crap," I said under my breath.

"What?" Sam looked over from her web surfing.

"I forgot, none of my jeans are going to fit anymore. I lost inches in my waist over the winter break." I kept looking through my drawer thinking something would pop up.

"Why don't you go to the boutique down the street? I would go but Tyler said he'll be here in five."

Tyler was her boyfriend of over two years. They met at a school football game. She got hit in the head with the football and he was there to make sure she was all right. They had been inseparable ever since. She always had a way of getting guys' attention. I didn't think she'd been single for more than two weeks in her life. I, on the other hand, always had a more difficult time finding good guys. The jerks were always somehow attracted to me.

"Okay, I'll see you later," I said as I grabbed my sweatshirt. "Do you need anything while I'm out?"

"Actually! Now that I think of it, we need some cucumbers."

"Again?" I groaned. "We just bought some." She used cucumbers twice a day on her eyes. She was convinced they made her eyes brighter and less puffy.

She shrugged.

"Okay then, I will get more cucumbers."

I walked a couple blocks to the boutique. It was warm out. One of the perks of living in sunny California was having a warm winter. I grew up in Boston where there was snow all winter long. When I was applying to schools, The University of California had emailed me, just an electronic email, but still it got me interested. I took a trip out here my senior year, with my older sister, Rachel, and younger sister, Jessica.

I fell in love with Althoridge, California the second I got off the plane. It was about thirty minutes south of Los Angeles. I decided right away I wanted to go to school and probably spend the rest of my life here.

The bell chimed as I entered the store. I skimmed the clearance racks looking for a size three. Nothing. It was only zeros and anything above a three. There was a boy who looked about my age who was scanning one of the shelves.

"Excuse me? Do you work here?" I asked him. He almost leapt halfway across the store. "Oh, I'm sorry, I didn't mean to startle you."

He smiled, "No, it's okay. It's usually the other way around. I'm usually the one startling people," He looked at me as if expecting a reaction from this. Then he put his hand in his hair and ruffled it a bit. "I'm Kyle."

"Chloe," I said as I smiled back. "Why?" He looked confused. "Why are you always startling people? Do you like to spy on them?"

He laughed, "Nothing like that. I guess I just catch people off guard a lot. Not that I mean to. But, I actually don't work here. I don't know who does, there's no one in here but us."

"Is this your first time in here?" He nodded. "That explains it. You see, Mr. Harper works here but no one usually comes in here in the afternoons so he mostly stays downstairs. He has the bell on the door but he's so old he can't hear it anymore."

"Then why did you think I worked here?"

"He hires college kids every so often. They usually last a week or two before getting bored. My roommate used to work here." He stared at me deeply, as if what I was saying was the answer to life. "So anyway, what brings you to town?"

"I uh…" he hesitated. "Vacation. With some friends. I'm from Burbank. You go to school at the University?"

I nodded. "I'm actually going to a concert tonight. I just came here to get a pair of jeans but I guess they don't have my size."

"Well, there are some other stores around here, right? I mean there has to be." He waited for me to respond. I shrugged. "I'll look with you. I was looking for a nice outfit myself, but nothing here really caught my eye."

"Sure. I think there are some more stores up the street." We left the store and started walking. I texted Sam; *Can't find my size. Going to look up the street. I'll text you when I'm on my way back.*

"Who ya texting?" He asked. "Hot date? Is he going to the concert with you?"

"Yeah, right. Me? Hot Date? Please." I crossed the street. Kyle was walking next to me, his hands in his pockets. "Oh, I know how that must sound. Sorry, that's like horrible that I just said that. I mean, I only just met you. Wow."

He let out a tiny giggle, "I don't have many dates, myself. I travel a lot. It's hard to find a girl worth the effort. Late night phone calls, trust issues, it just gets so crazy."

"You seem pretty trustworthy." We walked a few more blocks until we got to the next store and went inside. I had only been in this boutique once before, when my mom flew out to visit. She said I needed a new wardrobe. Sam came along, too, and of course agreed with her. Even though I felt like I was backed into a corner the whole time it was one of the best times I've ever had with my mom. Back in Boston, she never spent much time with me. She was in Public Relations and eventually had to move to New York, leaving my dad, two sisters and me by ourselves. Our parents were madly in love but they decided they just couldn't take my sisters and I away from our lives in Boston. So, my mom worked during the week and came back to Boston on the weekends. It was weird at first but we started to adjust. Once my older sister went to school in New York, it seemed more normal.

"Hello, can I help you two?" The lady behind the counter sat on a chair with her legs crossed eating a bag of potato chips.

"Actually, I'm looking for a size three jeans. Do you have any?" I said as I looked around the store. Kyle was already skimming the men's rack.

"We should have some in that section over there." She pointed to the back wall, all the way in the corner. It was so far from the rest of the store it must have been an old employee room.

"Thanks." I made my way over and started looking for my size. The lady started talking again, she was either on the phone or she was talking to Kyle, it was hard to tell. Her voice was muffled and the food in her mouth did not help. I finally found a pair and tried them on in the dressing room. They were snug but comfortable. I glanced at the price tag. Seventy. *Ugh,* I thought, *for one pair of jeans.* I walked out of the fitting room.

"How'd they fit?" The lady asked.

"Fine. I just can't afford these right now. But thank you so much for your help." I went to put them back on the rack.

"Hang on!" Kyle called. He sprinted over to me. "How much?"

"Seventy." I put them back on the rack. "It's just too much for one pair of jeans. I could buy four pairs at that price for the boutique up the street."

"But they didn't have your size. Hang tight." He walked back into the other room, to the lady at the counter. "My friend really needs these jeans. She only has thirty dollars though. We could go up the street, the guy there seemed so nice."

"Honey, why don't you bring those jeans up here. I think those were on discount anyways. Thirty it is." She shook the potato chip salt off her hands.

My mouth must have dropped open. "Kyle. What?"

"You heard her," he said. "Thirty it is." He smiled at me. I didn't know what they were talking about earlier but whatever he said or did charmed that lady into giving me a discount.

I paid, she bagged up the jeans, and we left. "I can't believe you just did that!" I nudged him lightly on the arm.

"It's nothing. I'm a charmer by nature." He stopped. "But I've got to get going. I have somewhere to be tonight and my hotel is that way." He pointed in the opposite direction we were walking. "And you have a concert to get ready for!"

"Oh, yeah." I honestly completely forgot about the concert.

"Well, I guess this is goodbye." I looked down at my feet.

"Which concert are you going to tonight? It's not Big Time Elevation is it?" "Yeah, actually it is. Why? Don't tell me you're going. Why in the world would you want to see a boy band?" I smiled a little.

"Oh, well, some of my friends are going so I thought I would stop by and see what all the fuss is about."

"Maybe I'll see you there," I said hopefully.

"Maybe," he replied. "Bye, Chloe." He walked away, and just like that he was gone.

Chapter 2

"I hope those jeans you bought were absolutely amazing because that took you two whole hours," Sam said as I walked in the room and tossed the bag on the bed. "Tyler was gonna stick around and wait for you to get back to say hello, but he had to get to the gym. I kept saying, no, she'll be back shortly, but then I gave up!"

I pulled the jeans out of the bag and held them up, "Well? Are they to your approval?"

"They certainly are!" She looked entranced as she got off her bed. "Which boutique did you end up going to?"

"*Sunside*. The one that we went to that one time when my mom came up."

She shook her head. "The expensive one. These must have cost a bunch!" She grabbed them, scanning every inch.

"No, not really. I mean, they did but I got a discount." I didn't want to add in the part about Kyle. Every time I mentioned a boy to her she would make a huge deal about it as if I could never obtain one, which was sort of true but I didn't need her reminding me.

"Amazing," she said as she handed them back to me and went over to her vanity. "Did you remember the cucumbers?"

"Oh my gosh, I completely forgot. I was so distracted."

"Distracted?" She glared at me. "That is so unlike you, Chloe! Tisk, tisk."

We started getting ready at about four. The show was at seven. Sam did her hair and make-up and then did mine. We changed into our outfits and drove downtown. The venue was packed, mostly younger teens, some little kids, not a lot of people our age.

"So, how does this work, exactly?" I asked Sam as she scanned the crowd, looking like a kid in a candy store. "Do we meet them first or do we watch the show then meet them?" This was new territory for me.

"A-ha," she said as she spotted a VIP entrance door. "This is where we go in!" We walked over, handed over our tickets, which got exchanged for VIP passes, and we headed inside. There was a long, dark hallway leading up to a big purple room. It was crowded so we waited in the hallway. "This is so exciting! My heart is pounding!"

"How does Tyler feel about the competition?" I asked sarcastically as I looked at the pictures on the wall, they were of other musicians who had performed there.

"He knows how it is. He loves Tasha Edwards, you know, that country girl that's our age. We saw her in concert last summer and he could not stop talking about her." She took out her compact mirror and adjusted her hair. "We can go bananas over whatever celeb we want. It's not like these people are going to want to date us so it's a safe zone." She closed her mirror and put it back in her purse.

We waited about fifteen minutes before a security guard came out and told us the band was ready. Everyone started freaking out when the line started moving. We were the last ones in line. I guess, we got there kind of late. We waited and waited, I tried to keep her calm, talking about school starting in a couple days, what classes she was taking but I could tell she was still distracted.

As we inched closer to the door, I asked, "What is so amazing about these boys that you can't even breathe normally?"

She sighed. "These boys might be the most talented people on this planet. They can sing, dance, and act. And they are so hot. Like, how can you go up to one and form a sentence when their hotness is staring at your face? Your normal, not famous, face."

I rolled my eyes, "Sam, they are normal people, like you and me. They just happen to have a job that involves people paying money to meet them." Which was such a weird concept to me. People paid hundreds of dollars to meet them. Paying to meet everyday human beings. But I tried my best to be supportive for Sam's sake. This was the highlight of her life.

The door opened and we were let inside. There was a curtain in front of us and the boys were talking to the people in line before us. We couldn't see them yet but we could hear them.

"Thanks for coming! We hope you enjoy the show!" One of them said.

"Okay!" Sam took a deep breath. "I am so ready for this."

The security guard pulled open the curtain, "These are the last two."

I could not believe my eyes. There he was! Kyle! He was a member of the band? Why didn't he say something?

"Kyle? How sneaky. How come you didn't tell me you were in the band?" I walked closer to him while Sam kept her distance, obviously, a little more than confused.

"I just wanted you to see the real me. I didn't know you would have VIP passes and not know who I was." He held out his hand to Sam, "What's your name?"

"I'm Samantha. You can call me Sam," She stuttered. "You know Chloe?"

He looked over at me. "We actually met this afternoon when she was looking for a pair of jeans. She kept me company. She also didn't know who I was." He laughed. "Well Chloe, this is Jake, Cam, and Luke."

"Hey Chloe, we heard so much about you today," Jake smiled. He had the most gorgeous brown hair and a stunning smile, one of the best I had ever seen.

"You heard about me?"

"Kyle, here, could not stop talking about you!" Cam added as he put his hands in his pockets. Kyle blushed a little.

Luke extended his hand out to Sam, "So how long have you been a fan?"

"Oh, well, probably since last year or the year before that. I just love your music. Your new album is addicting! I can't get it out of my head. I just had to meet you guys, but I guess we didn't even need to buy the VIP to do that." She looked at me. "Maybe we could hang out with you guys? After the show?"

"That sounds like a plan," Jake said as he slid his way over to Sam. "What is there to do around here?"

"There's a bar just around the corner that is always fun!" Sam said excitedly.

"Well, you guys, come back here after the show and we'll go from there," Kyle said as he motioned one of the security guards forward. "This is Sam and Chloe. They are gonna come back, after the show."

The guard took a sharpie out of his pocket, "Let me see your passes." We handed them over and he signed his initials on our passes. "Just incase I forget."

"This is too cool!" Sam practically screamed.

"So you guys can go on through this door, and we hope you enjoy the show!" Cam said as he escorted us out.

The show was amazing. I loved the lyrics, the melody, the dance moves. Sam was right, they were great! We were in the front row and every so often Kyle would smile or wink at me. *Does he do this to all the girls?* I asked myself. I barely knew him but I just couldn't take my eyes off of him. Sam kept bumping into the girls next to us, they had to be ten years old, but Sam didn't even notice, she was so into the music.

Once it was over, we went back to the door we came from. The same Security Guard was there and let us in. We hung out with them in their dressing room for a little bit and then started walking to the bar. There was a line out the door that stretched around the corner.

"Is it always this packed?" Jake asked as he stared at the line.

"Sometimes," I said as I smoothed my hair out of my face, the wind was blowing it everywhere. "Do you guys want to wait?"

"Sure," Luke replied. "It's not that bad."

"Are you kidding? You guys are Big Time Elevation! You can get in anywhere. You can just sneak into the front, flash those smiles and boom you're in," Sam said as she pointed to the front door.

They all looked at each other. I turned to Sam, "That's kind of rude. Just because they are celebrities you're going to say that to them?"

"Uh, please," she rolled her eyes. "A celebrity is a celebrity. I love you guys but once someone gets famous all the rules change. They don't get treated the same as us. Maybe we should just go." She glanced at her phone. "Tyler's calling me, I'll be right back." She walked across the street.

"Wow," Cam said as he pulled his coat tighter. "She got something against us?" The line started to move a little. A group of guys came out and started smoking.

"No. She just gets star struck, I guess. I don't know. I'm really sorry, though." I bit my lip. "I know you guys only want to have a good time. I know you don't think like Sam does about the whole fame thing."

Jake nudged Luke and Cam. "You know what?" He said. "I'm actually really tired. I could head back. What about you guys?" Luke and Cam glanced at each other.

"Yeah, we should head back, just us three. Kyle took a nap earlier, he's good," Cam smiled.

"Well, if you're sure. I really don't want Sam to ruin your night," I suggested as I tugged at my zipper.

"Yeah, it's totally fine! We'll see you around, Chloe. It was great meeting you," Jake said as he shook my hand and turned the corner with Luke and Cam. Sam was still on the phone, pacing back and forth.

"Well, it looks like it's just us," Kyle said. "And Sam." He adjusted the beanie on his head as Sam hung up and walked back over to us.

"Tyler wants me to go back to campus. He needs help unpacking, I guess…" She paused. "Where did the other guys go?" She looked around.

"You kind of scared them off," I nodded to the corner.

She shrugged, "You coming back or you gonna stay here?"

"She can stay here with me," Kyle said, looking at me. "I can walk her back. It's not too far, is it?" I shook my head. "Perfect. Well, it was nice to meet you, Sam. Have a good evening." He smiled.

"Yeah, great to meet you all," She turned away but I could hear her say, under her breath, "Weird ass day." I couldn't help but laugh.

Once we finally got into the bar, everyone seemed to be clearing out. It was around eleven, but it was a Sunday so not many people stayed out in general. I'd never been in this bar before but it seemed like all the other typical Althoridge bars. The bartender looked about my mom's age, there was a dance floor but no one near it, and to top it all off the bathrooms were labeled *Mares* and *Stallions*. The bars in town usually had the bathrooms labeled after animals, but horses, that was a new one. After a few drinks and Kyle getting me to dance with him on the empty dance floor, we headed back to my dorm.

"I can't believe it's one in the morning! You don't have class tomorrow, do you?" He asked as we kept walking.

"No. I would not be out this late if I had class tomorrow. We don't start until Wednesday. They give us some time to settle in." I looked up at the sky, I could make out a few stars but I couldn't see the moon. The sky seemed so black.

"I wonder what it's like. Going to college. I never pictured myself doing it because acting and singing has always been my life."

"Well, college is like high school, except you just have that class two or three times a week instead of five and you have so many classes to chose from. And there is so much freedom!" I paused. "Well, you probably know all about freedom. I can't really picture your parents coming to all your concerts. I mean they have to work, too."

"Yeah, I don't get to see my family as much as I'd like when I go on the road. But I still have people telling me what to do, my manager, the bands manager, my publicist. The list could go on forever," he sighed. "But, I'm not complaining. I love this life. It's the one I chose. You give up things to live out your dream."

"Like dating?"

"Hey, hey! I never said that." He smiled. "I just said it's hard to find a girl worth the effort. I love dating. I wish I could do it more but it's not as easy as it looks. Distance is tough."

"I know what you mean. I lived in Boston and then my mom moved to New York when I was thirteen so that she could pursue her public relations career. My parents weren't legally separated they just didn't want to uproot my life along with my two sisters. So, I know how ugly distance can get. I wouldn't wish it on anyone."

"So, if you found that one person you really cared about and they really cared about you, you're saying you wouldn't do the distance thing?" He twisted his watch around.

"I don't know what I would do. I wouldn't want to do that. There's probably someone out there who I wouldn't have to do the distance thing with. So I'll just wait for him." I coughed. I wanted to change the subject. Distance was always my worst enemy, something I couldn't get away from my whole life. It was still there. My mom still in New York with Rachel, my dad still in Boston with Jessica and I was out here, in California, the farthest away but it felt the closest to home.

Chapter 3

After Kyle walked me to my door, I crept inside hoping not to wake Sam up. But when I got in the bedroom, she wasn't there. She must have been at Tyler's. I didn't want her to question me about Kyle. I just wanted this one relationship in my life not under scrutiny.

I planned to meet Kyle for lunch the next afternoon at a café just near the boutique where we met. I hoped Sam wouldn't come back before then.

When I woke up, Sam still wasn't back. I texted her to make sure she was okay and I hoped in the shower. When I got out I had received a text but it was from my sister, Rachel.

It read: *Hey! Haven't heard from you since you went back to Cali the other day. Hope you're doing ok. Call me later.*

Rachel was always the one keeping my family in touch with each other. She always called us after she went off to school in New York, and I knew she made our mom call, too, because mom never called before Rachel got there. My mom rarely ever called anymore, though, not since she learned how to text. I'd usually get a text a week from her if I was lucky. Rachel, however, would send at least a text a day just to check up.

I texted back: *Went to a fun concert last night. Actually hit it off with one of the members. He's really nice. I'll call you later.*

I finished getting ready and attempted to do my makeup the way Sam did it last night, but I was not doing so well.

"Hey!" Sam said as she came into the room. "Going somewhere?" She walked over toward me and opened up a vanity drawer.

"I actually have a lunch thing with Kyle," I said sternly as I wiped off the eye shadow from my eyelid.

"It's called a date, Chloe! You should sound more enthusiastic." She pulled out an eye shadow kit that must have had twenty different colors. "Let me help."

She started doing my make-up and attempting to teach me, this time, how to do it. "Where were you, anyway?" I said casually.

"Oh, I just spent the night with Tyler. I actually fell asleep in his arms. It was *so* cute." She finished putting on my lip-gloss and stood up. "Totally forgot to text you to see if you got home okay. But it seems you got home more than okay! Three dates in two days, I can't believe it. I think this is it for you Chloe. I think he is going to be it!"

"Be *it*. What does that mean?" I stood up and looked for something to wear.

"You know. Be your next boyfriend! I can see it now, he's on tour and he calls you late at night and then…"

"No." I cut her off. "He's not going to be my boyfriend. We're just hanging out while he is in town and then Thursday he moves on to the next part of his tour. I probably won't even talk to him again after that."

She shook her head. "No. You are wrong. He really likes you. Why don't you see it?"

"I don't have to see it!" I said as I changed my pants. "There is never going to be anything between us. He travels. He's a celebrity. I'm a nobody. And besides, I can't do long distance, I told you that before."

"I just think you should at least talk to him about it. What have you got to lose?"

I waited outside the café on a bench thinking about what Sam said. *What have you got to lose?* I could lose everything. My morals, my sanity, my heart. Everything could just change the second I started dating him. But who was I kidding? He didn't even want to date. He couldn't find a girl worth the effort. What made me think I was that girl? I didn't even know what I was thinking. How could those thoughts even be in my head? I'd only known him for a day.

The last time I thought this much about a guy was when I was moving into college. I had a boyfriend, Ryan, who I dated most of high school. When we were looking at colleges, he wanted to stay local and I knew I wanted to go out to California. When I came back from my trip with my sister, I told him.

"I want to go to school there," I said one day after school. We were in his car, heading to my house.

"Why? Won't you miss me?" He gave me an adorable smile, the one that always made me smile even when I was mad at him.

"Of course I will miss you. You are my world. But there is nothing for me in Massachusetts. I need to go where I want to be. I want to go to school to be an event planner. I love the California parties. It's just where I picture myself for the rest of my life." It was true. I really wanted to live there. There was no other place in the world that compared to California. It was the right place for me.

After I moved out here, Ryan and I tried to continue dating but it was so difficult. Eventually, he was the one to break it off with me. It was painful at first but I eventually realized it was better for the both of us, in the long run. The relationship never would have lasted.

"How long have you been here?" I looked up. It was Kyle. He had on a backwards *Boston Red Sox* hat. Why was he so adorable?

"Not long," I glanced at my phone. I had been there for at least twenty minutes, but I had come early so it was irrelevant. "You like the Boston Red Sox?"

"Nah, I just like hats." He took my hand, "Shall we?"

We sat in the corner, in the back. They must have recognized Kyle and figured he wanted his privacy. We even got a curtain that closed us in.

"Well, this is comfy," he said as he made a funny face.

I started to laugh out loud. He laughed, too. "You are so entertaining. Do you know that?"

"I hear it from time to time."

When the waitress came over, she could not take her eyes off of him. She barely remembered to ask us for our orders. I was learning what it was like to be friends with someone famous. It must have been hard for him to always be recognized, to never have the chance to be someone new to other people. That must have been why he didn't tell me who he was when he realized I didn't know.

"She digs me," he said as he took a sip of his water.

"So, what are the guys doing today?"

"Not entirely sure. They said they were going to sightsee a bit, I guess. Jake has a friend who lives not too far from here so they might visit him, too."

"You aren't going with them?" I asked.

"We spend so much time just the four of us. It's nice to have even just a little break," He paused. "And I wanted to spend some time with you."

I blushed. "So, where do you guys head next on your tour?" The waitress came by with some bread. She stood there for longer than she needed to and then eventually walked away.

"Orange County on Thursday, San Diego on Friday. It's nice to have a break before OC, though. I could use some relaxation." He broke off a piece of bread and popped it into his mouth.

"How many shows do you usually do?"

"For this tour, we are doing twenty," he looked at me. "Seems like a lot but it's not so bad. Already have two out of the way, only eighteen more to go! We're going to all these different places, some we have been to before, some we haven't. It's a lot of fun." He paused as he took another bite of bread.

"I'll have to watch some of your television show now." It seemed like a polite thing to say but honestly it made sense. He would be gone, but I could still see him, on television.

He laughed. "I want to know what you think of it. You have to tell me the truth. I trust you to do that." Whoa, he trusted me? "Your opinion matters. And I don't say that to just anybody."

A smile spread across my lips. My heart started beating faster. Calm down, Chloe. You can't get excited about a boy, not this boy. This boy will be leaving in just a few days. He will be gone and you will never talk to him again. Don't put yourself through this, again. You can't handle it.

I tried to think of other things. I kept trying to change the subject, talk about his career or something and he would keep talking about me. Why wouldn't he stop?

After we finished our food, he insisted on paying for it all. I convinced him to let me pay for my half, eventually. I needed to leave before he said anything more to me that would make me fall for him. Before I said anything that I would regret.

"I…have to go." The words stumbled across my lips. I covered my mouth with my hand like I was erasing the words I just said. "I mean, I don't have to go, I just…have to…"

"Go?" His big, green eyes were looking into mine. They were melting me. I was going to say something. I felt it coming. I was going to say I liked him or he couldn't leave me, something stupid. I had to leave.

"Look, I had the most amazing time with you. I just can't stay." I looked around the street, looking for any reason at all to run.

"I had an amazing time, too, Chloe. Can I get your number? I never got it before so I was just wondering…maybe we could meet again tomorrow? I found a place this morning that I really want to show you."

I could give him my number. I wasn't going to say anything I would regret in a text message, right? I would have time to think about it. And that didn't mean I had to meet him tomorrow, I couldn't do that. This was hard enough. "Sure, you can have my number." I gave it to him and walked as fast as I could back to campus.

Chapter 4

"Hey! So, who is this new boy? I want to hear all about it!" Rachel said.

I stood outside my townhouse and switched my cell to the other ear. "All I said is that we hit it off. There's nothing else to tell."

"Please! I know you. You are so discrete. This boy is probably crazy about you and you don't even notice." She paused. "There are good boys out there, Chloe. Ryan was just one jerk in the world. But there are so many amazing guys!" She was referring to when Ryan and I decided to end it. He decided it was time to move in on my best friend from back home. Needless to say she was not my friend anymore.

"I know. I've dated some guys here. They were…okay. I haven't sworn off dating or anything. I just don't want to get involved in another long distance relationship. They never work. Look at Mom and Dad, they can't be happy right now." I sat down on my front stoop.

"Jessica is going to college in the fall and then Dad is moving in with Mom in New York. How can you say that didn't work? It took awhile but they are finally going to be together again!"

"It just makes no sense. I never understood why Dad didn't want to just follow Mom to New York, you know? Like normal people."

"What is normal? No one is really normal. Nothing is really normal. Everyone has their own rules they live by, this is just what our parents thought was best."

"Well, my normal does not involve dating someone who I never see. I just can't do it." I dropped my head down.

"Okay, I get it. But just hear me out before I go. If you see yourself in five years married and with kids to the best man you ever met in your life and you guys are together, not separated any longer, wouldn't those few years apart be worth the forever of being together? Just a thought."

She always knew what to say. I guess when you put it into those words it seemed worth it. After dating useless jerks for most of my life, having someone that's not always there but is always amazing seemed like a good thing. Didn't it?

I walked into the townhouse, and up to my room. Sam and Tyler were watching a movie. I let out a sigh.

"How was your date with Mr. Superstar?" Tyler asked enthusiastically.

"You told him?" I put my coat on my chair and sat on my bed. "Why must he know everything? Now the whole school is going to know."

"For starters, this school is huge, so the whole school won't find out. And Tyler's not gonna tell anyone. He keeps good secrets." She touched his nose lightly. I shivered.

"So me hanging out with a celebrity is a good secret?" I opened up my laptop and started the Internet. "Then, let me ask you, Tyler, since you are an outsider on this situation. If Sam had a job as a singer and she was doing world tours and she was gone more than you saw her would you still have started to date her? Now, think carefully before you answer."

He thought about it while Sam looked nervously between him and I. "I honestly don't know. She would be on the road and there would be guys all over her. And how can you even date someone if you aren't with them?"

"A-ha," I said. "That is exactly my point. Sam and my sister both think otherwise. They think it's worth it. But how am I even supposed to get to know…" My phone started ringing but I didn't recognize the number. "Hello?" I answered.

"Chloe! It's Kyle. Is everything okay? I know I should probably give you space but I just wanted to call and make sure we were okay. You seemed like you were trying to avoid me or something. Did I do something wrong?"

I mouthed to Sam and Tyler, "It's Kyle."

"Tell him what you are feeling," Sam said as she grabbed Tyler and left the room.

"No, of course you didn't do anything wrong. I just... I only met you yesterday, and so I'm worried." Silence. "I don't entirely know how you feel about me but to be honest I really like you. If you didn't travel all the time and were around to get to know me I could do this. But how can we even start something when I know you'll be gone in just a few days? How can you get to know someone like that?" More silence. "It's just like you said, how it's so much effort, you have to find the right girl. It's not that you aren't the right guy, because like I said I really want to try this. I just don't think the distance will work."

I heard him breathe. "I can get to know you. Today is only Monday so we have until Wednesday, when you go back to class. Then Thursday, I'll only be in Orange County, that's just twenty minutes away. I can come see you then, too. And then, after we go to San Diego, we have another week. That is two whole weeks together! And if you don't like me by then I will accept that and move on. But just give me these two weeks. I promise you won't regret it."

Two Weeks. Was that really enough time to decide if I could do the distance with him? Maybe. It was worth a shot. As Sam would say, *What do you have to lose?*

I ran my fingers through my hair. "Okay. Two weeks. But if it doesn't work we will just have to be friends."

"Ah! Thank you!" He sounded so excited.

"Wait, does this mean what I think it means?"

"What's that?"

"You think I am worth the effort of a relationship!" I smiled.

"There are a lot of things I think you are worth. Wait until you see."

The next day my housemates and I went to the campus gym. It was only a few blocks away from our townhouse. They went to the gym all of fall semester but I never started working out until a month ago.

My family had always been health conscious since diabetes ran in the family. However, after I moved out to California and started college I gained the freshman fifteen and never lost it. Every time I visited my mom in New York I wouldn't hear the end of it.

"You have a gym at school, don't you?" She asked just last month. I stayed with my mom the first half of vacation and then I stayed with my dad until I went back to school. We were sitting in the kitchen. She lived in a penthouse suite. It was really too big for one person but she said she needed the space.

"Yes, Mom, I have a gym. I just don't ever go. My schedule has always been really hectic," I said as I took a bite of one of her dry nutrition bars. She mostly had gross health food at her house. For breakfast she would drink a protein shake and eat one of these nutrition bars. I used to buy her eggs and toast when I would come up, but she would throw them away the second she saw them, so I gave up.

"No one is ever too busy for a nice work out. I get mine done in just thirty minutes every day. Can you believe it? Just thirty minutes to get this great shape." She was actually reading *Shape* magazine while she said this to me.

My mom hadn't changed at all since she was in high school. Same blonde-haired, blue-eyed, stick thin, tiny doll. She looked like a Barbie. I was surprised her Public Relations company even took her seriously. Everywhere we went together, the men would just stare. Part of the reason I never used makeup or cared very much about what I looked like was because of her. I was not going to compete with my own mother for attention. My sister Rachel was a spitting image of my mom. She was so gorgeous, my mom's mini me. Jessica and I looked more like our dad.

"Well Chloe, I really think you should try to work out. You've gained some weight in college. You look beautiful, I just want you to feel healthy!" She closed the magazine and went into the other room. "I have some work out DVDs that you can try. I don't use them anymore, they are just too beginner for me. You should have better luck."

"Gee, how could I refuse?" It was more of a statement than a question.

She smiled gleefully, "That's what I like to hear! You could even call Rachel and go to her gym with her, get a guest pass for these two weeks."

So that's what I did. I started working out to those annoying fitness DVDs and going to the gym with my sister. Once I started eating healthy, everything just fell into place.

"So, Sam tells us that you had a blast at the concert!" Erica, one of my housemates, said as she climbed on an elliptical machine. I went for the treadmill.

"Oh yeah? Is that all she told you?" I took a sip of my water before hitting *Start*.

"Uh, I think so? Sam, am I missing something? What else happened?"

These were my friends, my housemates. I had known them since freshman year. I could let them know what had been going on between Kyle and me. Sam would spill the beans sometime soon, anyway. "I met one of the guys before the concert. We're kind of dating now. Not official or anything but we are just testing the waters. See what happens."

"Wow. You're dating a celebrity!" Lindsey, my other housemate, said as she started up the treadmill next to mine. She was flipping through a gossip magazine.

"It's really not like that, guys. When I met him I didn't even know who he was. You guys don't even care for that band."

"We sure will now!" Erica said. "You have to invite him over. Is he still in town? We want to meet him! And tell him to bring his friends." I started walking faster.

"Are you still going to that *secret place* with him today?" Sam asked as she threw a towel over her shoulder. She could see the look on my face. I was getting embarrassed. "Sorry. We don't mean to be pushy. We are just so happy you found someone who deserves you. We care a lot about you." She smiled as she walked away.

"I know you guys mean well. I just want to take it slow with him. We are basically on a trial run for two weeks and then at the end of two weeks we will decide if we can handle this or not." I increased the speed. "But, I will keep you all updated."

"Oh my God! Wait! Is that him?" Lindsey flashed her magazine at me. It was a picture from Sunday's concert, the four boys on stage.

I nodded, "I guess I should start getting used to this."

Once we showered and got back to the dorm, I decided I should update my sister as well. I opened up my computer and started writing her an email.

So, Kyle, the boy we were talking about, called me yesterday a little while after we talked. He convinced me to give him two weeks of a trial run, I guess you could call it. That's how long he will be here before he goes off for the other tour dates. So hopefully it all works out. I just wanted to let you know, and please don't say anything to mom or dad yet. I really don't want everyone knowing about this before I even know what "this" is. Thanks.

Love, Chloe

As soon as I closed my laptop, I got a text from Kyle.

It read: *I'll be there in 15 minutes. Wear a good pair of sneakers.*

"Okay, you have to tell me where we are going!" I said as I adjusted my seatbelt. We had already been driving for about twenty minutes. "What if we get lost? You aren't from around here. What will we do?" I was nervous but excited at the same time. I had never been surprised like that before. I always knew what was going on. I always had control.

"Relax! Do you always get this stressed out? It's kind of cute." He glanced over at me but I turned and looked out the window. "We should be there very soon. And I know where we are going, we won't get lost. Trust me."

And in just five short minutes, there we were.

"Pacific Park?" It was an amusement park right on the Santa Monica Pier. It was around four o'clock so it was already starting to get dark and the rides were staring to be lit up.

"Yeah!" He said enthusiastically. "Is that bad?"

"No. I've actually never been here. I've been wanting to for years! But I never got around to it. How did you know?"

He shrugged. "I didn't. I just figured even if you had been, it's a great place to come back to."

"This is perfect." I was amazed. The fact that he thought this out, picked an amazing place for a date, and it was so beautiful! "I can't even thank you enough. You have been so good to me."

"You can thank me by having the time of your life, today! Let's go!"

First we went on the rides; the roller coaster, the scrambler, the plunge, and the Ferris wheel. Then we played some games; water races, ring toss, balloon popping, and plate breaking. Kyle won me a cute, stuffed giraffe. It was pretty big, too. Then we ate dinner. We stayed until closing at seven. It was the perfect date, the best I had ever been on. None of my other dates had ever been very creative. Dinner and a movie was probably the most I had ever done. Oh, I did go to one concert in high school, but that ended up being horrible.

We started walking along the beach, next to the pier. I could actually see the moon tonight. It lit up the whole sky and the water. Was this real? Was I really on a date with Kyle from Big Time Elevation? Did he really take me to the Santa Monica Pier? I just could not believe that was my life.

"What are you thinking about?" He asked as he looked over at me with a smile.

I hugged the giraffe tighter. "This just feels like a dream. I know that's cliché and whatever but…I can't even explain it." I paused. "It's just, nothing like this ever happens to me."

He smiled bigger. "Nothing like this happens to me, either. My life isn't black and white, I get to experience new things everyday but I've never found anyone worth sharing it with." Everything that came out of his mouth was just what I needed to hear. He really was a charmer. "But, don't forget. This is only day one. We still have twelve more days before I go."

I nodded. This snapped me back to reality. He was still leaving. I still had school tomorrow. This was just temporary. "Have you ever had a long distance relationship before?"

He thought before he said, "Yes. Just last year actually." He looked down at the sand and stopped walking. "Do you want to hear about it?"

I nodded.

"Well, the boys and I work for *Blinkeo* television network. We have the most amazing cast. We all became fast friends. I fell for my on-screen girlfriend, in reality. We both loved acting and singing and we had so much in common. The show was going great, we didn't have to do the long distance until her contract was up. She wanted to move onto her singing career. We both knew it was coming but it was just like a shot in the stomach. She would be on tour for eight months and once that season of the show ended I would be going on tour, as well. We tried to do the distance but she would be going home when I would go out on tour and vise versa. We literally never saw each other. We ended things in June, when we started our stadium tour. She told me she couldn't do it anymore." He looked at me for the first time since he started the story.

"Did you love her?"

"I did. We both loved each other. But things happen. We chose our careers over each other. I don't regret it." He walked toward the water and splashed me.

"Hey! That is freezing!" I dropped the giraffe and pushed him into the water. I started laughing so hard I couldn't stop. He grabbed me by the waist and pulled me down with him.

After we stopped laughing, he ran his fingers through my hair. "You are so beautiful," he said to me. His skin was glowing from the moonlight. I leaned in to kiss him but he pulled away. "Not here," he said as he took my hand and pulled me up.

"What?" I said a little bit embarrassed and confused.

"Trust me."

We got to his car, tried to dry off as much as we could, and then got in. He started driving, but not the way we came from. "Are you kidnapping me?"

"Chloe, trust me!" He reached over for my hand and wrapped it in his.

I closed my eyes. I never did anything spontaneous so this one time couldn't hurt. We didn't drive long before we came to a stop. I opened my eyes. We were up on a hill but that's all I could really see.

"Come on," he said as he got out of the car. I slowly opened my door and stood up. Either he was pushing me off the edge or he hired someone else to kidnap me from there.

"What are we doing up here?" I asked cautiously. I shimmied away from the edge.

"Don't you want to look?" He was pointing toward down the hill. I was facing the opposite way.

I turned around. "Oh my gosh," I said softly. We were looking at downtown LA, all lit up, so sparkly, so beautiful. "You really know your way around here, don't you?"

But he didn’t say anything. He took my hand and pulled himself toward me. His glowing, green eyes stared into mine. His breath was warm on my lips. He pushed my hair behind my ear and kissed me. It was so soft and romantic, the perfect kiss to end the perfect day.

Chapter 5

The next day, I started classes. Wednesdays were going to be my busy days. I had four classes, but that left just one class on Tuesday and one on Thursday. I planned this schedule last semester so that I would have Mondays and Fridays off incase I wanted to go home for a long weekend. I had a break for lunch but besides that I was in class nonstop from nine in the morning until three in the afternoon.

Sam started class at three, so I didn't get to see her. I hated having conflicting schedules with Sam. She was my best friend and it was hard to have a day without really seeing her. She wouldn't get out of class until seven so I invited Kyle and his band over for pizza and a movie.

I went back to the townhouse right after class and checked my email and saw that my sister had emailed me back.

Chloe, that is just wonderful! I am so happy you gave him a chance. You should tell Jess about him, I'm sure she would really like to hear about it too! Of course my lips are sealed, your secret is safe with me. Hope you have been having fun with him so far. I can't wait to hear more. Call me anytime! Oh, and Todd says hello.

Love from both of us!

Todd was her husband. They met during my sister's junior year of college. He was a bartender she was a waitress, they fell in love. Things came more easily to Rachel, it even seemed like she just got everything handed to her on a silver platter. Jessica, on the other hand, was more like me, quiet and not so good at obtaining men, at least, men that were worth having. Actually, thinking about Jessica made the men I had dated seem not so bad.

She was only seventeen, but she has had her share of boy problems. Her first boyfriend, when she just turned sixteen, turned out to be a kleptomaniac. After a month of things going missing around my dad's house, they finally figured out why. I never got the pleasure of meeting him. The second boyfriend however, I did meet.

She dated him around Christmastime of the same year, so I was on my winter break. Just a few days after I met him, Rachel and I were at the mall looking to return a few things when we saw him with another girl.

Her most recent boyfriend lasted all of last summer, actually, three whole months. Everything seemed to be going fine, she even brought him on a trip to New York to visit my mom for a week. We all thought he had potential, but then that one day…

I was sitting on the couch, minding my own business when he walked into the room, Jess was right behind him. "Does your sister ever get off her fat ass and do something?" They started walking to the front door.

"What the hell did he just say?" I said as I flung off the couch.

"Oh, I didn't think you would hear me. I tried to whisper," He looked a little surprised, like he had gotten away with saying stuff like this before and I was just making a big deal out of nothing.

"And so, if you whispered this to my sister that would make it okay? If I didn't hear you?" I walked closer to him and Jess touched his arm. "Jess! This is ridiculous. Does he always talk like this?"

She looked embarrassed as my dad walked into the room. "What is going on?" He said as he walked over to my sister and that jerk of a boyfriend.

"Nothing, Dad. It was a misunderstanding. We were just leaving," Jess said as she backed toward the door.

How long had this been going on? How long had he been talking to people like that? He must have been saying things behind all our backs. Did he talk like that about my sister?

"No! There was no misunderstanding. The kid said 'Does your sister ever get off her fat ass and do something?' I am quoting."

My dad looked so angry, I swore he was about to punch a wall, or that kid, if we were lucky. “You do not talk to anyone in my family like that. Get the hell out, now.” He paused as my sister started walking with him. “Jessica, don’t you dare move another inch. You are staying right here.”

The boyfriend walked out and slammed the door. Jess looked so different, not like I had ever seen her before. Like this boyfriend owned her, she was quiet but she wasn’t a pushover. It hurt that she didn’t stand up for me, she just let him talk to me like that. My dad had a very long talk with her about how she should not be dating someone who insults others, especially when they are doing it to people we care about. I still couldn’t believe that sweet, innocent kid had a mouth like that. He had seemed so genuine. He had us all fooled.

She broke up with him the next day, on the phone, since my dad forbid her to see him ever again. She was upset for a while. I could even tell when I got back to school and she would call me, that she was still upset. She just did not sound happy. I tried to convince her that no guy was worth feeling like that. I told her that there were great guys out there that would be lucky to have us, but she knew I was trying to convince myself of that at the same time.

I shook off the memory.

“Hello?” I heard someone in our living room.

I went downstairs. “Oh hey, Erica.” She was going toward the refrigerator. “How was your first day of classes?”

“They were actually really fun. Nothing to complain about so far. How about you?” She took a water bottle out and took a sip.

“Hectic. But I’m sure it will get better.”

“At least this is our last year, you know?” She paused as she took another sip. “I just can’t believe this is it! I’m gonna miss you guys.”

“Stop,” I said as I waved a hand at her. “You can’t start that yet. We still have four more long months ahead of us.”

“I know. It’s just going to be so weird not living here anymore. Not going to classes. How will we survive without each other?”

“We’ll meet new people. Everything will be okay. I can’t picture you not surviving.” We both laughed. She was the tough one out of the four of us. She played field hockey and was all about men and woman equality. She was level headed and never let her emotions get the best of her. It was strange to see her talk about emotional things.

"Well, anyway. I have a team movie night tonight so I won't be around. What are your plans?"

"Aw, really? I invited Kyle over. I thought maybe you or Lindsey would be around. You guys wanted to meet him." I shifted my weight.

"Seriously? You should have told me! I would have canceled the movie night thing. Too late now. Lindsey has a date, too, so she won't be here." She headed toward her room. "I'm sure we will meet him soon. If not we can always see him in the magazines!" She joked.

After a couple of hours, Kyle, Jake, Cam, and Luke came over with the pizzas. Kyle looked so cute in his flannel button down shirt, dark jeans, and Vans sneakers. I never really had a *type* of guy I looked for but if I had to choose, he would be pretty close.

"So, we brought a couple movies. Mostly violence. Hope that's okay?" Jake said as he put them down on the table.

"Wow. *Skull Crashers*, really?" I pointed to the DVD on top of the others.

"I had no part in this!" Kyle said defensively. " I picked up the pizza, they picked up the movies. We don't mind watching one of your movies. Do we, guys?"

They were already devouring the pizza as he asked. I heard a few groans but nothing else.

"It's fine." I said as I looked through the pile. "There's like five that they brought, so they can't all be that bad, right?"

Wrong. The one I picked out of their pile called *Horseshoes* actually had nothing to do with horses at all. It was just about a serial killer who would kill people with, horseshoes, no surprise. It wasn't terrible, though. Every time I would cringe or jump, Kyle would hold me a little closer. I couldn't help glancing over at the other guys, every so often, to see if it bothered them. They seemed to be too focused on the movie to even notice if a fire started in front of them.

"Well, I gotta hand it to you, Chloe," Cam said as he took his eyes away from the credits. "That was a tough one to sit through, but you did it. You're tougher than you look."

"Thanks? I think." I reached over Kyle to grab the remote when Sam walked in.

"Hey, guys!" She chirped as she made her way through the living room. "It's great to see you all again."

"Likewise," Luke said as he sat up off the couch. Although, he didn't look like he felt likewise. I guess Sam noticed, too.

"I really have been meaning to apologize about what I said the other day. You guys are just so hard to track down!" She walked closer to them. "I really am sorry, though. I judged you right away. And it's weird, too, because that is so unlike me to do, especially since you are my favorite musicians ever, and I just still can't believe I did…"

"It's fine!" Jake cut her off. He smiled. "We can all be friends. We like hanging out with Chloe so hopefully next time you can join us."

"And your boyfriend is more than welcome, too," Kyle added as he put his arm around me.

"You four are just so sweet! I knew you'd understand!" She turned toward the stairs. "I gotta start homework. Can you believe it, homework already?"

"We gotta head out, anyway. We are leaving early tomorrow. I mean five AM early," Jake said as he got off the couch and took the DVD out of the player. "Which is so not cool. It's only twenty minutes away!"

"Are you going, too?" I asked Kyle.

"I can stay a little bit longer. Just an hour or so." He smiled.

"Okay, man, we'll see ya later," Luke said as he walked toward the front door.

"Bye, guys. It was good to see you again," I called out to them as they walked out the door. I pulled a blanket over myself and snuggled next to Kyle.

"Will you come to the concert tomorrow?" He asked as he took my hand. "The guys really want you there. I really want you there."

"What time is it at? Is it seven, again?" He nodded. "I guess I could…"

Sam came running down the stairs. "Chloe, do you have lab tomorrow? With Mr. Lawrence? Doesn't matter what time."

"Uhm, yes. It's my only class. Why?"

"Just got an email from the president. Mr. Lawrence's wife passed away, like two hours ago. He won't be in tomorrow. All his classes are cancelled. Just thought I'd let you know." She ran back upstairs.

Kyle was smiling at me.

"Uh oh. What are you thinking?" I asked hesitantly.

"Now, don't blow off the idea, yet. Just listen first. Promise?" He asked with his beautiful smile.

"Yeah, yeah, I promise I'll listen first."

"Why don't you come on the road with me and the guys? You leave on the bus with us, tomorrow morning, we get to Orange County, do the show, Friday morning we head to San Diego for the next show. We could even stay in San Diego for the weekend. Jake's parents live there so we all stay at his house whenever we have a show. It will be so much fun if you come! Just a little adventure. Please?" He squeezed my hand tighter.

It did sound fun. But I couldn't get used to that. That was just a tease. That was a random coincidence that he had shows near the weekend and I had a canceled class. That stuff doesn't happen all the time and if I did it, now, I would just expect it to happen in the future.

"So, what did you say?" Sam asked after I explained the situation to her, later in our room.

"I told him I'd call him later." She gave me a look. "I couldn't answer then! I really needed to think about this." I sat on her bed next to her.

"There is nothing to think about. That's your problem, you think too much. Have some fun, do what your heart is telling you to do. It's just a few days." She took a scrapbook out of a drawer in her desk. "This is a once in a lifetime thing. I don't want you to regret not doing this." She opened up the scrapbook to the first page. It was a picture taken on the stage of a band with thousands of fans in the audience. I leaned in closer.

"Don't even tell me that's them. Where do you get this stuff? You are such a groupie."

"There are thousands and thousands of girls just like me who would kill to have the chance to go on the road with a band, this band in particular." She closed her eyes.

"I'm not dating him because he's in a band, this band in particular." I flipped to the next page of the scrapbook. "Is that a lock of hair?"

"Chloe, Focus! This isn't about my weird obsession with them and trying to act totally normal in front of them and failing miserably in hopes that my best friend will marry the man I thought was made for me." I raised my eyebrow. "This man is wanted by so many girls. You have no idea!" She looked at her hands. "And he only wants one. He wants you, Chloe. He wants you to be a part of his life, to share these special moments and memories with you. He's never done that with any other girl."

"For one, it is a little creepy that you know that," I paused. "But I never looked at it like that. I guess, it could be fun to go on the road with them."

She nodded.

"And can you please film every, little thing! I want a video journal when you get back!" She hugged me. "I love you and I only want you to be happy. I think Kyle can give you that happiness."

I pulled away. "I promise to film this trip if you promise to throw away that lock of hair! Who's is that anyway? Please, don't say it is Kyle's." I started laughing.

"You will never know! Now go! Start packing! You only have seven more hours until you're living the dream."

Chapter 6

I hopped on the tour bus at exactly five o'clock. Kyle handed me a coffee. "You sure know how to make a girl feel welcome." He looked fresh and awake, as if he never even went to sleep after he left last night. I could barely keep my eyes open, but I knew I couldn't complain since they were the ones who had a lot to do and all I had to do was watch. Sam had given me her video camera to film everything 'I felt was important' aka what 'Sam felt was important'.

The bus was huge and so awesome! There was a living room combined with a kitchen. Then, when you walked a little further there were bunk beds against each side of the bus. All the way in the back, there was a lounge with a big screen television. I had never seen anything like it before.

"What do you think?" He asked as he took a sip of his drink. "It's going to be pretty crazy staying with all guys on this trip but I think you will have a lot of fun." Jake and Cam were already in the back room playing video games and Luke was on his laptop in the living room/kitchen area.

"It's really nice. I can't believe you spent all of last summer on this bus." I walked toward the back room. "I really am looking forward to this. But I wasn't kidding on the phone last night, Sam really does want me to film, like, everything." I pulled the camera out of my backpack. He took it from my hands and turned it on.

He pressed record as he turned it toward himself, "Hey, Sam!" He waved. "Too bad you couldn't be here with us. Maybe next time." He turned the camera toward me.

"Ah," I said as I covered my face. "She sees enough of me, she doesn't need to have me on there."

"Sure she does. Without you there would be no recording." He kept filming.

"But I hate being on camera. Turn it off!" I turned my back to him.

"Okay, okay! It's off." He handed it back to me. "You don't like being on camera?"

"Or having my picture taken, really. I'm self-conscious, I guess. I know what I look like, I don't need a video or photo memory of it." I sat down on the opposite side of the couch that Jake and Cam were sitting on.

"Beat you again!" Cam said. "I'm starving. What's in the fridge?" He asked Jake as they both walked down the hallway.

Kyle sat next to me. "Having those images, though, brings back a clearer memory. You can remember things you didn't think you could."

"Says Mr. Magazine! You must love having your picture taken. You guys are always in the magazines. You always look great."

"I'm shy. I didn't used to like getting my picture taken, either, but it's growing on me." He took his phone out of his pocket. "Could we at least take one together, just you and me?" I shot him a look. "Please, Chloe? For me?"

I shrugged, "Fine! Just because no one will even be looking at me in this picture, everyone will just look at you."

"I don't think so." He held the phone out and took a picture.

"See! I look horrible," I said as I looked at it. "But, this is just for you, okay? No one can see this picture!"

"If you insist."

I never liked taking pictures, ever since I was about ten. My school photo, that year, ended up looking horrible. Worse than horrible. I got gum stuck in my hair, that morning, and I never told my dad. So I went to school, with gum stuck in my hair, trying to maneuver it out all day. At lunch, my friend, Nadine, told me the only way to get gum out of my hair was to put peanut butter in it.

So I did. I took the peanut butter off my sandwich and put it in my hair. I didn't really have enough to get the gum out so I ended up having peanut butter gum hair. Then, it was picture time. I tried to put my hair in a bun or ponytail to cover the mess I made but it was no use. Everyone called me *PB and Gross* for the rest of the year.

After that, I swore off getting my picture taken. There were probably five pictures of me in the whole house, from after that incident. I knew it was just a childhood photo and it was silly. I didn't have peanut butter and gum in my hair anymore, but I couldn't explain it, it was just a phobia.

After we watched some television and talked for a bit, we were there, in Orange County. We got off the bus and walked into the lobby. I looked up at Kyle. He had a hat and sunglasses on, probably trying to stay inconspicuous. The other guys looked the same. If anyone recognized them they would probably be wondering why in the world *this* random girl was with them. I was wondering that myself.

We walked up to the front desk. There was barely anyone in the lobby. A young girl, probably a little younger than me, was on her laptop and there was an older couple, about my parent's age, reading an itinerary.

"Hello and welcome to *Razton's*. Do you have a reservation?" The lady behind the counter greeted us, as if we were in an infomercial, so fake and corny. Then she looked between the boys, like she recognized them but couldn't put her finger on it. Her nametag said *Fiona*.

The guy's manager stepped around us, to the front. "It should be under Wayne Thompson. We have ten rooms and one suite."

"Wow!" I said quietly to Kyle. "Did you guys reserve a floor?"

"There's a lot of us," He said as he shifted his bag to his other shoulder. "Crew stays here, too. The guys and I all stay in one suite, though. It's fun. You'll stay in the suite with us. There's like three bedrooms."

The manager, Wayne, got the room keys and we all headed toward the elevators. "Do I know you guys from somewhere?" Fiona called after us.

"No!" All four guys yelled back, in unison. I chuckled.

We got inside the elevator. "You guys are on floor twenty. The rest of the rooms are on floor nineteen. That bimbo couldn't get us on the same floor, even though I told them on the phone four months ago!"

"It's cool, Wayne," Jake said as he patted his shoulder. "We'll try to behave."

Wayne got off on floor nineteen and we headed on up to twenty, the last floor in the building.

The doors opened and we all hopped off. "Have you guys stayed here before?" I asked as we walked down the hall looking for Suite 2080. The halls were lined with turquoise wallpaper with white sailboats. The floor was a gold carpet. Some kids ran past us. It was only six in the morning. What in the world were these kids doing up so early and with full energy?

"Nope. Never stayed here," Cam answered. "We've never done a show here, but our twitter followers kept asking for it. They signed a *twittion* and got like seven thousand people to sign it. So, we figured we'd give it a shot."

"A *twittion*?" I asked confused.

"It's a twitter petition," Kyle answered. "We really listen to our twitter followers. They have a big part in where we go on tour. This show tonight is sold out."

We kept walking. "Does this hallway ever end!" Jake said more as a statement than a question. We were only passing room number 2048. I looked back to where the elevators were. It was so far away I couldn't even see them anymore.

"Maybe it's one of those hallways that you just keep walking and you can never get out of. If you try to go back to the elevators the same thing happens, you just keep walking and you never go back to the real world!" Luke said. We all laughed.

"Let's hope not," I said as I kept looking at the numbers.

We finally reached the end of the hall to Suite 2080. It was the last room, facing the long hall we just walked. "I seriously don't want to walk down that hall again, it took like five minutes," Jake said as he put the key card in the door. It blinked green and he opened it. "They really got to put an elevator down this end, too."

We all walked into the room. It was a wide hallway, a short one, though. The hall led to a huge living room, with windows that went from the ceiling to the floor. To the right was a beautiful kitchen, with a counter to sit at and a dining table off to the side. I couldn't believe I was staying here, even if it was just for one night. It was amazing.

“Me and Jake will take this room off of the kitchen,” Cam said as he entered that room.

“Luke and I can take this room,” Kyle pointed to the room closest to the hall. “And you can take that one over there. It’s the biggest.” He smiled at me.

I walked over to the room farthest away from all the others and opened the door. *Wow*. I had never seen a hotel bedroom that big. A king-size bed was on the left wall and on the right wall was a beautiful balcony, overlooking the pool.

I opened up the door and went outside. It was about seventy degrees. No one was in the pool area. It probably hadn’t opened yet.

I felt like I was in a dream, everything was so surreal. This was *so* not my life. Staying in a suite with four members of a famous band. Me, living like a celebrity. It was so foreign yet it felt so comforting. I felt safe when I was with Kyle, even though it had only been five days. It was the best feeling in the world.

Chapter 7

The guys headed off to rehearsal at eight thirty. They had a studio rehearsal with their choreographer somewhere downtown. I went into the living room and sat down at the computer desk. The computer screen was bigger than the television in my dad's house.

I loaded up the Internet. I wanted to watch some interviews of the guys, get to know them more. I felt like I knew them all but I needed some more reassurance.

I watched a few videos of the guys at radio, magazine, and miscellaneous interviews. They talked about their albums, television show, life on the road, and basically anything you would want to know about them.

Jake did most of the talking for the band. I could tell when I first met him he seemed like the one who stood up for the band, not like a leader but more like the voice of them. Cam would make jokes but he also said a lot of heartfelt things. Luke was very flirty, and always made comments towards the girl fans.

Kyle was just like himself, the one he showed me. Nothing different, he was perfect in every way. There was a video on the right hand side of the screen. I clicked it.

It was some girl named Kourtney. She had pretty blonde hair that was in big spiral curls. Her makeup was flawless and her skin shimmered and glowed each time she moved her face. She was talking about her career, how she loved acting, but music was her passion right now.

Just as I was about to click out of the video, because it had no relevance to me, I heard her say something that caught me off guard.

"We were together for a while. Once I started going on tour, though, it was hard on me, not seeing him everyday." She adjusted her hair. “I wanted it to work. I think we both did.” She took a long pause, like she was going to cry. “We gave up each other for our careers. We are just too young to be serious.” Okay, she had to be talking about Kyle.

I searched her name online. There it was in fine print. Kourtney was the girl Kyle told me about. It felt more real now. Now I knew what she looked like, what she sounded like, and what her thoughts on the situation were.

I leaned back in the chair. How could I compete with that, with her? She was more his type than I would ever be. I was simple, definitely not Hollywood gorgeous. What was I thinking, coming on this trip? I shouldn’t even be here. I should just go.

My phone buzzed. It was Kyle.

“Hey,” I answered trying not to sound frazzled.

“We just finished rehearsal. We have to shower at the hotel real quick and then we have some time before the radio interview, so we are all gonna grab some lunch. Do you want to come with us?” I heard the guys all saying *yeah* in the background.

I hesitated. “Uhh, I’m not sure. You know, I don’t want to be in the way. Maybe I should go.”

He laughed, “Chloe, you’re not in the way. I invited you to come, remember? We all wanted you to be here. We’ll be there in ten. You are coming with us. That’s an order, young lady.”

Right on time, they were at the hotel ten minutes after we hung up.

“I’m showering first! I take the quickest showers,” Luke said to Kyle as he headed into their bedroom. I was sitting on the couch, channel surfing.

“There is another bathroom, doofus,” Cam said as he headed into his room. “I’ll shower first, Jake. You have too much hair.”

I giggled. “There is a bathroom outside of my room, too. Go for it,” I said as I pointed to the door.

“If you don’t mind,” Kyle said to Jake. “Cam is right, you do have too much hair.”

“Go ahead, but I sweat more than you. Poor Chloe has to smell me,” Jake said as he sat on the loveseat. I laughed out loud.

“It won’t take long. I don’t shower like a girl,” Kyle yelled back before getting to the bathroom and shutting the door.

"Here, pick something," I said as I handed him the remote. "I can't find anything good." He flipped through the guide and landed on a snowboarding network. He leaned back and put his arm across the back of the loveseat. He crossed one leg over his knee. "Snowboarding?" I asked.

"Kyle didn't tell you? We are all obsessed. It's our favorite sport. We do it as much as we can, with the extra time we have, which isn't much." He kept his eyes on the screen.

"Can I ask you something? About Kyle." I sat up from the couch and looked over to the bathroom door.

"Sure, anything." He shifted his glance toward me.

"Well, I came across a video of Kourtney, his ex-girlfriend, and I couldn't help but wonder why he was hanging out with me after he had such an amazing girlfriend. I'm nothing special. I don't get it." I looked down at my hands. They were shaking a little. I looked up at Jake.

"You are special! You are the first girl that has ever come on tour with us, ever! We have all dated here and there but no one has actually stayed with us while we were on tour. Not even Kourtney." I heard a shower door slam.

"I'm out, Jake. It's all yours," Cam called from the bedroom.

Jake leaned forward. "Chloe, I can't say I have ever seen Kyle this happy. Don't compare yourself to anyone. Kyle really likes you, it doesn't matter about anyone else." He stood up and went into his room.

Jake was right, I shouldn't worry about who Kyle had dated before me. Kyle wasn't obsessing over my old boyfriends. I just had to take things slower and not jump to conclusions. I was really bad at that.

I went back to the remote and flicked through a few more channels. When I finally decided on one, my phone rang, the caller ID said *Home*.

"Hello?" I said as I turned down the volume on the television. A show was ending on *Blinkeo* and Big Time Elevation's show was next.

"Hey! It's Jess," she said with an excited squeal. "I just wanted to call and check in. See how school was going?"

I focused on the television screen. "School is good. How about you? Decided where you want to go next year?"

"Not entirely sure. I really liked that one in Northern California but I don't know if I will like being away from everyone." She sighed. "All of my friends are here, in Boston. But I know that dad's moving to New York after I leave so, I guess, it doesn't make much difference."

The boys' show started. They were all on the screen talking about girls. "It is weird being away from home but you get used to it, and it ends up being really fun. Once you make friends, it's not so lonely anymore." Kyle came out the bathroom wearing a fresh pair of black jeans and a t-shirt. He walked over and sat next to me on the couch. He glanced over at the television and chuckled. I couldn't resist laughing, too.

"What's so funny?" Jess asked curiously.

"Oh, nothing. I'm just with one of my friends," I answered. Kyle was still looking at the television.

"Oh, okay. Well, I didn't mean to bother you. I can call later," She said bashfully.

I got up and walked over to the kitchen. "No, it's fine. I'm here, I can talk." I leaned over the counter.

"I was just wondering if it would be all right with you if I stayed with you for a little bit during my winter break? Maybe I could look at your school again or something."

"Yeah! That sounds great. Email me the dates and I'll get back to you." I looked over at Kyle. "It would be great to have you here. There's so much you haven't seen. So many people you haven't met. I can't wait!"

"Cool! So I'll talk to you later," she sounded excited.

"Definitely! Bye." I hung up and walked back over to Kyle.

"Okay, haven't you seen these episodes like a million times already?" I sat next to him and curled my legs underneath me.

He put his arm around me, eyes still glued to the screen.

"Actually, I only saw this one once. It just premiered last week."

"I see. So, what's this one about?" I rested my head on his shoulder. It felt nice to finally have someone I could do that with.

"In this episode, Valentine's Day is coming up so Jake, Cam, and Luke are all worrying about finding dates. Jake likes the new girl but she secretly likes Luke. Cam's character was in a magazine saying he had a girlfriend but he really didn't, so every girl he asks says no."

"And what about your character? Does he want a date for Valentine's Day?" On the screen was Kyle. He was by the pool, sitting in a lounge chair.

"He wants the girl to ask him. The other guys think the guy has to ask the girl and my character is convinced it doesn't have to happen like that. He's proving to them he can get a Valentine's date without asking." As he said this I could feel his head shift toward me. I knew he was looking at me.

"So what ends up happening?" I asked, still watching the screen. A few girls walked by his character at the pool but they didn't stop. "Does he get a date?"

"Yes, he does. The girl that asks him actually ends up being the one in the magazine that was supposedly Cam's girlfriend. Then, once all the girls see that the magazine story was fake Cam ends up finding a date," he said as I looked up at him. "Then, the new girl asks out Luke but since he knew that Jake liked her Luke turns her down. The two of them end up not having dates. It was one of my favorite episodes."

He flashed me his adorable smile as he pushed the hair out of my face. He kissed me gently on the forehead and then on the lips. His lips tasted sweet and the kiss felt magically, like an out of body experience. His hair was still wet from his shower and his hands were cold against my skin.

Just as he was about to kiss me again, Cam came storming in the room. "You guys ready to go?"

Chapter 8

We ate at a corner restaurant, facing the ocean. It was just the four guys and myself. Their 'people' were going to meet us over at the radio station.

We had a lot of fun, just talking about how they met, stories from on the road, and everything in between.

Sam had texted me to remind me to film everything. So far I had filmed the tour bus, a tour of the hotel suite, and us walking to this restaurant. Not that interesting, but to her I guess it was.

Once we finished eating, we walked about ten more blocks to the radio station. It was so much warmer than it had been earlier. I didn't even need the lightest of sweatshirts.

Jake said it was perfect weather to go surfing. Too bad there wasn't enough time. He planned on teaching me once we had those few extra days in San Diego, though.

We got to the radio station and the boys went into the interview room. It was a big room with three long tables, one for the interviewer, one for the boys, and the other was for the music software. There were microphones and waters set up on the boys' table.

I waited in the special area outside the room and looked through the window into the studio. I could see everything perfectly.

Jake, Cam, Luke, and Kyle all had bright smiles as they introduced themselves to the interviewer. They sat down at the long table and put their earphones on. They all talked for about twenty minutes before the red recording light went on. I put a piece of gum in my mouth.

“This is 101.7, Orange County’s number one for today’s hit music,” the guy said. “I am here, now, with the boys of Big Time Elevation. How are you guys doing?”

“Pretty good,” Luke said. “We’re stoked to be here. This is our first time performing here. The show is tonight and we actually have a CD signing at four.”

“We can’t wait to meet all the fans out here!” Jake added.

They went on for about another thirty minutes, here and there, in between music and commercials. They talked about their new album, how the first couple dates of the tour were, and more general stuff about them individually.

“Kyle is seriously the messiest out of all of us. He even admits it,” Cam said as he patted Kyle on the shoulder.

Kyle laughed. “I know. They are always on my case about it. But we’re on the road and I just don’t care. Life isn’t long enough to worry about being clean.”

“Well, anyway,” the interviewer said, I had learned at this point his name was Nick. “We have a few fans calling in to ask you guys some questions. Here is George.” Nick pressed a black button off to the side.

“Uh, it’s Georgia,” the voice on the line said.

“Right,” Nick said, adjusting some paperwork in front of him as his assistant, who looked younger than me, came to whisper something in his ear. He nodded.

“I had a question for Kyle. I just watched your newest episode, the Valentine’s Day one. And I was wondering if you had a girl you were spending Valentine’s Day with?” Georgia coughed really loud and the room grew silent. Kyle looked over at me. I smiled hesitantly.

“You know, all four of us try to date as much as we can. We are in our early twenties so it’s normal.” He thought for a minute. “I have someone I would like to spend Valentine’s Day with. Hopefully it works out.” Did that just happen? Did Kyle just refer to me over a live broadcast? I must have been dreaming. He really wanted to spend Valentine’s Day with me. I couldn’t believe it.

The guys got a couple more callers. They would take turns answering, depending on what the question was about. One kid actually called and asked what toothpaste they used, like it mattered.

"Okay, we got one last caller on the line," Nick said. "Her name is Keegan, I think. If I have it wrong, kid, don't get offended."

"Yeah, that's my name but I'm a guy."

Nick turned off his microphone as he stood up. "Uh, these kids! Like who cares who you are? You could be tiny freaking Tim and it would make no difference. This isn't television. I need a drink." He walked into the hallway.

"What's up, Keegan?" Jake said as he adjusted his earphones.

"It's not really a question, more of a suggestion. But I think it would be really awesome if you guys made some videos and put them online. Show your fans what it's like to be on the road with you guys! It would be so cool."

I snapped my gum. It was loud, I guess, because everyone in the whole studio turned to look. I shrunk in my seat.

"Keegan, we actually have that in the works right now. You are right on target. We were thinking the same thing. Maybe we can post one as soon as tomorrow!" Jake said as he drummed his fingers on the table. "Thanks for calling!"

"So, that about wraps it up. We really appreciate you guys calling in. Make sure to come to the album signing at *Placid Records* downtown today at four!" Kyle said looking around. He moved the microphone away from him. "Where did Nick go? How do we go off air?"

Without thought, I hurried into the room and clicked the big red button. The guys all stared at me, even some of the crew members.

"What are you doing?" The assistant said to me with a sharp tone. She kept pressing down her skirt like she was trying to deflate it. "I'm not even supposed to touch the buttons."

"I know how to work a radio station control room. My dad works in one." I pressed another button and music started playing through the earphones. "I just put on a song. It will be over in a couple minutes so you should probably get your boss." I motioned to the other room.

She walked out of the room at record pace. I turned back to the guys who were getting out of their seats.

"That's pretty cool that your dad works at a radio station!" Luke said as he put his cell phone in his pocket. "Kyle told us he's from Boston, right? Maybe we could do an interview there sometime."

"That would be so cool. I love Boston, I actually went to school there for a little while," Cam said as we all started down the hallway. "What radio station?"

"It's not really a big one. WZL 99.9." I pushed the button for the elevator.

Cam pulled on his ear. "Wait! That's the one I always listen to, every time I'm there. They don't play the same five songs on rotation, I love it!"

I smiled. I didn't think that many people even listened to my dad's station.

"I totally remember, now! One time, I was listening and there was a little girl talking. I think her name was Jessica. She sang the whole alphabet before anyone got hold of the microphone. It was so funny."

"That's my sister." The elevator door opened. "She is actually coming to visit in a couple weeks. Maybe you guys could meet her."

Oh crap. What did I just say? I would have to explain the story of how I knew four famous guys, *again*. And I wasn't entirely sure I wanted to let Jess know about Kyle, yet, anyway.

I felt like if I told too many people it would jinx it, everything would be over with. And I wasn't sure how Kyle felt on the subject of informing people of our relationship status. For all I knew, the three guys were the only people he had told.

Once we got downstairs, we headed down the street toward the music store. We went through the back alley to the back entrance. Once they got seated and situated, the line started moving inside.

I stood off to the side and watched. It was so amazing how many people looked up to those boys. Boys who I had spent so much of my time with these past few days. They were just normal people like the rest of us, but, I guess, some people didn't see it that way.

One mom came with her two younger children and was completely swooning over Jake. She would have stayed there all day if security didn't push her out the door.

Four younger girls came in, each with a shirt of a different boy's face on it. The back of their shirts said *You Elevate Our Hearts*. Cute.

And then, there were two girls, probably my age, that went right over to Kyle, they barely even said hello to the other guys. I couldn't help but feel a little jealous. I knew Kyle wasn't my boyfriend or anything like that but it was just weird to see someone I was dating being looked at like that.

I made sure to film as much as I could and after two hours of crying, screaming, and everything in between the guys packed up to head over to the venue. We took the bus, since it was on the other side of town.

"How are you holding up? This day's been pretty hectic. I'm sorry we haven't had much time together," Kyle said as he held my hand. We were sitting at the kitchen table.

"No, don't worry about it. Today has been really fun. I can't believe you do this, like, everyday." I looked out the window. It started to rain. "It seems so exciting. You must love it."

"I do. I really do. Every day is something different, something new." He took a deep breath. "I just wish I could spend more time with you. I'm really starting to fall for you."

I blushed. I was starting to fall for him too, seeing all those girls swoon over him may have jump-started the process. But I wasn't ready to tell him, yet. "Don't do that, yet. We still have one more week until you leave. Let's just take it slow until then. We won't make up our minds about each other until then."

He looked out the window, too. "But I've already made up my mind." He looked back at me. "Just do me one thing?"

"What's that?" I looked him in the eyes.

"Watch us backstage tonight. I'm going to need you there."

Chapter 9

It was halfway through the show and I was getting tired. I made sure to film every so often and reply to Sam's text messages that I was doing so. This was one of the longest days I had ever had, waking up before sunrise, after not getting much sleep, didn't help. I was looking forward to getting back to the hotel and crashing.

I sat down in a nearby chair and closed my eyes. The boys had just finished one of their high-energy dance numbers so I was sure a slow song would be next. I took a deep breath. I tried to block out all the noise and relax when I heard Kyle.

"There is someone here, tonight, who means a lot to me. I haven't known her all that long but I know she is going to be something special to me. Chloe, will you come out here?"

Huh, what? Cam, Jake, and Luke came over to me and took my hands. "What is going on, guys?" But they didn't answer.

"Everyone, say hi to Chloe!" Kyle took my hand. Everyone said *Hi, Chloe* at the same time. Whoa, that felt weird, thousands of people recognizing me and saying my name. No, really, what was going on?

Jake, Luke, Cam, and some of their band members pulled up five stools to the center of the stage. "So, Chloe doesn't know, but the guys and I were working on a song this morning. A brand new song that no one has ever heard before!"

"You guys are going to be the first to hear it, how does that sound?" Cam said as he sat down on one of the seats, Jake and Luke followed. The crowd went nuts, clapping and screaming, I even heard a few *I love you*'s.

Kyle took my hand and helped me onto the stool in the middle. He leaned away from his microphone and said to just me,

"Chloe, I wrote this for you, with the help of the guys." One of the band members handed him an acoustic guitar and he took the seat next to me.

I couldn't even explain to you the way I felt when he sang me the song. The other guys were singing, too, but I knew it was really him telling me how he felt, in a song.

He sang about how we first met, the concert when I realized who he was, Pacific Park, the cliff where we first kissed, and how each moment had meant so much to him. He sang about yesterday, when we were all watching the movies, and how all he wanted to do was hold me for the rest of time. The chorus sang:

I'm young and I'm crazy, but I'm crazy for you.
There's not a thing I would say, or I thing I would do,
To keep you from being mine.
I want you until the end of time.

It was the most amazing thing anyone had ever done for me. And he did it in front of thousands of people! Someone had to have recorded that. It would end up on youtube by the morning. I just could not believe he did it.

"You are unbelievable! So you didn't even have dance rehearsal this morning?" I asked Kyle. It was an hour after the concert had ended. It was almost midnight and Kyle and I were snuggled up on the couch in the hotel room. The other guys were in the kitchen, eating.

"Yes, we did have dance rehearsal. We just didn't have it for three hours," Kyle said as he adjusted his shirt.

"I still cannot believe you did that!" I playfully hit him. "You really caught me off guard. I had no idea you were going to do that."

He stood up in front of me. "So, Chloe, girl of my dreams." I giggled. "I know we said we would wait two weeks but I can't wait any longer. I want you to be my girlfriend. I don't want to pretend we're friends." I looked over into the kitchen, the guys were looking at Kyle now. "I want you to be my girlfriend. The guys want you to be my girlfriend. Even the fans want you to be my girlfriend."

I stood up to face him. “Okay, now you are just jumping to conclusions. None of the fans ever said that.”

He nodded his head. “Yes, they did.” He walked over to the big computer screen and typed something. He pulled up youtube and there was a video of the guys singing to me, just from a few hours ago. He scrolled down to the comments. *They are the cutest couple,* one of the comments read. *If she isn’t his girlfriend by next week I’ll be crushed,* was another. The last comment on the page was a really long explanation of why Kyle needed the best girlfriend ever and if I wasn’t that then she would find me.

“The last comment is a little creepy though,” I pointed to it. “I don’t want to deal with crazy fans if I am dating you. People are going to know who I am now. Everything’s going to be so different.” I pulled my sweatshirt tighter around me.

“Chloe, I’m not going to say you’re wrong, because you’re right. It is going to be really different. But I really want it to work. I really want you.” He wrapped his arms around me and pulled me close. “I’m willing to do anything I can to make you feel like this is right.”

“It already does feel right.” That was true. I felt like I belonged in his arms. I felt like I belonged when I hung out with all four of the guys. I felt like I belonged when I went up on the stage next to them. To anyone else, that would be so nerve wracking and such a rush. But for me, it felt like something I could manage. I wanted this to be a part of my life, as difficult as it may be. For right now, this was something I wanted to do.

“Okay,” I nodded. “I want to be your girlfriend. We can try this.”

“Yahoo!” Jake practically screamed. He ran over to us, Cam and Luke followed. They wrapped their arms around Kyle and me, squishing us closer together.

“The fans aren’t even as crazy as it seems. And no one can even see your face really on the video. No one will recognize you,” Cam said as he pulled away from our group hug.

Luke glanced at him and made a face. “What he means is you don’t have to worry, right now, about the fans. You’re just a friend of the band, if that’s all you want people to think. We don’t want you to feel uncomfortable going out in public.”

"I think for right now it's best that we kept it a secret," Kyle said as he pulled me over to the couch. We both sat down. Cam sat down at the computer. Jake and Luke went toward the back balcony. Kyle was looking out the balcony window.

"Yeah, that sounds like a good idea." I let my arms fall as I sank into the couch. No one needed to know right now. He was focusing on his tour and I needed to focus on graduating college. No one could really understand how we felt about each other besides us, anyway. Right now there would be too much judgment. On the outside, we seemed like an odd match, a superstar and a college student.

Kyle grabbed my hand and held it tight. I was starting to see that we fit better together than I ever imagined.

Early the next morning, we headed back onto the bus. We had about an hour and a half drive to San Diego. We were staying at Jake's house, right along the ocean. I was excited to see how the other half lived. I had already seen what a celebrity hotel room looked like, I couldn't wait to see a house.

It was around eight in the morning when we arrived. We drove up to the front gate. I couldn't see anything past it. Once the gate opened, we drove down a long windy path until finally there was a house. Wait, was this a house? It looked more like a place to throw cool parties. It was very white, square, and modern. There were edgy, blue windows in random spots, on different levels.

The guys hoped off the bus and headed to the back yard, I followed. The backyard led right to the beach. There was a pool to the left with a Jacuzzi inside it. There was a huge waterfall over to the right. And a little farther back to the right was what looked like a guesthouse.

"We stay here," Kyle said as he pointed to the guesthouse. It was probably the size of my actual house.

Jake unlocked the door and let us in. We went up a half flight of stairs into the living room. It was decorated just like the outside of the house, modern. There was a gold record plaque from the boys' first album above the mantel. Jake pressed a button and the fireplace lit up.

Luke and Cam headed toward the hallway, where there was another flight of stairs, which was very fancy. It reminded me of the *Titanic*.

We all went up the stairs. “Cam and Kyle’s bedrooms are on this floor, then up another floor is Luke’s and mine,” Jake said as he put down his suitcase. “You can have one of our rooms and we can sleep on the couch.”

I didn’t want to put any of the guys out. They had already been so sweet to me this whole trip.

“Or you can stay with me?” Kyle suggested. “My room has a couch that I can sleep on. You can take the bed.”

“No! I’ll take the couch. You guys have been so great. The couch is fine for me.” I adjusted my shirt strap.

“Okay. Let’s put our stuff away. We have another interview in two hours so, Chloe, you can come or stay, whatever you want.” Kyle said as he took my hand and led me down the hall. The other guys went to their rooms. “There’s the beach and the pool. He also has a movie theater and game room inside the main house if you wanted to do that.”

“Wow. That sounds awesome. I’ll stay here. I should film some of this for Sam, she would die.” We stepped into the bedroom. The walls were a light shade of green and the floors were hardwood. There was a queen-size bed and a massive sofa in a little nook in the corner. There was a flat screen hung on the wall along with a surfboard above the bed.

Kyle flung his suitcase onto the bed and opened it up. The room smelt like clean laundry and lavender.

Jake popped his head in the doorway. “We’re gonna take a quick dip in the ocean. You guys want to come?” I could hear Cam and Luke in the background, they were laughing so hard I thought they might burst.

Kyle glanced at me. “Yeah! Sounds great,” I said to Jake. “Meet you down there in a few.” Jake smiled and headed back down the hall. He yelled something at the guys as I heard footsteps heading toward the front door. Cam let out a big yell and the front door slammed shut.

After we put on our bathing suits, Kyle and I headed out to the backyard. Jake was already surfing. Cam and Luke were swimming.

I took the camera out of my backpack and pressed *Record*. "So, Kyle, tell us, what are you looking forward to most about this tour?" The wind and waves were so loud I could barely hear myself.

"I can't wait to meet the fans and, of course, sing the new song we wrote." He winked at me.

I laughed as I dropped the camera. "They can't know it's me filming! We're being secretive remember?" I pushed a lock of hair behind my ear. "Just keep it simple. No hints that you have a girlfriend."

I put the camera back up to him. "Tell the fans why you're going on this tour, what you want to accomplish."

He scratched his head. "Hm, Okay. Well, I hope to meet as many beautiful girls on this tour as I can." He paused. "How was that?"

"Much better!"

After about an hour, we all headed back inside and the guys got ready for their interview. I stayed in Kyle's room and uploaded the videos onto his laptop. My phone rang. It was Sam.

"Hey, Sam. What's up?" I clicked the icon to edit movies.

"How is it going? Are you having the time of your life right now?" She asked with a squeal. She didn't wait for me to answer before saying, "I saw the video of last night, the show. Where they sang to you!"

"Oh yeah, I figured you would sooner or later. It was amazing. I couldn't believe they did that. I was in total shock." Kyle came into the room and put a blue flannel shirt over his black tee.

"So? Did he ask?"

"Did he ask what?" I replied even though I knew what she was referring to. Kyle put a finger to his chest and mouthed "Me?" I nodded.

"May I?" Kyle asked as he took the phone from my hand. "Hey, Sam." I went back to editing the video. "Yeah, we just wrote the song yesterday morning. I'm so glad you liked it." A long pause. "Do you want to tell her?" He mouthed to me.

"I guess so. She won't tell anyone but Tyler. But just remind her not to tell anyone but Tyler." I started clipping pieces of the video out. There was a clip on the tour bus that Cam shoved a whole breakfast sandwich in his mouth. I figured the fans didn't need to see that. And then there was a clip backstage from yesterday's concert when one of the VIP girls threw up after meeting the guys. Yuck.

"Yes, Sam. It's official. Chloe and I are dating. But you can't tell anyone." Kyle adjusted his collar. "Well, yeah, actually she said he was the one and only person you could tell. We are trying to lay low right now. We're not telling anyone, yet. Great, thanks. It was great talking to you, too." He handed the phone back to me.

We talked for a little while and then hung up. She decided she *had* to see me tonight, so she was coming to the concert.

I was still editing clips of the video when Cam yelled to Kyle that they were leaving. "You sure you want to stay here?" Kyle asked as he rubbed my arm.

"Yeah. I have to finish editing these videos and get ready for Sam. Have fun, though." He kissed me and started heading out the door.

He turned around before saying, "I'll miss you."

I nodded. "I'll miss you, too." I couldn't believe I was already saying it.

Chapter 10

Once the guys came back from their interview, a couple of hours later, the five of us got ready and headed out to meet Sam for an early dinner. We got there a little late and saw Sam had already gotten us a table.

"Well, it's about time, you guys! I thought you were going to stand me up," Sam said as she stood up and leaned into me for a hug.

"Oh, well, you know how celebrities are. We're all the same," Cam joked as he sat down. We all laughed.

After we all sat down and ordered, I noticed a lot of people were looking at us. They must have recognized the guys.

"Chloe, I couldn't believe it when I saw that video you uploaded today. Well, the one on Big Time Elevation's page," Sam said as she took a sip of water.

"Why?" I asked confused as I looked around the table.

"Well, earlier Kyle said you didn't want anyone to know the two of you are dating." She shrugged.

"Right. That hasn't changed. What are you talking about?" A look of worry crossed her face.

"The video. It has you two talking at the beach. You said something like 'They can't know it's me that's filming. No hints that you have a girlfriend.' So you basically defeated your purpose. Now everyone knows he has a girlfriend." She said it so matter-of-fact, like it was no big deal.

"I didn't put that in the video! I edited it out!" The guys all looked at me.

Sam shook her head, "It's in there, all right. And it already has like over a million views."

No way. This could not have happened. I specifically took that clip and deleted it from the video, didn't I? "Oh my God! What do I do now? I never meant to put that online. We didn't want anyone to know."

"Relax!" Sam said as she touched my hand. "No one knows who you are, your face wasn't in the video. They just know he has a girlfriend."

"But we didn't even want anyone to know that at all," I said as I turned to Kyle who was sitting on the other side of me. "I am so sorry. It's all my fault, I can't believe I did this."

He ran his fingers through my hair. "It's okay, Chloe. We'll figure it out, don't worry."

"Yeah, don't feel bad. Mistakes like this happen all the time," Jake chimed in as he took some bread out of the basket in the middle of the table.

"We have PR people, it's their job to fix stuff like this. It will all be taken care of," Luke added.

That made me feel a little better.

Kyle pulled out his phone, "Just gonna check twitter." He paused, "Oh man."

"What?" I asked as I impulsively grabbed his phone and looked at it. There were tweets piling into his account. Some said they were happy for him, a lot of them said bad things about him having a girlfriend like they weren't fans anymore. One said 'How could you abandon your fans like this?' Like what? He hadn't even done anything.

"How could having a girlfriend turn some of your fans against you? That makes no sense at all." I said as I handed him back the phone.

"They were never really fans then," Kyle said as he put his phone back in his pocket.

"Some of the people that call themselves fans get mad at us for the dumbest things," Cam added as the waitress came over with our food. "One time, I cut my hair and I kid you not, some girl tweeted me that I was a different person and she couldn't be a fan anymore. How totally insane is that?"

"Fans that do stuff like that aren't really fans. They are just waiting for something to change on us and then they will leave, it will happen sooner or later. So whoever is saying to Kyle that they aren't fans anymore would have left eventually." Luke said as he took a bite of spaghetti.

Everyone started eating but I wasn't hungry anymore. "There's more love than hate, Chloe. And I know once we introduce the fans to you they will love you," Jake added.

"And anyone that doesn't can deal with me," Sam said as she patted me on the back.

Once we were done dinner, we headed over to the arena. We went in the back entrance and took the elevators. Once we got up to the main level, we made our way to the dressing room.

Sam and I went for a walk while the guys got warmed up and ready. We walked down a long hallway and up a few levels of stairs. Once we reached the top, there was a balcony facing the stage overlooking the whole arena.

There were so many seats and the show was sold out. I could picture all the girls singing and cheering. It was crazy to think that they would all be there to see my boyfriend. Well, not all of them, some of them probably liked the other boys, too. But Kyle was a fourth of the reason why every girl would be there tonight.

And now half of them didn't want him to have a girlfriend. What was his PR rep going to do? How could she possibly fix this? *This* felt unfixable.

"Maybe I should just come forward. Tell everyone I'm the girlfriend. I can't delete the video, people have probably already made copies of it," I said as I leaned against the balcony railing.

"No, not yet, it's not the right time. You're thinking too much about it." Sam glared across the arena. Maybe I was but I couldn't help but think about it.

We went back downstairs toward the guys' dressing room after a while. Once the VIP ticket holders started arriving, Sam and I continued walking around the building, exploring.

"So how are you and Tyler doing? I haven't heard you talk about him this whole trip." I said as we walked toward the floor seats.

"It's going great. Nothing new, except I think he might be like cheating on me or something." She pulled down her shirt and fluffed her hair at the same time. She proclaimed this as if to say he might be catching a cold.

"Uhm, cheating? Why would you think that?" We started walking closer to the stage. The floor was clean. There was a man mopping in the back corner, he must have been doing that all day.

"Well, pretty much, like, every Saturday he says he's going shopping with his sister. But, like, he hates shopping and he hates his sister so he could come up with a better lie than that if he wants to play circus." As we got to the stage Sam pulled herself up and sat on the edge.

"Have you considered he actually may be shopping?"

"No." She said as she whipped out her cell phone. "Ah crap, tomorrow is Saturday isn't it?" She started typing a bunch of buttons.

"I doubt he is cheating on you. He loves you. You guys have been together for two years!"

"Uhh, are you listening to yourself? Two years. That is a long time, long enough for two people to get bored," she said, still looking at her phone.

"Are you saying you're getting bored?" I raised an eyebrow as I looked over at her. I glanced over at the mopping man but he was gone.

"Things are complicated." She put her phone down. "Okay, it's not complicated but I feel like he is about to break up with me and I just wish he would do it already. If he is gonna hit me he needs to do it fast before I die a painful death." She put her head down.

I had never seen her this upset about anything. She never let her guard down, not even around me. She was always so put together. I guess underneath it wasn't like that at all. I took a seat next to her on the stage.

"Sam, I can't imagine what you're going through but I know Tyler and he seems like a genuine guy. I don't think he would string you along for this long if he was just going to break up with you." A few workers starting heading to their food booths. "I've known a lot of messed up relationships, trust me, I know how to spot them. Yours is not headed in that direction. You've just got to talk to him." She ran her fingers through her hair.

"If you don't think he is shopping with his sister then say something to him about it." I couldn't imagine her, of all people, holding back from speaking, especially calling someone out, like she did with Luke, Cam, Kyle, and Jake the first time we met them. But maybe her romantic relationships were different.

She sighed. "You're right. I should just talk to him about it." She lifted her head up. "I just didn't want to hear it from him if he was cheating." She smiled. "Thanks."

Kyle came running toward us from behind the stage. "Chloe! Come with me, I gotta talk to you."

I followed him backstage. "Shouldn't you be with your fans right now?"

"No." He turned around to face me. We were smushed between the drums and the wardrobe rack. "Just talked to Nancy, my public relations rep."

"Oh," I said questionably. "What did she have to say?" I could hear some girls behind the curtain talking to Jake.

"She said if we don't want anyone to know that we are dating, right now, to just leave it alone. Don't confirm or deny anything. Take the video down and don't speak of that part. She said you could edit the video again, without the girlfriend part, if you wanted. She just wanted you to send it to her first so she could review and put it up." He adjusted his backwards baseball hat. "That's what you want right? You don't want anyone to know?"

I blushed. "Well, not right now. We haven't known each other very long, you know? After a month or two, I guess, we could tell your fans, if they really would want to know." I paused as I looked at his facial expression. He looked so attentive and sincere. It was a look I was not used to seeing. I smiled as I looked down.

"What?" He asked with a reciprocated smile. "I really want to do this your way. However you want to go about it. If you never want to tell people about us, if you want to tell them right now…"

I shrugged. "I don't know anything about dating in Hollywood. I don't know what it will be like for you once *you* announce you have a girlfriend. I don't know what it will be like for me when your fans find out I'm *your* girlfriend. All I can envision is having to go into hiding." I giggled.

He pulled me close to him and wrapped his arms around me. His skin was so soft, like he had just shaved, and he smelt like citrus, so yummy. "You will never have to go into hiding for anybody. I don't know what it's like being on the other side of this, dating someone in this business. However..." He paused. "Cam's ex could tell you all about it, if you wanted to talk to her."

"Who's she?" From all the videos I watched I didn't remember seeing anything about Cam having a girlfriend, at least not while in the band.

"Her name's Sasha. They went out for over a year. Just broke up last summer actually, when we got back from the tour. Anyway, I'm sure she would love to talk to you. She kind of went through the same thing you're going through now." He kissed me on the forehead and pulled away. "She'll be here tonight after the show. I gotta get back though. I'll see you after the show. Where are you and Sam going to watch?"

I grinned."Oh, we have a place."

Chapter 11

"Okay, do you see the one way over to the left? About ten o'clock. She has a bright red shirt on and she has a hat, totally blocking the view of whoever is sitting behind her," Sam said

"Oh, God, I see her. That's a good one, but wait! Two o'clock on the right that bright, bright, neon blue shirt. I think there is a picture of Kyle's face on it," I replied.

We were sitting up in the balcony that we had found earlier that day. It was a nice hide out to pick out the girls in the audience who we thought were the most obsessed with the boys. We had found one girl earlier that had a huge poster that said *Roses are Red, Violets are Blue, I snuck into this concert, how bout you?* We were pretty sure security took the poster away, maybe her too.

The boys had just finished a song and were now starting to put the stools onto the stage.

"Oh my gosh, this is it, isn't it?" Sam said as she held her hand to her heart.

"Sam, don't get your hopes up. They probably only sang it last night to change things up. They aren't going to sing it every night for the rest of the tour."

"Hey everybody! How are you all doing?" Cam asked with enthusiasm. "We are going to slow it down a bit and sing a new song we just wrote yesterday. We hope you guys love this song as much as we do."

Sam smiled ear to ear. "Told ya!" She took out her camera. "I can't believe I missed this opening night. My best friend getting serenaded by her rock star boyfriend."

"Okay, that camera better not be on right now." I raised a finger at her.

"Pshh, I wouldn't do that." She pressed down a big button and a light on the camera turned red. "Okay, now I'm recording."

Once the show was over, we headed backstage again to meet the guys. I had told Sam earlier about Sasha and how she was going to be here. I was a little nervous to meet her, even though I had no idea who she was. Even Sam didn't know and that was a shock.

As we walked down the long hall, toward the dressing room, I started getting a twinge of nerves. It reminded me of the time Ryan first came to visit me in California, my freshman year. He flew over for Valentine's Day weekend. Before he arrived, I got so nervous. The last time I saw him before that had been when I went home for winter break. Everything had been fine with us, nothing out of the ordinary. However, once February came around it just started to feel different.

Before Christmas, we would talk on the phone every night before we went to bed. Even with the time difference it had worked out okay. But then after a couple of weeks since I had gone back to school he was coming up with reasons why we couldn't talk each night, always a different excuse. One day it would be because he had an exam the next morning so he couldn't stay up. Another reason was because his phone bill was too expensive. So when he had called me a couple of days before Valentine's and told me he wanted to come visit I was more than surprised.

I had no idea why he was all of sudden interested in communicating let alone going out on a limb to make our relationship work. Once he got here, my nerves didn't calm down much.

"You're shaking," Ryan said as he sat on my bed. My dorm freshman year was nothing to brag about. Everyone had the same set up. It wasn't the worst of dorm rooms but it definitely was not the best.

I walked over to the window and opened it. "I'm fine. It's fine. Are you hot? It's hot in here."

"No. I'm not hot. It's not hot in here." He gave me this look that I would never forget as long as I lived. He had never given me a look like that before, and it made me feel even worse about myself than I already had at that moment. It was a *What is wrong with you?* look mixed with a little bit of *I'm so glad I'm about to break up with you.* "I get that you're freaked out. I don't know why. I just came for a simple visit. Yet, you're sweating so much I don't think you'll have any left in you by the end of the day."

I took an ice pack out of the freezer and held it in my hand. "I'm just confused, I guess. After not talking on the phone for like a month you just all of a sudden think it's a good idea to come and visit?" I put the ice pack on the back of my neck as I took a deep breath. It took everything I had in me to say those words and then I felt like I was going to pass out.

"I thought I should see you before I made a final decision." He looked down at his hands and then his phone started beeping.

"Make a final decision about what?"

His phone kept beeping. It sounded like it was getting louder and louder.

"Answer the phone, already!" I practically screamed.

"I think we should see other people." The beeping stopped.

I sat on my windowsill. I didn't say anything.

"I didn't want to break up with you if I wasn't absolutely sure about it. I needed to see you first."

"Well, you just wasted your time and money. Get out, now"

I never talked to him again. It wasn't like he had cheated on me or anything like that. He had just come to break up with me in person. Would I have been just as upset if he broke up with me on the phone? Would I have wanted him to wait until I got home? I just never had the urge to answer another one of his texts, calls, or messages. Any way he tried to communicate with me I didn't want any part of it.

And then he went after Nadine, my oldest, best friend since we were two. But it wasn't just him to blame, it was her, too. She had given me a lot of bad advice over the years but when she told me to accept the two of them being together, that was when and where I drew the line.

"You know she's just a person," Sam said to me, now, as we both stood outside the dressing room door. "And if Cam dated her she must be fabulous."

I looked down at my hands that were visibly shaking. "I don't know why I'm so nervous. I don't know what she could say that is scaring me so much."

"I get it, it's ok. You don't have to explain to me."

But I needed to explain it to myself. Why was I so nervous? Maybe it was the fact that this girl could tell me dating a celebrity was horrible, worst experience of her life. But maybe she was going to tell me the opposite. That it was the best thing she ever did. But if that was the case, why were they broken up? I just wanted to stop asking myself questions and get them answered.

Sam opened the dressing room door and we both walked inside. Sam headed over to the table full of food. There were mini pigs in a blanket, a huge salad bowl, and lots of desserts to choose from. Of course Sam went for the salad and took a seat at the table in the corner of the room.

As soon as I took a seat on the couch the guys came out of their wardrobe room. They were all wearing comfy sweats and had water in hand.

"How was the show?" Jake asked as he sat next to Sam at the table.

"It was amazing!" Sam said as she shoved a fork full of salad into her mouth. "Loved the new song." You could barely understand the words.

"You guys did a great job, as usual," I said as I sat on my hands to keep them from shaking.

Kyle sat next to me. "Where did you guys sit? You could have stayed backstage with us, best seats in the house," he said as he kissed my cheek.

"Debatable," Sam said as she pointed a sharp finger at him. "Our seats were bomb."

"We actually found an amazing view before the show started. It was way up high on the top balcony, there aren't even seats up there. It's so high but we could see everything!" I said as I itched my ear. I knew it was a mistake to move my hand the second I saw Kyle's face. My hands were still shaking. I put my hand back under my leg. "So, when will Sasha be here? I'm dying to meet her."

"*Literally* dying," Sam said as she took a sip of water.

"Oh, well, she should be here soon. She was watching from the audience. I'll call her to see where she is," Cam said as he took out his phone and walked out into the hall.

"Are you all right?" Kyle asked me as he put a hand on my arm. "Sasha's really nice, you shouldn't be nervous. Is something bothering you?" He had a deep look of concern in his eyes, total opposite of that look Ryan had once given me.

I exhaled loudly. "I'm fine."

Once Sasha got there we hit it off instantly. She was tall, dark, and gorgeous. She looked like a model. I sometimes would catch myself staring at her and I would force myself to casually look away. I had never seen beauty like hers, how could Cam hide her? She was hilarious, too. She had such a great personality, it made me relax a little and almost forget why she was here to talk to me.

"Don't get me wrong Cam is coordinated. But that one concert he fell off the stage! I could not stop laughing. I don't think he ever forgave me." Sasha winked at Cam who was now sitting at the table with Jake, Sam, and Luke. Kyle, Sasha and I were sitting on the couch.

"That was just one time! It never happened again. My shoelaces were untied," Cam said as we all laughed. He stuck a fork in his piece of chocolate cake.

I was really surprised to see the way Sasha and Cam got along. They were so playful and friendly with each other I couldn't help but wonder why they had broken up at all.

"Okay, but enough about that. I know why you really wanted to talk to me. Let's take a walk." Sasha stood up and motioned to Sam. "You too! Guys, we'll meet you back at Jake's house later, okay?"

"Have them back by midnight!" Kyle said as Sasha, Sam, and I headed out the door.

Once we got to the exit door, we stepped outside. The air was nice and cool, no humidity. It was perfect. We started walking down the main street. There were still a bunch of girls waiting outside the doors, probably waiting for the guys to come out.

"Who are they?" One of them asked.

"I don't recognize them. Who cares?" said another one.

Ouch. Sasha winced.

"How long did you and Cam date?" Sam said to break the ice.

"About fourteen months. Although don't tell Cam I kept track. I always made fun of him for knowing the number of days we dated." She smiled as she looked down at the ground.

"If you don't mind me asking, what was it like? Dating him, being famous and all? I don't know how much the guys told you about me but…" I paused.

"You're dating Kyle," Sasha said as she looked at me. "I know. Kyle told me. He's really excited about it. He just wants you to be comfortable about it, that's why he wanted me to talk to you."

I nodded.

"Cam and I fell in love really fast, about two months into it. I wanted to see him all the time but I wanted to be careful about letting the world know about us." She put her hands in her pockets. "I would go to some local concerts with him, just like you are doing. I would stay backstage and really wouldn't let any fans see me with him. I wanted our private life to be private. I didn't think it was necessary to bring his fans into it."

She paused as we crossed the street. "After like six months of dating we really talked about coming out with our relationship. I gave it a lot of thought. It actually took me a month to decide I definitely did not want to be recognized. And that was that. Cam was okay with it."

Sam was watching Sasha carefully, probably wondering the same thing I was. "Were you happy? How come things ended?" I asked.

"I guess those two questions have the same answer. No, I wasn't happy. I wasn't around Cam as much as I wanted to be, and I could have been. If only we both just told the world we were dating I wouldn't have felt so alone. I hated walking by the fans and hearing 'Who's that girl?' I hated not being able to hold his hand in public. I hated not being able to tell my own family I was in love for the first time in my life. I regret the decision I made to not speak up about us, I was afraid of how it would change my life."

We turned a corner and went down a side street. "This is my car," she said. We all got in. As she closed the door she said, "I don't regret my decision to end it. I love Cam, I always will, but this life isn't cut out for me. All I really want you to know is that you should do what feels right to you. Don't put in mind what other people might think because in the end it's your life."

"Amen, sister!" Sam said from the back seat.

"I hope this helps your decision. I know it's not much but it's something to consider," Sasha said as she started the car.

"I can't even tell you how much this helped. I've done enough considering," I said. "I know what I'm going to do."

Sasha dropped Sam and I off at the driveway.

"You sure you don't want to come inside?" I offered.

"Yeah, it's past my bedtime. Hope to see you two again!" She said before she drove off into the darkness.

Once we headed back inside, Jake offered Sam to stay the night, she accepted.

"Don't think that because you think Tyler is having an affair that gives you permission to have an affair. And don't go after my boyfriend's friends!"

She smiled gleefully, "Did you just say boyfriend? Oh, what is the world coming to?"

"You can sleep on the couch," I said as I went to the closet to look for extra sheets.

"She can sleep in my bed," Jake called from the kitchen.

I almost burst out laughing. I tried to contain myself as I shook my head at Sam. "Don't even think about it. You are not doing this. Don't make me call Tyler."

"Oh relax, I'm not hooking up with anyone! I'm a loyal girlfriend."

I finally found some sheets and pillows in the way back of the closet. I handed them to Sam. Jake walked out of the kitchen. "She's just gonna sleep on the couch but thanks for offering." I shot Sam a look as I walked toward Kyle's room. "Goodnight, Samantha." She rolled her eyes at me.

Kyle was already lying in bed, it looked as if he had already fallen asleep. I slid off my high heels and skinny jeans as I quietly made my way over to my suitcase. I pulled on a pair of boxer shorts and turned around to see Kyle smiling at me.

I jumped. "Crap, Kyle! I thought you were asleep. You scared me." I put a hand over my face.

He grinned even bigger. "I was going to sleep on the couch over there but I figured it would be more cozy sleeping next to you." He placed his hands under his head but kept his eyes locked with mine.

I crawled into the bed and sat with my legs crossed as I pulled my hair into a loose ponytail. "You know, I'm actually not that tired. I could stay up for another couple of hours."

He glanced at the clock. It was already one. The moon reflected off the pool water and was shining onto the bed. He pressed his lips together. "I guess we could stay up, we get to sleep in tomorrow," he said it almost as if he had just remembered. He propped his pillow up and leaned back against it. "So, how was Sasha? What did you guys talk about?"

"Girl stuff," I said simply as I propped my pillow up as well. "Mostly what it was like to date in this industry. How it affected her. It really got me thinking *What am I getting myself into?"* Kyle looked tense. I could tell he was worried about what my answer to that question would be.

"Don't worry," I said as I nudged him in the arm. "Nothing bad. She just said how much she wished she put herself out there and didn't care what anyone thought about her. Let people talk, it's what they do best." I shrugged.

Kyle nodded. "I get it. She wanted to keep things private. She didn't want to be in the limelight." A look of confusion crossed his face. "But she said she wished she did?"

I nodded. "She didn't like taking a backseat to not only Cam's career but basically his life." I understood the feeling. Now that I was officially dating Kyle I couldn't imagine him being asked by people if he was dating anyone and him answering 'no'. It would be too painful for me. She may have been able to do it for fourteen months but I didn't think I could do it for another second.

"I don't want to take a backseat to your life. I want to be right up front with you." Kyle sat up. "I'm not saying I'm ready to tell your fans I'm your girlfriend but I'm not going to hide. I want to be there for you. We'll tell the public when we feel it's right. As long as this is all okay with you."

He grabbed the back of my head and pulled me closer. He kissed me softly, his lips tasted sweet, I could never get tired of that taste. He pulled back, our lips still touching ever so slightly. "It's okay with me."

Chapter 12

After spending, what seemed like hours, talking about everything you could imagine, the two of us finally fell asleep. He told me about his family, which consisted of his mother, father, and two older brothers. He had always wanted a younger sister, so he could watch over and protect her. I told him about my older and younger sister, what it was like living apart from our mom.

I had never gone into detail with anyone before about how the distance really affected me, not even to my own family. I kept the pain hidden. I really felt that it made things easier that way. Being upset about it all the time would just put a burden on everyone. But for some reason, I had no problem telling Kyle all about it.

He didn't judge. He just listened. I could tell he was really hearing me because he would occasionally ask questions about little details I had said. He didn't try to offer advice. He knew I just needed someone to listen. He was good that way. I never had to tell him what I wanted, he just knew.

Once I started falling asleep, I could feel his body so close to mine. The feeling of being so close to him was unexplainable. It was so reassuring to know he was right there. I knew in the future there would be lots of times where he would be so far away so I knew to treasure the moment.

The next morning, when I woke up, Kyle was still asleep. I threw on some sweatpants and headed out into the hallway. Sam was sitting at the kitchen table, looking out the window, her back facing me. I stood next to her, leaning against the counter.

"Are any of the guys up?" I asked.

"Yeah, Jake is out surfing already. He's been up since like seven. He's been out there all morning." She rubbed her hands over her eyes. "I think Luke and Cam went to get some bagels or something. I was on the phone when they were telling me. I couldn't really hear." She sighed heavily.

"Are you all right?" I asked as I sat down at the table next to her. I glanced at her face. Her eyes were red and puffy. She looked like she had been crying. "What's wrong, Sam?" I pulled her close and wrapped my arms around her.

"It's Tyler. He called me about an hour ago. He said, 'We need to talk'. Just like that." She started sobbing. "He's gonna break up with me. He told me to meet him at *The San Diego Zoo* at like two today. He knows I love animals why would he chose there?"

"Maybe he's not going to break up with you. Maybe he just has something he needs to say," I said as I handed her a napkin. "Maybe he just doesn't want you to hang around the guys anymore or something."

She shook her head. "No, that's not it. I told you he's having an affair. He is probably going to tell me today. 'I love her, I want to be with her, and it's over between us'." She started to cry.

"Well, I'm not letting you go alone."

"Go where alone?" Cam asked as he and Luke walked through the front door. They had paper bags in their arms. I assumed it was bagels as Sam thought. They both walked toward the counter.

"Sam's upset because her boyfriend wants to meet her at the zoo today," I said as I stood up and walked toward the counter. I turned on the sink and started to wet a paper towel.

"Why are you upset about that? *The San Diego Zoo* is awesome!" Cam said as he opened up one of the bags and took out a bagel. He held it out to Sam but she shook her head.

"She doesn't eat bagels," I said to Cam quietly. He shrugged and put it in the toaster.

"He's going to break up with me there. Why would he do this?" She started to sound less depressed and more angry. I handed her the wet paper towel.

"Chloe's right, you aren't going alone. We will all go with you. We'll make a day out of it. It will be fun. You won't even think about him," Luke said as he sat down at the table and started buttering a bagel.

Sam half smiled. "You guys are too adorable. Good thing we found them, Chloe."

It was nice to see that since we met the guys their friendship not only benefited me but it was also starting to help Sam as well.

After Kyle had woken up, Jake had come inside from surfing, and we all had eaten, with the exception of Sam, we headed to the zoo. Since Sam left her car downtown yesterday, Jake stopped by to drop us off. Luke and Cam went with Jake in his car and Kyle and I went with Sam in her car. She was still upset and in no condition to be driving so Kyle took the wheel.

Once we arrived, the line to the ticket booth went on for what looked like miles. However, Jake had bought our tickets online so we just had to get to the entrance, which still looked a little tricky. The guys all had on hats and sunglasses, trying to stay incognito, but it worked. In no time we were inside and no one had recognized them yet. It was kind of fun to look out for people who might recognize them, little kids, their mothers, teens. So far they were in the clear.

Sam was still shaky, just as bad as I had been the night before. The guys kept trying to take her mind off of it. They would tell her jokes or stories of girls they once dated, a lot of them were really funny but nothing made her any calmer.

"We're supposed to meet him over at the *Polar Rim* where the Polar Bears are," Sam said as she pointed to her map. It was the complete other side of the zoo. "He couldn't have picked something farther away! Who does this? Who plans the event of breaking up with someone?" She squinted as she looked around.

"It's this way," Luke pointed toward where the monkeys were. "There's a sign for the *Polar Rim*."

We passed through the *Lost Forest* and the *Panda Canyon* before we saw the sign for the *Polar Rim*.

"Ugh, he just texted me. He said he sees me and he'll be right over." She handed me the map. Her hands weren't shaking anymore. "Is it too late to bolt?" She ran her fingers through her hair and adjusted her top. "Do you see him?"

We all looked around although the guys didn't really know who they were looking for.

"Sam!" Tyler came around a corner. He looked nervous, really nervous. He was wearing a polo shirt and blue jeans. His hair was swept to one side and his teeth looked extra white. Kyle, James, Luke, and Cam stood still next to me. "Oh, hey. I didn't know you were all going to be here." He adjusted his posture. "Hey, Chloe, good to see you." He shifted his glance to the guys. He whispered, "You guys must be Big Time Elevation. Nice to meet you."

He shook each of their hands. Sam looked impatient as she shifted her weight, her arms crossed.

"Well, we will just be over here looking at the polar bears or something. If you need anything, Sam, just holler." I gave her a supportive wink as I pulled the guys over toward the big pool where the bears where.

"Okay, I don't think they are going to break up," Jake said as he put his hands on the railing in front of us.

"Nah, me either," Cam added.

Kyle and Luke looked at each other and shook their heads.

"Wait, so none of you think he is going to break up with Sam?" I pushed a piece of hair, that kept flying in the wind, behind my ear. They all shook their heads simultaneously. "Well, what do you think he's doing?" They all obviously knew something that Sam and I didn't.

"They've been going out for like two years, right?" Luke asked as he looked over at Sam and Tyler.

"Yeah," I answered still not getting it.

"And he's been acting weird, she said," Kyle said, now looking over at Sam and Tyler, too.

I started to say, "Yeah, but what would that…"

"Are you serious?" Sam screamed. Everyone looked over at her. Tyler was down on one knee. Oh, now I got it.

"You mean everything in the world to me and I can't picture my life without you being there every second of every day, forever," Tyler said as he pulled out a ring from his pocket.

"Of course I'll marry you! Duh!" Sam squealed as he slipped the ring on her finger. Everyone started clapping.

I turned back to the guys. They all had secretive smiles on their faces. "How could you all have possibly known this? And why didn't you tell us?"

"First of all, it was so easy to see, from an outsider's perspective," Jake started as he adjusted his sunglasses. "She thought he was acting weird but then he tells her he needs to talk to her. Here, at the zoo, of all places. She told us the other night at dinner how much she loved animals. After dating for two years I don't think the guy would break up with her at the zoo."

"But he could have been doing any number of things. Why would you assume he was proposing?" I asked as Sam came strolling over to us.

She flashed her ring in front of me. "Can you even believe this? I am engaged! Guys, did you see this coming?"

They all looked at each other. "Nope, not a clue," Luke said as he looked away quickly.

"I just came over real quick to let you know that me and Tyler are going to spend the rest of the day together, if that's all right with you? I'll give you all the details tomorrow when you come back!" She gave me a quick hug and danced over to a food station where Tyler was.

The guys started laughing. "Stop it!" I playfully hit Kyle. "I can't believe you let us think the worst."

"How could we tell you? He was going to propose. You think it would be better if she knew and wasn't surprised?" Cam said.

They were right. Tyler probably did all those things to make it seem like he was doing anything but getting prepared to pop the question. It was so funny that all four of the guys had the feeling that Tyler was going to ask her. Was it a guy thing or was it just like they said, an outsider's perspective? Either way, my best friend was getting married.

After a couple of hours at the zoo, only a few kids had recognized the boys. All of them asked for autographs and a select few asked for pictures. I had stepped aside whenever this happened. Kyle would offer an apologetic smile but it was okay with me. I didn't feel left out, this was just part of his career.

Besides, it only happened a couple of times. If it was every kid in the zoo, I would have felt worse.

Once it started getting dark, we went back to Jake's. We all swam in the heated pool for a while and then Kyle and I went out to the beach. It was still bright enough to see so we went for a walk. The stars were all so clear. I couldn't imagine the last time I looked up at the stars and could see them all. In Althoridge, there were so many lit up buildings it was impossible.

The water was so crystal clear I could see the rocks at the bottom. I looked over at Kyle who was walking at pace with me. He was looking straight ahead at the never-ending shore.

"I love the beach," he said as he pulled his hands out of his pockets. "Especially at night. It's perfect."

It was getting colder and I was shivering a bit. Kyle noticed and took off his sweatshirt. He put it around my shoulders without saying a word.

"Thanks," I said as I put my arms through it. I pulled it tightly as I zipped it up to my chin. Kyle chuckled. "Aren't you cold?" I asked him. We were both in our swimsuits still. I had pulled on a pair of shorts and Kyle had put on a black wife beater. His biceps were glowing in the moonlight.

He shook his head. "I'm okay." He took my hand in his as we kept walking. His fingers locked perfectly with mine as he squeezed my hand, but not too tight.

"So where are you guys staying this week? You said you have it off, right? No tours?" I looked at him. He was still looking straight ahead.

"We're staying at Jake's this week. Then we head out to Pennsylvania on Friday and have a show there on Saturday." Now, he was looking at me. "We can work it out this week, you and me. I can drive down to see you when you aren't in class. I mean, I really don't want to take you away from your schoolwork, though. So whenever you want me there, I'll be there."

"Well, I don't have class tomorrow and Tuesday I don't have class until three. So I guess I could stay until Tuesday morning. I don't have homework because I haven't had the class yet so you lucked out." I smiled at him. "But this is going to hit us hard on Friday when you leave, after spending so much time together.

I'm going to have withdrawals." We were coming to a bunch of big rocks in the sand, ones that would be difficult to climb over. Kyle sat down on one. I sat next to him, still holding his hand.

"I know. It is going to be really hard. We'll be gone for three weeks." Yikes, that was a lot longer than I thought it would be. "We can do it, though." He pulled out his phone. "Let's figure out the dates and when we can see each other."

Once they got to Pennsylvania they had shows Saturday until Wednesday. After the show on Wednesday they had Thursday off and would be performing in New York on Friday and Saturday and would have off on Sunday. Then on Monday they would be in Boston.

"Wow, that worked out well. I could totally visit you that weekend in New York and stay with my mom. Then I could go with you to Boston and stay with my dad. What are the odds?"

"I know, I can't believe how that worked out. Good thing you have off Fridays and Mondays," he said as he looked back down at his phone.

For the other two weeks, they performed on and off all over the country. Then on the last Saturday of the tour, they had one more show in Northern California.

Those two weeks would be difficult but I would be so busy with school I probably wouldn't notice. At least, I hoped. A cold breeze blew through my hair. I shivered.

"Are you too cold? We can go back inside," Kyle said as he put his arms around me. He rubbed my arms to try to make me warmer.

"No, it's not so bad," I said as I looked up at the sky realizing this was just where I needed to be.

Chapter 13

The next afternoon, Jake tried to teach me how to surf. I had fallen more times than I could count but he never gave up on me. Kyle, Luke, and Cam were on Jake's deck making burgers and dogs for lunch. Cam was out earlier, surfing a little, but he told me that his surfing wasn't as half as good as Jake's.

Every time I stood on the board I could feel how bad my balance actually was. Jake tried to give me some exercises to help. He would hold my hands as I would lift my legs to the side, bend my knees, and walk heel to toe but I didn't think any of it made much of a difference.

After doing exercises for about an hour on land, we moved to the water. Every time I fell into the ocean, I could hear Kyle cheering for me before I peeped my head above the water. Once I would get back to the shore, he would shout encouraging things with his adorable smile. I loved how attentive he was to me, something I was still getting used to.

"Hey, guys, the food's ready!" Cam called from the deck.

"Be right up!" Jake answered. "And good job today, Chloe."

We all grabbed food and sat at the picnic table on the deck.

"So, Jake, if you don't mind me asking, where are your parents?" I asked as folded my napkin onto my lap.

"They were actually out of town for the weekend but they should be back later this evening. You'll get to meet them."

"They'll love you," Kyle said as he filled his cup with lemonade. "We all consider each others parents our own parents. If that makes any sense. So Jake's parents our are parents, too."

"And they'll love me?" I asked.

All the guys nodded as they started eating.

I took a sip of lemonade before I said, "Do your parents ever visit you on the road? They must be so proud of you guys."

"They usually come to the local California shows and then every so often they will fly out and see us wherever we are," Luke answered.

The sun was starting to burn, the guys noticed, too. Jake put up the umbrella in the middle of the table. It shaded us all pretty well except the corner of my face. It wasn't too bothersome, though.

"My mom is coming out to the shows in Florida because that's where I was born, she loves to go back," Cam said. He was done his first burger and reaching for his second.

"And my mom won't be able to make it to any of them I don't think," Kyle said. His tone was sad. "My grandfather has been sick so she has been staying with him."

Out of all the things Kyle and I had talked about the last couple of days he had never brought that up.

Before I could ask anything Kyle said, "He's okay. He will be fine. She just doesn't want to leave him alone right now. He just had a stroke a couple weeks ago so he still needs some help." I knew he could see the look of worry on my face. He put his hand on mine and squeezed it. "It's okay. I promise."

"You know," Jake said changing the subject. "We should really give Chloe a nickname. She's hung around us for like a week now, she deserves one."

"What?" I said as I shot Jake a look. "You guys don't even have nicknames for each other why would I get one?"

"Oh, we do," Luke said as he raised his eyebrows. "You just haven't heard them yet. We try to keep them a secret."

"Chloe, Chloe, Chloe," Cam said as he tapped his chin. "You know, I think Kyle should do the honors, he knows her best."

Everyone was now looking at Kyle. The sun was starting to cover more of my face, now. "Do any of you have a pair of sunglasses I could borrow?" I asked as I shielded my eyes.

A look of realization crossed Cam's face. "That's it!" he shouted. "That's what we'll call you."

"Really? You're going to call me sunglasses? That's like one of the worst nicknames, ever."

"No! Your nickname should be Glow. Like Chlo Glow. It rhymes," Cam said as he adjusted his backwards baseball hat.

"Where did you come up with that?" I asked curiously, still shading my eyes. Kyle offered me his own sunglasses since he was completely in the shade. I took them and put them over my eyes. "Was it just because the glow of the sun was in my eyes or something?"

"No. When you're around everyone lights up. Everyone's always in a better mood. You are just so friendly. It's hard to explain. Guys?" Cam said.

"Yeah, Cam's right. As cheesy as it sounds, Glow fits you," Jake added.

I glanced at Kyle, who was smiling at me. "I agree. I like it. Glow."

"Okay, so I'm Glow. Are you going to tell me what your nicknames for each other are?"

"Not a chance!" Luke said.

Kyle turned to me. "You'll find out soon enough."

After talking at the table for another hour, we headed inside to the game room in the basement. It was filled with bright colors and tons of arcade games. There was also a big television where the guys were playing video games. After five minutes of playing, the nicknames came out. Jake's nickname was apparently Jets, Cam's was Costa Rica, Luke's was Luigi, and Kyle's was King.

I didn't know what these nicknames meant but it was funny to hear them say it to each other. They were having a blast playing this game where two of them were driving cop cars and the other two were driving city buses. I didn't really understand how the game worked but I was having just as much fun watching as they were playing.

Luke had this hilarious dance he would do every time he got a point. It was like the Macarena mixed with break dancing with the occasional back flip, and yes, there was enough room in this game room to do back flips. Cam would sing a song every time he got excited about something but the only words in the song were *yeah* and *dominating*.

When Kyle or Jake won points they would just scream really loud. Kyle would turn to me after each scream and apologize. I got it though. It was a man thing.

I heard someone coming down the stairs. "What are you guys doing inside right now? It is gorgeous out!" A skinny lady with high heels said as she got to the bottom of the steps. Her blonde hair was piled onto her head with a clip and she was wearing a power suit.

"Hey, Mom!" Jake said as he threw down his controller and went over to her. He gave her a big hug. He was almost twice the size of her. "We were outside but we came in for some *Road Rage*!"

She glanced at the television and then at me. "Chloe, right?" What? How did she know my name? "Jake already told me about you on the phone. You are so adorable!" I stood up from the couch as she came over toward me and gave me a hug. "You can call me Melody, I'm Jake's mom."

"Wait, Jake told you about *me*?" I said as she released from the hug. She smelt like jasmine and clean laundry.

"Yeah! He told me all about the song they were singing the other night about you and how you and Kyle are a thing now." She winked at me. "I had an image of you already in my head but you are so much more adorable than I pictured."

"Call her Glow," Cam said from the background although I had no idea where he was.

"Oh, you boys and your nicknames. Did they tell you what their nicknames for each other were?" She nudged me in the arm.

"Uh, not exactly but I know what they are, now."

She laughed as she turned to Jake, "Dad's upstairs bringing in the groceries would you guys mind helping? I want to chat with Glow!"

Jake nodded and the four of them headed upstairs.

Melody took my hand and pulled me over to the couch. Her hands were so soft they felt like porcelain. "I just wanted to talk to you a little bit. From what I hear from Jake you have been hanging out with the guys a lot?"

I shrugged nervously. "Well, I only met them last weekend but since then I guess I have been hanging around them a lot. They are all terrific guys and it's always really fun when we're all together."

Melody smiled, her teeth were so white it made me squint. "I've never seen Kyle so happy and I've known him for a while now, probably five or six years. He was dating that other girl, oh, what was her name?"

"Kourtney."

"Oh, yes, her. She was a drag let me tell you. She worked with the guys on the show and they would all come back here and say how much they couldn't stand her! Well, all of them but Kyle, he obviously liked her if he was dating her."

"So, none of the guys liked her?" I asked as I adjusted a couch cushion behind me.

"I mean, it wasn't that they didn't like her they just couldn't stand her. That sounds bad doesn't it? Well, in any event, they all eventually told Kyle they didn't like her, not until after they broke up, though." She paused. "I don't think Kyle was half as happy with that girl as he is with you. Jake tells me everything and he told me all the guys love having you around. You're really special. I mean the guys even gave you a nickname, already. They don't give those out to just anybody." She winked at me.

I didn't really know their whole system of nicknames. I just figured it was a right of passage, when you hung out with them you got a nickname. It made me feel special to know that they didn't give them out as frequently as I thought.

After I was introduced to Jake's dad, Kyle, Luke, Cam, and I played charades in the living room while Jake helped his parents in the kitchen. Luke and I were on a team and Kyle and Cam were on a team. So far I was doing pretty well, Luke had guessed all of my charades and I had only missed one of his. Kyle could barely get any of Cam's.

This was the first time I was in Jake's actual house, besides the basement where the game room was. The living room was so big and the ceilings were at least two stories high. It was painted beige and there were pictures of Jake from all ages hanging on the walls. He was a little bit chubby as a kid but so adorable. The couch we were all sitting on was so soft and comfortable I melted into it every time I sat back down.

I was trying to keep the score on a piece of paper but it was getting so confusing. They had this whole weird point system. If someone guessed their partners word in thirty seconds or less they got thirty points. If they guessed it between thirty seconds and sixty seconds they got twenty points. But then if they guessed part of it in the first thirty seconds and the rest of it in the last thirty then they got half of the half point. I eventually gave the paper to Kyle to figure out, it was causing my head to hurt.

Once Jake had yelled to us that dinner was ready, we all went into the kitchen. Everything was laid out on the island in the center of the room. There was so much food, more than I had ever seen. There were burritos, casseroles, pizzas, sandwiches, chicken fingers, fruits, and vegetables. It was all so beautiful and colorful. My mouth dropped open.

"It's okay, Glow, we eat a lot," Cam said as he grabbed a plate and started putting food onto it.

"Yeah, this will all be gone in thirty minutes," Jake's dad said as he laid out some napkins.

I took a plate and grabbed a sandwich and some fruit. Once we all sat down at the table together and started talking, it really felt like I was part of this family. Not just Jake and his parents but all of the guys. This was a place they came to feel at home and I was here with them. It had been a long time since I felt at home.

Once my mom left, it never really felt the same. I had always looked forward to the day when my mom and dad would move back into the same house but then they decided my dad would move to New York and that would never feel like home to me. The New York apartment was always her house, it was never mine, or my dad's, or my sisters'. I never thought I would really feel at home again, until now. I felt like I was a part of something that mattered and I didn't want it to go away.

Chapter 14

The next afternoon, I packed up my things to head back to campus. Jake's parents were already at work and the guys were all in the guesthouse living room watching a television show. I didn't know exactly what it was but the main girl kept mentioning crickets on her porch. I couldn't gather if it was a metaphor or if she really did have crickets on her porch, which made no sense because she lived in New York City.

"All right, I'm gonna get your bags into the car. I'll be right back," Kyle said as he picked up my suitcases and headed out the front door.

I looked out the window as he started walking past the main house to the driveway. It was pouring outside, the sound of the rain hitting the windows was echoing through the room.

"Is he going to tell her he can't sleep without her in his life either?" Cam asked the boys while still focusing on the screen.

I walked over toward the back of the couch. "So, the whole crickets on the porch thing means she can't sleep at night?"

They all nodded their heads without looking away from the show.

"And what is this show called?" I asked.

"Runners," Jake answered. "It's like our favorite show of all time. Kyle's not much of a fan, though. He doesn't like shows about pretty boys."

I laughed. Pretty boys? I thought everyone on television was a pretty boy. Kyle, Jake, Luke, and Cam were prime examples of this.

"So, you don't think of yourselves as pretty boys?"

They all shot their heads around and looked at me.

"You think we are pretty?" Jake asked as he batted his eyes.

I laughed. “Uhm, yeah. Everyone on television is usually pretty, unless the role specifically calls for someone ugly.”

“Everyone, huh?” Cam said with a sinister smile.

I didn’t know where they were going with this. “You know, I don’t know what you…”

Kyle walked through the front door and interrupted, “We should go, now, before it starts to downpour.”

“Okay, bye, guys,” I said as they all stood up. I hugged them each individually as they told me how much they would miss me. We all exchanged numbers so we could keep in contact.

“And don’t forget to tell your dad we want to be on his radio show! We’re in Boston in two weeks,” Cam said as Kyle and I started to walk toward the front door.

“I’ll let him know.”

Kyle and I got into one of Jake’s cars and started driving. After about ten minutes, I got a text from Cam. He sent a picture of himself as a teenager. He had braces and acne. I closed the picture and put the phone on my lap. Not a minute later, it started buzzing again, it was a picture message from Jake. It was a picture of him as a kid at the beach. He was so chubby and adorable, just like the pictures that had been in his house. Before I could exit out of that picture, Luke sent me one, too! It was a picture of him as a kid wearing an American flag sweatshirt and glasses.

“Okay, I give up!” I said out loud as I threw my hands up in the air.

“What’s wrong?” Kyle asked as he looked over at me. The rain was still coming down hard.

“Cam, Jake, and Luke all texted me pictures of themselves as dorky kids. I don’t get why?” I started laughing as my phone buzzed again and I started getting more pictures. “I mean, these pictures are hilarious and they just keep sending them.”

Kyle smirked. “You didn’t by chance say anything to them about being good-looking did you?”

“What does that have to do with this?”

“Whenever someone they are friendly with tells them they are hot, handsome, cute, pretty, gorgeous, you name it, they send them those pictures." Kyle started laughing too. "They really are funny pictures."

I glanced down at my phone again. Cam had most recently sent me one where he looked about four and he was climbing a wall in his tighty whities.

"They just want everyone to see them as human beings. You know? They don't want you to see them as anything but your friends."

"Okay," I said as I put my phone down on my lap again, it stopped buzzing. "I understand that. I don't see you guys as anything celebrity-like. You know that right? They are all my friends and you're my boyfriend." I paused. "Is that weird that I just called you that?" I bit my lip. "I called you my boyfriend to Sam the other day but that was different."

He grabbed my hand. "I like when you call me that. I like calling you my girlfriend. I'm proud to say you are my girlfriend."

"But would you prefer to have a nickname or something? I feel like I should give you a nickname. You gave me one, it's only fair."

"Okay. What should it be?" He asked, his eyes on the road.

I thought about it for a couple minutes, neither of us said anything. I had no idea what to give him as a nickname. There was nothing you could pull out of the name Kyle, really.

"You don't have to think of something now. One day something will just roll off your tongue and that's what it will be."

Once we got to campus, we said our goodbyes and he headed back to San Diego. I would see him again tonight, after my class was over and I finished my homework. I opened the front door to our townhouse and headed upstairs to my room.

"Mom, for the millionth time I'm not pregnant. We love each other and want to get married. Is that so hard to believe?" Sam was on the phone lying on her bed, looking at the ceiling. There were magazines sprawled out all over the floor. I walked over and picked one up, they were Bridal Magazines.

"No, Mom I have classes tomorrow. Yeah, I have classes Thursday too. Just come home this weekend then. No. Okay.

Goodbye, Mother." She hung up the phone. "Can you believe her?" She turned to me as she sat up.

"She thinks you're pregnant?" I flipped through the pages of the magazine. The dresses were really bizarre.

"Yes! She doesn't think people want to get married in college unless they are knocked up. As if," she said as she took a stack of post-its off her desk and sat on the floor. "I was first trying to look for a theme I liked. Romantic, edgy, floral, modern, it's hard to choose. But so far I like this." She picked up a magazine and pointed to a picture of a function room.

It was decorated in all black and white, nothing else. The tablecloths were white with black silverware. The flowers were all white. It was really beautiful.

"Wow. I really like that one."

"And then I was thinking, if we end up doing that theme then we have everyone wear colorful clothes. No black, no white. Me and Tyler are the only ones in black and white. So that means the guys have to pick a different color tux, but nothing outrageous. I was thinking more along the lines of navy blue, gray, khaki colored. You know, something like that?" She put a post-it on the picture of the black and white room and set it to the side. "And we both talked about it, we want you to be our wedding planner."

"Really?"

"Of course, who else?"

I was flattered. I obviously had no real experience at planning any kind of event. And after four years of school, I wasn't exactly positive what kind of event planning I wanted to do. There were non-profit events for charities and stuff like that. And then there was wedding, funeral, and party planning. And then there was the type I had been considering recently, concert planning. A concert planner would arrange all of the tour dates and venues with the help of a team. I had thought about it once freshman year but I never really considered doing it until I went with the guys on their tour dates. It seemed like something that I could really be interested in.

"So you're already thinking about this stuff?" I asked as I sat on the floor across from her.

"You can never be too prepared. And besides we both decided we want a summer wedding." She flipped through the pages of another magazine.

"I'm sorry, do you mean this summer?"

She nodded. "It's perfect. We're graduating in June. We're going to get married in July. Then we will both be focused on finding jobs together and it will be *amazing*."

"Where are you guys going to live?" I asked. Tyler was from Colorado. Sam lived in Laguna Beach. She had always said how much she loved living near the beach and she couldn't imagine living anywhere far from it.

"Tyler and I talked about it. He loves the snowboarding, I love the beach so we figured we would live in Colorado during the year and then in the summer we would stay in Laguna. Is that stupid?"

"No, it's not stupid but what are you going to do when you get a job? You can't just not work in the summer," I said as I picked up another magazine. I didn't want to think about Sam moving. Colorado was so far away. I didn't know what I would do without her.

"Well, I was thinking I could work as a *school* psychologist September through June in Colorado and then I would have the summer off anyway." She slapped another post-it on a page with bridesmaids' dresses.

"And what about Tyler? Doesn't he want to be a cop? He can't just leave for three months, Sam."

"Actually, he can," she said as she wrote something down on the magazine page. "He already talked to his dad, who's the chief in their hometown. If he works Monday through Friday every week, doesn't take vacation or holiday days, he could leave for the whole summer."

Well, at least I would see Sam during the summer. That was better than her being gone forever. We would still have three months, it was exactly opposite of what we had been doing these four years at school.

"We're gonna make it work, Chlo. It won't be easy but summer is for vacationing! And I can't go twelve months without seeing my best friend."

I smiled. "So, are you thinking about using that hideous dress for the bridesmaids?"

I headed to class at three. It was a finance class so after it was over my brain started to hurt. As much as I wanted to be an event planner I hated the financial side of things. If I had a team of people helping me I think I would be much better at my job. But I really needed to think about it more. Was I only thinking about concert planning because of Kyle's job or was it something I would have wanted to do anyway? I really didn't know much about it. I would have to get some information, maybe from their tour manager.

Once I got back to the townhouse, I checked my email. Jess had sent me her vacation schedule. It was in just three weeks. She wrote that she would fly out on a Saturday and head back on Friday. That was exciting, to have my little sister come and visit me out here. Of course, Kyle would be done the tour by then and Jess would be another person to find out that I was dating a celebrity.

I was probably being too harsh, though. It was one thing to hide my relationship with Kyle from his fans but to hide it from my friends and family, maybe it wasn't necessary. I didn't think anyone who cared about me would expose the relationship.

Kyle had texted me that he was on his way. He was driving from Jake's house to have dinner with me and then spend the night. Sam was downstairs attempting to make Tyler dinner. I could hear her groan every so often. She didn't cook much, probably because she wasn't very good at it. But she was trying to prove to Tyler that she would make a good wife. I think she was trying to prove it to herself, too.

I walked downstairs to see a mess on the counter and Sam sitting on the couch. She was wearing a cream colored dress that was speckled with spaghetti sauce. There was an apron hung over a chair that was also covered in sauce.

Sam had a wine glass in hand. "I can't do it. I'm going to be a horrible wife."

"Sam," I said as I walked toward the couch. "Not everyone is a good cook. That doesn't make you a horrible wife." I sat next to her trying to keep my distance so I didn't get sauce on me.

"Easy for you to say. You can cook and you're good at it." She turned toward me and took a sip of wine from her glass. "You're good at everything, Chlo. It's amazing boys aren't lining around the block for your milkshakes."

I laughed. "I don't know where you come up with this." The doorbell rang. I got up to answer it. "I'll help you cook and I bet Tyler will, too. This is probably him, right?"

I opened the door. Wrong. It was Ryan. Ex-boyfriend Ryan.

Chapter 15

"Hi Chloe," he said stiffly as if he was unsure why he had come here in the first place. I sure as hell was unsure why he was here.

His hair was short, much shorter than when I was dating him. And he looked more muscular than the last time I saw him, too. But what was he doing here?

I didn't say anything. What was there to say? I couldn't even stammer out a 'hello'.

"Can I come in?" He asked as he put his hands in his back pockets.

"What the hell?" Sam said as she ran toward me. "What are you doing here, jerk off?" She looked at her empty glass of wine. "You're so lucky this is empty or it would be all over you right now. What the hell do you think you're doing here coming uninvited? Even if you were invited you shouldn't show up, ever. No one likes you here!"

He looked kind of startled as if he didn't know what he did wrong. As if he forgot he came all the way to visit me at school freshman year just to make a "final decision" about breaking up with me. As if he forgot that shortly after he broke up with me he started dating my best friend, Nadine.

"Ugh." Sam rolled her eyes and walked back to the kitchen.

I stepped outside and closed the door behind me. "Sam doesn't really want you inside." I looked down at my feet. I hadn't even started getting ready to go out with Kyle, yet. I figured I would have had time. "What are you doing here?" I slowly looked up to meet his gaze. He quickly looked away.

"I needed to talk to you. I didn't think I would be unwelcome here. What did I do wrong?" He shifted his weight. Was he kidding right now or did he seriously not know that dating my only friend three years ago was wrong? For all I knew they were still together, married, and had triplets.

"You really don't know?" He was still looking off into the distance. "Could you stop being a coward and look at me?"

He slowly shifted his eyes toward mine. "It's been three years since we broke up, I thought you would be okay with me now. I'm not proud of what I did but I kept sending you emails to say how sorry I was. I thought you would have gotten them or something."

"I have not gotten a single email from you since the day we broke up. Stop lying." The wind was whipping my hair. I tried to put it behind my ears but it was no use, it wouldn't stay.

"I'm not lying. I really did email you a bunch of times to your AOL email."

"Uh, I haven't checked that since high school. You should have called me if you really wanted to talk. And you shouldn't have just shown up here like this. I really don't have any interest in talking to you." My hair was still whipping like crazy, I could barely see.

He took the hair from my face and moved it away. "Please, just hear me out. Can I at least come inside? It's too windy out."

I swatted his hand away. "Go home, Ryan. We have nothing to talk about." I walked toward the front door and opened it. I waited for him to say something else but he didn't. I went inside and shut the door.

Sam came running toward me. "I'm okay, Sam, it's okay." She wrapped her arms around me.

"What did he say to you?"

"I wasn't really listening. I don't want to talk to him. I don't know why he came. I don't want to talk to him to know why he came. I just want him to go away."

Sam pulled away. "Did he leave?" She ran toward the window and looked outside. "Yeah, he's gone."

"He's gone."

I went back upstairs to my room and attempted to get ready. The thought of Ryan coming here to visit kept bothering me, though. Why the hell did he think now was a good time to talk to me? I just didn't get it. But at the same time I didn't want it to bother me and I wanted to shove it to the back of my head.

My phone buzzed. "Hello?" I answered.

"Hey, it's Kyle. I'll be there in ten minutes."

Oh, crap. I still wasn't even close to being ready. All I had done was lay out a few outfits on my bed and braided my hair to the side. "Ten minutes?"

"Yeah. Do you need more time? I could…"

"No, Kyle, it's fine. I just was preoccupied. I'll be ready by the time you get here." I picked up a hot pink, one-shoulder shirt lying on my bed. It was what I originally planned on wearing but it was all wrinkly. I'd have to iron it, and there was no time for that. I sighed as I set it back on my bed.

"What's wrong?" I could hear him lower the volume of his music in the background. "What are you thinking about?"

I couldn't lie to him. I really didn't want to bring the whole ex-boyfriend crap into this new relationship but since Ryan happened to drag himself into my new life, literally, I had no choice. I didn't want to worry Kyle, though. "It's not a big deal. I'll tell you about it over dinner." I picked up another shirt on my bed. It was a strapless aqua colored top that Sam had bought me on my twenty first birthday. I guessed that it would look all right with a pair of jeans.

"Okay," he said, "don't rush or anything. Take your time."

I put on the aqua-colored shirt and slid into my boutique jeans. Sam, of course, helped me put on some makeup. By the time the doorbell rang I was ready.

"Hey, you look great," Kyle said as I opened the front door. I looked over Kyle's shoulder thinking Ryan would still be there. No sign of him. Good.

"Thanks, let's go. No need to stick around." I shut the door tightly behind me and started walking down the path to the main road. Every time I heard a noise I looked around. I had a feeling that Ryan was still there but that was silly, he was gone.

"You sure you want to wait until dinner to tell me what's bugging you?" I was walking a little bit ahead of him, now. I hadn't noticed. He reached for my hand and held it as we continued walking. His hand was so smooth and relaxed. My hand was a mess and shaking like crazy. There was no way I could wait until dinner to talk. "I hate seeing you like this and not know what's wrong. I don't like not being able to help. Maybe that's too old fashioned but I want to be able to help you."

I couldn't look at him. He always knew what to say. Okay, once we got to the car I'd tell him, just incase Ryan was still outside. I didn't know what Ryan's motives were. I stuttered out, "Yeah, yeah." Like that even reassured him of anything. It probably made things worse. I knew where he usually parked and it was probably about a two-minute walk from my townhouse. It had been about a minute so I still had another minute to kill.

I could feel his eyes beaming through me. I kept looking forward. "So, where are we going to eat?"

"Uh, I thought you could pick. Remember, I don't really know the area." I could see him smile out of the corner of my eye. He was trying so hard and I wasn't giving him anything to work with. All right, good, there was the car.

He opened the door for me and I got inside. I made a huge sigh of relief. But why did I even think Ryan was following me? If I cared this much I should have just done something when he came to my door. I didn't know it even bothered me. Not talking about it was not helping.

Kyle got in the car and before he started the engine I said, "Okay, there is something totally bothering me and I didn't want to make a big deal about it because it's not a big deal. I didn't think it was bothering me but the more I don't talk about it the more I think about it, and I just want to stop thinking about it."

I thought Kyle would have a shocked expression but he looked at me calmly. It reassured me that I was doing the right thing by telling him. "I'm all ears."

I started off telling him about Ryan, how we dated and he came here to break up with me and then date my one and only best friend shortly after. I told him how he had just shown up on my door today and I didn't even ask him why he was there after going so long without talking. I told him how it bothered me that Ryan said he wrote me emails but I had no idea what they said. "Is it weird that I really want to know what they said?"

"No," Kyle said. We were still sitting in his parked car. "It would be weird if you didn't want to know what they said. You need closure with him. He never gave you that. He broke up with you out of the blue. You need reasons that he never gave. You were probably too upset then to want to know why, but I think it's time for you to find out."

Maybe he was right. I never knew why Ryan had stopped trying to make our relationship work. I never knew how Ryan seeing me and saying nothing had confirmed to him that our relationship was over. And I never knew why he thought it was a good idea to date Nadine.

"So, what should I do? I don't have his number. How should I get a hold of him?"

"I think if he came all the way out here, it was for a reason. And he probably won't leave until he does what he came to do." Great, that just confirmed my fears of him following me. Kyle must have noticed the look of worry on my face. "Don't worry, Chloe. I don't think he's going to hurt you. Maybe he just wants to talk, too. Either way you both need closure, I think it's for the best."

After we ate, we headed back to my dorm. Sam was going to be at Tyler's for the night. She was already gone when we got inside. We headed up to my room. Lindsey and Erica were out again, they were hard to keep track of. I usually didn't see much of them at the beginning of the winter semester. Erica was always busy with sports and Lindsey was the captain of the cheerleading team. Once the middle of March came around, I would see more of them.

I flung off my flip-flops and started to take off my earrings. Kyle was looking around the room. He stopped when he saw the poster of the band that Sam had on her closet door. "It's weird to see this in person. Like, I know we have fans and I know they collect stuff but it's so strange to actually see it." She got the poster the night of the concert when we both had VIP. If this poster was in our room before the concert it would have completely changed the way Kyle and I first met each other.

"I can't imagine walking into Jake's room and seeing a poster of me and Sam!" Just as I started getting used to the fact that I was dating someone famous, I got another reminder of how abnormal it was. I couldn't imagine what it felt like to be on his end of things, to see a poster of him and his friends hanging in his girlfriend's bedroom. I guess there were just some things that we both would never get used to.

I took off my necklace and bracelets and opened up my dresser. "Did you bring anything to sleep in, Kyle?"

"No, I just figured I'd sleep naked." He winked. "No, actually I forgot my backpack in the car. I'll go get it."

He left the room, went downstairs, and outside. I pulled off my jeans and slipped into a pair of shorts. I took off my top, carefully hung it on a hanger, and put on a short sleeve shirt. As soon as I lay down on my bed my phone rang.

"Hello?"

"Hi, it's Mom. Are you busy?"

"Not at the moment, why?" I put my phone on speaker so I could put my hair up.

"Okay. I need to just get everything set for your sister when she comes to visit. We need to clarify a few things." She cleared her throat. "Do you have a pen?"

I finished putting my hair up and grabbed a pen and notebook from my desk. "Yeah, Mom. What do you need to clarify?"

"Well, you're picking her up from the airport on Saturday at two forty two PM. Let's see…that's the nineteenth."

"Mhmm." I had this date in my head because it was the last day of Kyle's tour. My sister was going to have to find out about the relationship because I was going to have to see him sometime that week. Two weeks without him wouldn't be easy.

"All right. Well, what did you have planned to do that week, Chloe? Did you think of activities and restaurants? Maybe you could even take her to your gym." She was typing something on the computer. "Hmm, there seems to be some interesting things to do around your campus, I see."

"Mom, don't worry. I have it all figured out." I really didn't have it figured out but I didn't need to. I had been living there for four years. I knew all about it. My mom just liked to be cautious and have everything planned to a T. Especially, when it came to Jess. She felt bad about not being there for so much of her teen years. She tried to compensate with having things be perfect.

I heard the front door and saw Kyle walking back upstairs. "Couldn't find my bag, I guess I will be sleeping naked."

My eyes shot to my phone, which was still on speaker. I hit the notebook to my head.

"Uhm, Chloe? Who is that?" My mom asked with a tone of embarrassment. My mom wasn't one to get mad at things like that. If she thought I was doing it with a boy she would be thrilled. She'd be happy I was getting action or whatever. That's just the way she was. But when she didn't know about a boy she took it personal, like I was purposely not filling her in on my life. I understood where she was coming from but sometimes she didn't understand I needed to keep some things private.

Kyle looked at the phone. "Oh, great."

I shook my head at him. "Mom, this is, uh, my friend, Kyle."

"I was just kidding, Ma'am. I'm not really going to sleep naked. Just a joke," he said into the phone.

I put the phone off speaker.

"Who is Kyle, Chloe?" She sounded genuinely interested, this time.

"Mom, I just told you. He is a *friend*." Kyle looked at me as he sat next to me on the bed. "Mom, I gotta go."

"Gotta go hook up with your friend, Kyle?" She laughed.

"Mom!" I laughed, too. "If I tell you he's my boyfriend will you leave me alone?"

"I will. If you tell me about it tomorrow."

"Fine!"

We said goodbye and I hung up. Kyle was now lying down on my bed, his head resting on my pillow.

"She seems cool," he said.

I lay down next to him. "She really likes to know about my dating life. Which has been non-existent for the past three years, so this news just…" I motioned to a brain exploding, "blows her mind."

I rested my head on his chest and he wrapped his arm around me.

"It's actually a relief to tell people you're my boyfriend. Holding it in feels worse." He rubbed my arm. "You know what, Kyle? Maybe this is it! Maybe it's time for the next step."

"What's that?"

"I think I'm ready to tell everyone about us."

Chapter 16

"Really? It's only been a couple days."

I sat up. "Well, I don't mean everyone. I mean my family." He sat up, too. "I thought that keeping us a secret wouldn't be so hard and I thought it really was what I wanted to do. Don't get me wrong, I'm not ready to tell your fans. But, I am ready to tell my family. Rachel already knows, my mom now knows, and Jess and my dad will find out when I go to Massachusetts."

Kyle looked at me and then over at Sam's poster.

"If you don't want me to tell them exactly who you are I won't."

He looked back at me. "No, it's fine. Is anyone in the family a fan of the band?"

"Not that I know of. My mom and dad probably know who you are but they deal with famous people all the time, they don't get star struck. I'm not too sure about Jess, though. I haven't ever heard her mention you."

He nodded. "Then it will be a piece of cake, no big deal." He smiled. "Sam was probably the hardest to convince that we were just normal people so if we got past that we can get past this."

The next morning, I headed to class. Kyle left early to get back down to San Diego. The guys had planned to do a surprise acoustic show in Disney the following night. Althoridge was just about twenty minutes from Disney so I planned on going. I texted Sam mid-afternoon to see if she wanted to come but she had already made plans with Lindsey. Erica was busy, too, with practice.

Just when I thought I would have to go by myself, Tyler texted me.

It read: *Sam told me you were going to Disney tomorrow night to see the guys perform. Still need a date?*

I answered: *Yeah actually that would be great. I'll meet you outside my place at 5pm.*

Tyler and I never really spent too much time together. Of course, I had hung out with him and Sam on multiple occasions but I had only hung out with him one on one a couple of times. We did spend a lot of time together junior year, in September, because we were planning a surprise party for Sam. It was a lot of fun.

We rented a hall and had a DJ. Her family was even able to come because they lived so close.

I didn't know too much about Tyler, though, just what Sam had told me. I should have probably learned more since he was going to be my best friend's husband.

He got there at five on the dot and insisted on driving. The car ride was quiet. Just small talk about classes and of course Sam and the wedding.

Kyle had told me to meet him outside the park, on the main road before the entrance, at five thirty. It was five twenty-five now.

"They should be here soon," I said as I glanced at my phone.

"Are you nervous?" Tyler asked as he put his hands in his pockets.

Why would I be nervous? I was just going to be out in a public place with my famous boyfriend where there would be thousands of fans. They would see Kyle and me, together. Maybe make assumptions, maybe not. Maybe they had seen the video of me onstage, maybe not.

"No, I'm not thinking about it." I looked away from him.

He laughed, "Thinking about what?"

"Oh. Just thinking about if his fans will recognize me or if they know I'm his girlfriend. Maybe they won't and maybe they don't. But I'm not thinking about it." I could hear the nerves in my voice. I wasn't fooling anyone.

"Well, Chloe, I'm not exactly an expert on this but if you don't want anyone to know about you and Kyle we don't have to go in, or we can stay far away."

He really was trying to make me feel better and I did appreciate it. "But I can't be like Sasha! I don't want that!"

He looked really confused.

"What I mean is, I don't want to hide behind him. I'm not ready for his fans to know that I'm his girlfriend but I'm not willing to stand to the side and not be a part of his life." I exhaled loudly. "I just want to go in and listen to my boyfriend play music. If they recognize me, cool, if they don't, even better. But I can't let this stuff get to me, it will just ruin my relationship." I really believed in what I was saying. I already decided after I talked to Sasha that I didn't want to be in the background of Kyle's life, I wanted to be part of it, no matter what that meant for his fans and me.

"Then, I think you're ready to go in," Kyle said. He was standing right behind me and I hadn't noticed.

"Kyle!" I playfully hit him. "Don't sneak up on me! You scared me half to death."

"I'm sorry!" He put his hands up in surrender.

Cam, Luke, and Jake were on the other side of the entrance. "Okay!" I said. "Let's go!"

Once we got inside, we went toward Main Street and their guitarist sat down on a bench. He started playing and the guys joined in one by one. More people would walk up to them and realize who they were. Their bodyguard was standing next to the bench and he screamed, "It's Big Time Elevation!" After that they were swarmed with girls.

Tyler and I stood next to the screaming girls. The guys would bring some of them up to sit next to them on the bench. It was starting to feel more normal to have girls scream over my boyfriend. None of them even looked at me, which I was more than thrilled about. I tried not to think about it too much but then every time a girl looked in my direction I could feel my heart speed up a little bit.

The guys ended the set and said goodbye to everyone. A bunch of girls swarmed to get autographs but their bodyguard politely turned them away.

"Sam keeps texting me. I should head back. Are you okay getting a ride back?" Tyler said as the girls started to disperse.

"Yeah, the guys can give me a ride back. Thanks so much for coming. I enjoyed the company." I smiled at him.

"Anytime, Chloe. Take care." He headed toward the exit.

I turned around to see no more girls in a close proximity. Just a few near the main stores.

"Well, that was totally awesome," Cam said as he waved goodbye to their guitar player.

"What'd ya think, Glow?" Jake asked as we started walking toward the castle.

"It was amazing. You guys did a great job. It's so nice that you do this."

"We like to give back to the fans as much as we can," Luke said.

After walking for a few minutes, Cam, Luke, and Jake decided they were going to the right to look for some rides. Kyle and I were going to go straight through the castle and he would take me home after.

"So, I've been meaning to ask you something," I said as we passed the 'Peter Pan' ride. "You mentioned something about your grandfather the other day but you've never said anything else about him. Do you not want to talk about it?"

"I don't mind. I just don't usually talk about him that much. I was never really close with my mom's dad." A group of little kids ran by us, with their mothers chasing after them. "My grandfather never believed in me, really. When he found out I wanted to be a singer and actor he just shut the door on me. He didn't even talk to me, he told my mom it was stupid to let me do this."

"That must have been hard."

He nodded. "I couldn't believe someone I had looked up to for so long would just lose faith in me and discourage my dreams."

"Did he ever tell anyone why he felt that way? Why he didn't want you to be a singer or actor?"

"No. But I have a pretty good guess. My grandmother used to be on Broadway, many, many years ago. My mom wasn't even born then. But she told my mom stories about how it ruined her life. My grandma changed a lot when she was done with it. She was a totally different person, and was completely miserable." He paused. "But that was her. And that was Broadway so many years ago! It's like he doesn't get that that's not what I'm doing at all. He didn't even give me a chance to explain." He glanced at me. "But I haven't seen him since the stroke, I'm nervous to. I mean, my mom says he's doing okay but I still feel like I should see him."

I reached for his hand. "Any time you want, I'll go with you."

"That means a lot." He kissed my forehead. "Thanks."

We walked toward 'It's a small world'. The line was short. It was still January so there were no tourists.

"This was my favorite ride. When I was ten, my family went to Disney, in Florida. I was obsessed with this ride. I would just keep getting back in line after I got off. Rachel stayed with me the first three times but then she got sick of it." I smiled looking at the outside of the ride. "I did that for five straight hours. I probably went on it a total of twenty times. They couldn't tear me away. It just felt like the safest place in the world."

"My favorite has always been 'The Tower of Terror'!"

I laughed. "I've never been on it. Is it scary"

"Nah, it's super fun. You just go up really high and then drop down really fast."

"That doesn't sound so bad."

"But then they open the top windows and you can see all of the theme park."

I cringed. "Okay, that seems bad! What if you fall out the window?"

"You don't. I don't think anyone has. We'll go together, sometime."

I smiled. Having something to look forward to was nice. I had never really planned anything exciting since I was little. While in California, I just lived a normal life, nothing too exciting. I had only been to the California Disney once, sophomore year when Rachel came to visit. But even then I wasn't too excited about it. Rachel liked rollercoasters and I hated them. I loved spinning rides and Rachel would get sick. So I knew that when we went together it wasn't going to be the best of times. It ended up being okay though, we actually had a lot of fun.

After Kyle and I went on 'It's a small world', just once, we went on a couple other rides before he drove me back to school.

"So, I'll see you next week in New York," Kyle said as he walked me to my front door.

"Yeah, and I'm gonna talk to my dad this weekend about having you guys on the show." I looked up at him. "My mom would probably love to meet you if you have time."

"Of course. I'll make time." He kissed me on the forehead. "This week will fly by. And I'll call you every day. We can video chat, too, so I can see your gorgeous face." He rubbed his hand up and down my cheek.

"I'll see you next Friday." We kissed and I hugged him as tight as I could.

"Bye, babe," He said as he let go and started walking toward his car.

I woke up the next morning with a voicemail from my mom. She was wondering why I still hadn't called her back since the last time we talked when she found out that I did, in fact, have a boyfriend. Sam was still asleep. She had class in a couple of hours so she needed her rest.

I went downstairs, sat on the couch, and called my mom.

"Finally! What do you think you're doing not calling me back? You agreed to call me on Wednesday!" She said.

"I'm sorry, Mom, I was busy. That's no excuse, I know, I should have called you. Sorry." I looked out the window.

"So tell me about the boyfriend! You've only been at school for two weeks, how did you manage to snag one, already?"

"Well, I didn't really *snag* him. We just met a couple days after I flew back, here, for school. He's really sweet."

"What else? Give me the juice!" In regards to relationships this was my mother's favorite line. *Give me the juice.* If a relationship seemed interesting to her she was all about it. She kept mum about pretty much everything else except romantic relationships.

"Not much else, Mom. I didn't tell you because I didn't want you to make a big deal out of it. It's not a big deal. He's a guy, I'm a girl, and we're dating. The end." I kept looking out the window. I thought I saw someone pass by but I couldn't tell who it was.

"Chloe, forgive me, but you haven't had a boyfriend since Ryan and I just want you to be happy. You're the next one in line to get married, keep that in mind."

"Mom!" I shrieked. "Stop talking like that. I'm not thinking about marriage. I'm only twenty-one. Just because Rachel got married right after college doesn't mean I will. Please, Mom, don't start with this."

Now, I was sure there was someone outside but why didn't they knock? Were they eavesdropping on my conversation with my delusional mother?

"Chloe, I'm really not trying to make you upset," she said with a serious tone. "When will I get to meet him?"

"Uh, actually probably next week. He'll be in New York. I'll be there, too." I started walking toward the door. "I'll call you back later today, Mom, okay?"

"No, I'll be busy with work the rest of the day. Just email me."

"Okay." I hung up as I reached for the door and snatched it open.

Nobody was there. I could have sworn someone walked by. Our townhouse was sort of on a dead end. It was just grass on one side of the house, no way to get to the road. So whoever walked by was still around here. They didn't walk back in front of the house, I would have seen them.

"Hello?" I called out. I started walking outside toward the back of the house.

"Is there someone here?"

Sure enough as soon as I turned the corner to the backyard, Ryan was there. He was wearing a black t-shirt and blue jeans. He was holding an ipad, sitting at our patio table.

"What are you doing here?" I said as I stormed over to him. "You can't keep coming around here uninvited. That's called trespassing."

His dark brown hair was glistening in the sunlight and his blue eyes were staring straight at me.

"I've just been wanting a chance to talk to you. That's all I was trying to do. Please, give me a chance?"

"Where have you been sleeping? If you say out here I might just scream."

"No, I was staying at a hotel. I've just been coming around here to catch you. You blew me off before I could even explain." He stood up from the table and started walking toward me.

"*Don't* come any closer." I put my hand up. "I'll listen."

"I came here for you. I came to tell you that I need you in my life again. It doesn't feel right without you." He reached his ipad out for me to take.

I took it. On the screen was sent emails from his email address. There must have been a hundred sent to my old email. I opened the first one, dated three years ago.

Chloe,

I made a mistake when I left you. I was immature and stupid. I thought that I needed someone with me, not someone that lived a plane ride away. I thought I could cope without you. I realize that dating your friend was wrong. But I just wanted a piece of you with me at all times. This is ridiculous I know, and I don't expect you to forgive me or forget what I did. I just want you to know how sorry I am.

Love,
Ryan

"Do you still feel this way?" I asked him as I looked up from the screen. He was still keeping his distance but I could tell he wanted to move closer.

"I wouldn't be here if I didn't. I just needed to tell you in person how much I miss you."

I stood there for a moment, thinking. Thinking about that day he broke up with me, about the day I found out about Nadine, about how he just showed up out of the blue, years later, to tell me he made a mistake.

"Why are you doing this now?"

He shrugged. "My life is useless now. I have nothing. I couldn't even focus at school so I quit. I'm working for my parents' restaurant. I've just come to realize how empty my life is without you in it."

"I don't know what to tell you," I said as I handed him back his ipad. "I'm really happy. I'm in a good place right now. I found a guy that wants to make me happy and will do anything to keep it that way." I adjusted my shirt, just remembering now that I was still wearing my pajamas. I tried to pretend I knew the whole time.

"So you *are* dating that guy!" He had a sense of realization to his voice.

"I'm sorry, am I missing something?"

"I saw you with that guy last night. I thought maybe he was your boyfriend but I thought, *no way*. I didn't think you would go out with someone like that."

"Someone like *what*, exactly?" I put my hands on my hips.

"A celebrity! I know that guy. He's from that band. My sister loves them…ah I can't think of the name but that's not important. How could you date someone like that?"

"First of all, you don't even know him. Second of all, who are *you* to make assumptions about *my* life?"

He put his hands up. "I know, Chloe, we haven't talked in years. It's my fault, though, can we just move past this?"

"No!" I practically screamed. "Ryan, I don't want you in my life at all. I want nothing to do with you. I don't care how sorry you are. The only thing I wanted to know was why you did all those things to hurt me, it just made no sense."

"I didn't mean to hurt you. The distance was just hurting me too bad. I didn't know what you were doing and I felt like I just lost you."

"But you didn't. I was there and willing to put myself on the line for you. I was the only one trying to make it work." I shivered as I looked at the ground. "Then, you went after Nadine."

"Chloe, I really am sorry. Dating Nadine was just a way of being close to you still." He stepped forward, hesitantly. "I didn't come here to defend my actions because I know they were all wrong. I take blame. But I wanted to see you and…I don't know, just seeing you I thought would help me figure out what I wanted."

I looked up at him. "Well, last time seeing me didn't help with much."

We stood there quiet for a minute.

"Well, Ryan, I need to get inside, I have things to do today. If you have nothing else to say then I think you should go home and get on with your life."

It seemed like a harsh thing to say but honestly the last thing I wanted right then was Ryan following me around because he thought he still needed me.

"But, Chloe, you belong with me! You shouldn't even be with this guy, he isn't like us, trust me."

I glared at him. "You need to just go back to Boston. I live here, you live there. We've been over this before, it's kind of the reason you dumped me in the first place, right?"

"Yeah, but you don't really want to live out here the rest of your life, I know you. You'll want to move back to Boston."

I shook my head. "No, Ryan, I don't. I'm living here. You need to just accept it." I sighed.

He took another step closer. I almost stepped away but then against my better judgment, I stayed where I was. He was only about arms-length away and his eyes looked pained.

"Chloe, I've grown a lot since I last saw you. I don't want you to get hurt and I'm only thinking about you. This guy you're dating, he's eventually going to leave you. You aren't part of that world."

"Ryan," I said as I took a step closer, this time. "There was a point where I thought that." I smiled. "But, now, I know better."

He looked disappointed as if he knew what I was saying was right.

"You can do whatever you want but if you really do care about me at all, you will let me be happy. You won't interfere with my relationships, ever, no matter who it's with."

He nodded. "You're right. I just want you to be happy. But just know that I'll be around, in Boston, if you need me." He started walking toward the pathway, to the main road. The sun was starting to shine brighter through the clouds.

Just when I was about to head inside he turned around slowly and smiled as he said, "And if that kid ever breaks your heart, I know where to find him."

Chapter 17

The following week, Sam and I started making plans for April Spring Break. We planned a week in Maui at the most gorgeous resort. We had both been saving up since freshman year and hadn't gone on any other vacations. We both knew that Senior Spring Break would be the one that would be most important.

After freshman year, Sam and I had planned on moving in together once we graduated. But now that she was going to be getting married this summer, it changed everything. I was starting to worry about who I would live with. But I couldn't tell Sam that, she was so happy. I would eventually figure something out and find someone to live with. It just wasn't the right time to start looking.

Kyle and I video chatted every day and he called me after each concert. It was now Wednesday and he was in Connecticut. I was flying out to New York tomorrow, after my class. My plane wouldn't leave until nine at night so I would get to New York at about six in the morning, Eastern Time. The jet lag would probably throw me off a little bit but I had done the back and forth from New York to LA so many times that I was used to it.

Once I arrived in New York, Friday morning, I grabbed my bags in the terminal and headed outside. I hopped in a cab and headed to my mom's apartment.

I was pretty well rested. I fell asleep at about eleven, California time, which was two in New York time, and I slept the rest of the flight. I didn't need much sleep. I had always been really good with a few hours. I was still tired but I could manage until later.

Kyle was probably still asleep. They left Connecticut yesterday at about nine in the morning because they had some interviews and then another CD signing in Long Island. After the CD signing they headed west and stayed in the city for the night. The guys' hotel was in Times Square, literally, which wasn't too far from where my mom lived. My mom was about sixteen blocks from Times Square or a five-minute cab ride. He said he would come over to visit around noon.

Since the guys were performing tomorrow night too, they booked their interview and CD signing for tomorrow. It worked out so that we could spend most of the day together.

I got to my mom's in about thirty minutes. She would be home since she left for work at about seven thirty. I rode up the elevator to the twenty third floor and knocked on the door.

"Oh, Chloe," she said as she opened the door. She looked around the hallway. "Is the boy not here with you?"

I rolled my eyes. "No, Mom, he'll be here at noon, when you're at work." Her face went from excited to disappointed in all of two seconds. "Mom, he's coming by tomorrow, too, you'll see him then." I stepped inside and put my bags on the floor next to the couch.

She headed over to the kitchen toward the latte machine. Yeah, *latte* machine. "Well, what are you guys gonna do today?" She started the machine.

"I don't know. Probably walk through Central Park or something, grab a bite to eat."

"He has a show tonight, you said?"

"Yeah, it's at Radio City at seven I think. But I'm meeting him over there at like six." I opened the fridge. Of course there was barely anything in it.

The latte machine started making noise. "Oh, okay," my Mom said as she ran her fingers through her ponytail. "Well, I'm gonna hop in the shower, I just got back from a great run in Central Park. You kids have fun tonight. I probably won't be back until late. We're working on snagging a new client, if we get her it will be huge!" She grabbed a mug, put it under the machine, and pressed a button.

"That's great, Mom. I think I'm going to take a short nap before Kyle gets here so I'll see you later. Good luck with the client." I picked up my suitcase and started heading toward the guest room.

"And don't forget to call your sister. She's already called me twice this morning to remind me to remind you to call her."

Rachel lived five blocks from my mom. It was a five-minute walk. I was surprised she wasn't here already, waiting for me. She had been texting me all week about how she couldn't wait to see me and how she really wanted to meet Kyle. She worked at a preschool right around the corner from her apartment but she had Fridays off.

I put my suitcase in the corner of the room and looked out the window. My mom had to have one of the best views of New York City. It was weird to think that my dad would be moving in here in July. This had always felt just like my mom's place. Or maybe they would move to a different apartment. I wondered how my dad felt about it.

I set my alarm for eleven thirty and fell asleep. When I woke up, I showered and got ready. I really was getting better at the whole makeup thing and I didn't feel like a clown anymore when I wore it. I didn't put too much on anyway, just some eye makeup, blush, and a little lip-gloss. I didn't have a need to put on foundation and all that other cakey stuff. I was lucky enough to have even toned skin and I hardly ever broke out.

Just when I finished clipping my necklace clasp my Mom's house phone rang, it had to be Rachel.

"Hey," I answered.

"Hi, Chloe! I'm so glad you answered. Did Mom tell you to call me?" Rachel said.

"Yeah, but I just got up from a nap, I'm going out with Kyle soon," I said as I looked at a post-it note that was on the counter. It was a list of things to pick up at the food market. I guess my mom hadn't had time to get there. It had a lot of my favorite foods on it.

"What were you guys planning to do?" She sounded more excited with every word.

"Central park, food, something simple. We can stop by sometime if you want?"

"That would be great! I've been looking forward to meeting him and I can't wait to see you. Whenever you guys want just stop by, I'll be here all day. Todd's at work so it's just me."

"Okay. I'll text you when we start to head over. It will probably be around three."

Right after we hung up, Kyle called me to let me know he was downstairs. I quickly grabbed my purse and got on the elevator. My heart started beating faster, which was ridiculous. It had only been a week since I saw him, but I guess that's the longest we had ever been apart so far.

Once I got to the lobby, Kyle was sitting on a couch playing with his phone. He didn't see me.

"Well, hello there," I said as I stepped closer.

He looked up and smiled. He stood and gave me the biggest, best hug I had ever gotten. It's hard to explain, but if you ever got a hug you would want it to feel like that. I just melted in his arms. He kissed me.

"I missed you," he said as he brushed the hair out of my face.

"I missed you, too." I couldn't help but smile. I felt like I was floating. Here I was, with the most amazing guy and he was telling me he missed me. I couldn't remember the last time a guy ever said that to me. Oh, wait. Ryan did just the other day. But that was different. I didn't miss Ryan, it was one sided. I missed Kyle and he missed me, and there was this electric feeling that I had when he was pulling me closer. With Ryan it was like we were opposite magnets pulling apart.

"You look beautiful." He took my hand and we started walking outside.

"Thanks." I blushed. Quickly changing the subject I said, "So, I thought we could walk around Central Park and then find something to eat."

"That sounds perfect to me. I have never walked through there before." We got outside and crossed the street.

"Me either! I feel like I should have by now. My mom has lived here for eight years, and I come around here enough." I thought about that, my mom living here for eight years. I seriously couldn't believe it had been that long. If I missed Kyle after one week I couldn't imagine how much my parents missed each other.

"When is your dad moving here?"

"July. I was just thinking earlier about how weird it's gonna be when this is actually my parents' home and not just my mom's. Like when I come home for Christmas this is where it will be." I shook my head. "I just can't wrap my mind around it. It's so weird. I do like the city a lot but I just can't picture my *home* being here."

He nodded as we crossed another street. "I'm sure it will be weird for your dad, too. But eventually, over time, things will start to feel more normal, again. Just like when your mom first moved here and you didn't live with her anymore. I'm sure it's easier to deal with now than it was when it first happened."

"Yeah, you're right." I smiled.

We walked to the *Boathouse* restaurant and ate there for lunch. Once we were done eating, we headed over to my sister's.

"So, I told my dad about you guys. I talked to him on the phone yesterday," I said as we walked toward the street.

"Awesome! What happened?"

"I told him about the four of you and how I had become friends with you," I hesitated. "Then I told him I was dating you."

Kyle looked at me. "What did he say? Was he okay with it?"

"Actually," I said as I looked down at the ground. "He was. He said he knew exactly who you guys were. He always gets requests to play your music and he would love to have you on the show. He's really looking forward to meeting you." I smiled.

"Wow, that's great! The guys will be happy." He took my hand. "I'm glad he's okay with us." I could hear the relief in his voice. I guess meeting your girlfriend's father is scary. I remember Ryan being scared to meet my dad. My dad was pretty laid back, though. He and my mom had never had any rules for my dating life. I was pretty lucky. They were harder on Rachel but that was probably just because she was their first, they learned a lot from her.

We stopped in front of Rachel's building. "Well, this is it." I turned to face Kyle. "My sister gets overly excited about things, especially about boys, boyfriends, that sort of thing. She might ask you a million questions but whenever you want to leave or something just let me know, just say you have to get ready for the show or something."

He kissed my forehead. "I'm sure she's not that bad. And besides, I can handle it. You mean more to me than anyone and if this is your family they are a part of my life, too."

I smiled. "Why are you so adorable?" I kissed his lips.

We rang the bell and Rachel let us in. We took the elevator to her apartment on the fifth floor. It had been a long time since I had been to her apartment. Everything looked different, even Rachel. She always had this pep about her but today it seemed even peppier.

Kyle and I were still holding hands as we sat on her couch. She had gone to the kitchen to get us something to drink.

"Is there something in particular you'd like?" Rachel said as she popped her head from the kitchen counter. Her apartment was an open floor plan, so no matter what room you were in you could hear or see everything else.

"I'll just have water," I said as I slid back into the couch.

"Me too," Kyle said as he rubbed his fingers along mine.

If I were in his shoes, meeting his family, my hands would be shaking, just like they were before I met Sasha. I was terrible at meeting new people, but Kyle was so natural at it. I guess, that was one of the things that drew me to him. He always seemed so at ease.

I pulled my knees into my chest and curled up into Kyle. I rested my head on his chest as he kept rubbing my fingers. I could feel his heartbeat in my ear, steady as ever.

I glanced at the coffee table in front of us. It had three picture frames on it. One of them was Rachel and Todd, I think from last summer. The second one was of Todd's family, his mom, dad, and brother. The last photo was of my family. The picture was taken at my high school graduation party. Mom, Dad, Rachel, and Jess were all there. It was one of the best times I had ever had with my family. But they had to practically tie me down to get me in the picture. It came out pretty decent, though.

"Okay, here you go," Rachel said as she came around the corner. She stopped and tilted her head. "You two are so adorable!" She squealed. She handed us the glasses and sat on the recliner across from the couch.

"Thanks," Kyle said as he took a sip and put the glass on a coaster before placing it on the table. "You have a great apartment. I never knew New York City apartments could be this large. I thought they were all teeny tiny."

"It's funny you would say that." She started to say as she fluttered a golden blonde lock of hair off her shoulder. "Todd is a contractor so he got the landlord to agree to knocking down two other apartments to get this one. So this is basically three apartments! Of course, Todd also had to upgrade the landlord's apartment as well but it was well worth it!"

I cleared my throat. My sister could go on and on about any topic you gave her so I needed to change the subject before she started talking about china patterns for two hours. "So, why don't you ask Kyle about the band? I know you wanted to know all about it."

Her face lit up. She asked him a lot of questions, ranging from their music to their television show. I almost forgot Kyle was an actor, too. So far, I had really only seen the music side of his job, except for that one Valentine's episode.

It was around four o'clock and Kyle had to head back to the hotel to start getting ready for his show. As we walked toward the door Rachel leaned into me for a hug as she said, "It was great to see you, Chlo. I know it's not convenient to come all this way just to visit me but it means a lot." I smiled as she leaned in toward Kyle for a hug. He gladly accepted. "Kyle, it was so nice to meet you. I look forward to seeing one of your shows someday."

"Well, you're more than welcome to come to the one tonight. It starts at seven. Chloe will be there, too," Kyle said as he rubbed my back with his hand.

"I'd love to come! If that's okay with you, Chlo?"

"Of course. Come to mom's place at five forty five and we'll take a taxi down."

Kyle and I started walking back to my mom's apartment.

"I like your sister. She seems pretty incredible," Kyle said as we stopped at the crosswalk. "You're just like her."

"What?" I practically screamed. "Are you nuts, we are nothing alike!"

"Hello, outsiders perspective, remember? You can't see it because you're in the situation. But you and Rachel are like," he said as he interlaced his fingers together. I glared at him. "Glare all you want but I think so, and it's not a bad thing. Did you hear me say I thought she was incredible?"

"You think I'm *incredible*?" I asked as we crossed the street. "Incredible could mean a lot of different things. Like incredibly terrible, incredibly exhausting, incredible?"

Kyle started singing a verse from 'I could not ask for more'.

"Really? Edwin McCain?" He nodded. "That doesn't answer how incredible I am!"

We were outside my mom's apartment. There were a lot of people and I thought some of them were recognizing him.

"I gotta go, babe. I'll see you before the show," he said as he pulled me tightly into him. His arms were wrapped around my waist. He moved his hands into my hair as he kissed me, passionately. These kisses were starting to stir up different feelings inside me. Each time he had kissed me had felt better and better but this time I wanted more. I didn't want him to stop. I wanted him then and there.

Our lips parted but I kept him close to me. "Babe, I really do have to go. I'll see you in, like, an hour." His eyes were locked with mine. I was biting my lip, couldn't he tell I wanted more? Or maybe I just wasn't thinking clearly. The kiss was just good, better than the rest. It was New York. It was getting dark and romantic. My emotions were doing this to themselves.

But what if I was thinking clearly and I was ready for this, ready to take our relationship to the next level? People always said, when you think it's right you're supposed to go with it, not plan everything. But it was bad timing. He had a show in three hours. Maybe it wasn't right. There should be a manual for that stuff!

"I…I…think people are starting to recognize you," I managed to stutter.

"I think you're right. Which is why I have to go, now," he said as I held him tighter. He laughed.

"No! You can't go. I'll just be alone in my mom's place. Let me go with you, please?" I gave him the best sad puppy dog eyes I could.

"What is this about?" He raised an eyebrow.

"I know I'm being weird but I can't talk about it out here in front of everyone." I took my eyes off of his and looked around. Great, there were even more people surrounding us and there was a whole cluster of kids in the corner gawking. But I didn't let go of him.

I could see Kyle still watching me out of the corner of my eye when I heard him say, "Okay, let's grab a taxi."

Chapter 18

We took the cab to Kyle's hotel, where all the guys were staying. They each had their own room this time. Kyle was on the tenth floor. Once we got there, he opened up the door and we walked inside.

"Okay, spill," Kyle said as he smirked at me. "I don't have a clue what's up with you."

"I don't either, really, but just after we kissed outside my mom's building I got, like, a flood of feelings." I took off my jacket and threw it on the sofa.

"What kind of feelings?" Kyle asked as he took off his shoes and walked over toward me. We both sat down on the bed.

"Everything has been totally normal and I haven't thought about anything. But then tonight, you kissed me and I just…"

"Wanted more?" He finished for me.

My eyes lit up. "Yes! Did you feel that way, too?"

He nodded as he put his hand on my knee. "I love kissing you, it's like one of the best feelings ever. But tonight it was different. I didn't want it to stop."

"Bad timing, though," I said as I looked at the ground. "It's already four thirty."

He stroked his fingers up and down my thigh. "Do you think you can hold it until tonight, after the show? We can do things to get out of that…zone."

"But I don't want to get out of it!"

"Babe," He said as he turned my face toward his. I loved that he was calling me that. My heart sped up every time he had done it today. It made it that much harder to tone down my desires. "I'm sure this feeling won't go away for good. I'll do the show, we'll come back here and we'll just ease into it. All it took was one kiss, right?"

I nodded. "But you can't touch me, it's turning me on." I took his hand off my leg and off my face and put them on his lap. "Ahh, why could this amazing kiss have waited to appear until after the show?" I threw myself onto his bed.

He got up and walked across the room. "Think of it this way, once the concert is over, we have all night to be together and I don't have that radio interview until noon, so we have time to sleep."

I closed my eyes and tried to think of other things. I thought about the guys and what they were doing, what my sister, Jess, would be doing, my dad, my mom. "Uh, nothing is working!"

Just as I said that I felt a heaping pack of cold fling on me. I opened my eyes, it was an ice pack. "Really? An ice pack? You think that is going to help?"

"Yeah, put it on your stomach, it will take your mind off of anything," Kyle said as he took some clothes and headed into the bathroom.

I did as he said and put the ice pack on my stomach. "Why my stomach?" I asked.

"Because your head would just give you a brain freeze and your stomach is in between your heart and your…you know," he said through the door.

"How do you know so much about this?"

"I've heard stories."

"From?"

"Who do you think?"

"Jake?" I guessed as I stayed on my back staring at the ceiling. I was afraid to sit up. I thought the feelings would come back again.

"Good guess," Kyle said as he came out of the bathroom.

"So Jake tells you about how he puts ice packs on his stomach when he wants to not have sex."

Kyle burst out laughing. "No. I've heard stories *about* this from him. Do you really want to go into discussion about this?" He came over and sat next to me. I was still staring at the ceiling. I could feel him move his hand closer toward mine.

"Stop!" I practically screamed.

"Sorry, I forgot!" He shot up from the bed and walked away.

I sat up. He was scrolling through his cell phone. "I think I know what I want to call you."

He looked over to me, phone in hand. "What is it?"

"K," I said as I took the ice pack off my stomach. "I want to call you K, like the letter K."

He looked back at his phone as he smiled. He kept scrolling.

"Did you hear me?" I flung the ice pack at him. He looked up just in time to catch it but kept scrolling.

"Kyle, I came up with a name for you. That wasn't easy for me. It took me like a week. And you have nothing to say about it?" I walked over toward him.

"You wanna see something?" He held out his phone for me. I had seen this before, it was his twitter page.

"What am I looking at?"

"What's the last tweet say?" He almost touched my shoulder but then he caught himself.

"It says 'You glo like no other, baby' but you spelt glow wrong." I looked up at him. He had a grin on his face. You glo like no other, baby. "Are you referring to me? I'm glo?"

"You're my glo, baby!" He said as he reached his arms up. "I really wish we could touch, right now!"

"So you posted that on twitter and no one knows what it means."

"Except Cam, Luke, and Jake, obviously. It's just my secret message to you. And it's my way of sharing with my fans without actually sharing." I could tell not touching me was killing him. He started walking backwards.

"That's so sweet! Thank you."

"And I changed your name in my phone to 'Baby' I hope that's okay. You're my baby. I just feel…right when I call you that. Is it okay?"

I nodded. "It's okay with me, baby."

I texted Rachel earlier to meet me outside Radio City around six since I wasn't at my mom's apartment like I thought I would be.

We met the guys in the lobby and started walking. It was snowing outside. Kyle was the only one who seemed to care. He looked sad, though, and his hand looked lonely. So I made an exception. I took his hand in mine and instantly he was another person. He squeezed my hand for appreciation.

"It's only a couple blocks. Like two, I think," Cam said as he led the way.

"I can't believe we are actually playing here, tonight," Luke said as he pulled his coat tighter. "This is like so surreal."

"It's gonna be totally awesome!" Jake said enthusiastically.

"You're lucky you have someone to share it with," Cam said as he nudged Kyle.

"No way. You guys have this to share with each other. Kyle isn't sharing this with me. Heck, I'm sharing this with my sister," I said. "This is one of the most amazing moments of your career, tonight. Don't think about anyone but yourselves. And the fans I guess cause you wouldn't be here without them."

Once we got inside, they headed toward their dressing room.

"I'm gonna go wait for my sister outside. Have a good show guys!" I said as I stopped in the dressing room door.

"So, you know where you're sitting?" Cam asked as he walked toward the food.

"Yeah, I'll be in the middle, close to the front. Your security guard gave me the tickets."

"Okay, well be safe, baby, and if you need anything just call or text any of us," Kyle said as I leaned in to kiss him. That surprised him, too. But it was fine. I was cooled off, now.

"Really? You guys are calling each other *baby*?" Jake called out.

"Really, Jake? Stomach ice pack?" I yelled back as I headed down the hall. I could hear them all laughing as I opened the *exit* door.

After I found my sister, we made our way to our seats. We were in the tenth aisle. I loved being able to see the show at different views each time I watched it. And, of course, I loved seeing my boyfriend having the time of his life up there.

Rachel loved it all. She was still a teenage girl at heart and would bop around as much as every other girl around us. Halfway through the concert, they set up the stools on the stage and I knew what that meant. My song.

But this time they performed it I was amazed. Almost every girl in that arena was singing along. They knew the words to this song, *my* song! Thousands of girls were singing about me and they had no idea.

Rachel had known about the song because Kyle had told her about it earlier. Once it was finished, she said, “Words did not do that song justice. That was amazing! Hang onto him, he’s a keeper.”

I glanced back up, onto the stage. At this point, they usually got changed and ready for their next set. But they were still sitting on the stools. What were they doing? I thought they were done with the surprises.

“So, Kyle, here, has requested we do a special acoustic cover for you all, tonight,” Jake said as the girls started screaming.

“Would you guys like that?” Cam asked as he waved and blew a few kisses to the audience.

The crowd was nuts. The other two shows were nothing like this one, this place got so loud!

“Have any of you guys heard of Edwin McCain?” Luke asked. There was uproar in the crowd, full of awes. “I think they like him, Kyle, let’s do this.”

Kyle started playing his guitar as well as another member of their musical band. And what came out of his lips? None other than ‘I could not ask for more’, the song he was singing to me earlier. Did he know earlier he was going to sing this or did he plan this after? Was this about our plans we had for tonight? Was he sending me a sign? Was this song for me?

I couldn’t help but cry. I was so emotional from earlier, along with the melody, the lyrics, my boyfriend singing, what felt like, just for me. But it was perfect.

Chapter 19

When the show was over, Todd picked Rachel up outside and I headed backstage to see Kyle.

All I kept thinking about, since he sang that song, was how badly I wanted him. I mean, really wanted him. The worst want you could have. The kind of want where you couldn't even think of anything else. Rachel could have told me that tomorrow aliens were abducting her and I wouldn't have even heard.

But nothing else mattered now, as I opened the dressing room door, it was just Kyle and me. And Kourtney?

What the hell was she doing here? She was sitting across the table from Jake. I didn't even see any of the other guys.

"Uh, hi?" I said as I walked into the room.

"Hey, Glow, this is uh…Kourtney," Jake said frantically as he stood up. "She came to see our show. She was in town."

"Glow?" She asked as she stood. She actually seemed kind of intimidated by me, which surprised me. Well, it was surprising that I was even meeting her at all. I thought I never would have to. But when I had pictured her in my head I thought she would be stand-off-ish.

"Chloe," I said firmly as I shook her hand. "Kyle's girlfriend. So, did you enjoy the show? What brings you to town?"

"I'm in town on business so I thought I would just stop in and see the show." She looked around carefully. She looked like she was hiding from her parents and was out past her curfew.

"Kourtney?" Kyle said as he walked in the room, without a shirt on. "What a surprise. What are you doing here?

"We've already established she's here on business, came to see the show." And she was getting one all right. This was the first time I had seen Kyle shirtless. Why did I have to share this moment with Kourtney?

Luke and Cam walked in, also shirtless. Staring blankly at Kourtney. Uh, I couldn't deal with this. I walked out into the hall and toward the exit.

"Babe, wait, don't go," I heard Kyle say behind me.

I turned around, almost out the door. "I just need some fresh air. This is a little too much for me right now."

Kyle moved closer but he was still far away. "Baby, don't go. You're coming back with me. Let me just get my stuff." He pointed back to the room.

"I don't think it's such a good idea anymore. I'm really not in the mood." I crossed my arms over my chest.

"Come on, Chlo, don't be like this. I didn't know she was going to be here. I swear," He said as he moved closer to me.

"I know. I'm not mad at you I'm just…mad. I can't believe that of all nights that I could meet her she picks this one to show up."

"Please, don't let this ruin our night. You know I sang that song just for you." He smiled so perfectly I couldn't help but smile, too.

"You did? I didn't know if you guys had just planned that a while ago or something," I said as I looked down at the ground.

"No. I told them, when you left to sit with your sister, that tonight was really special for you and me. But they already knew that after you said that thing about the stomach ice pack."

I giggled.

"So don't let her showing up ruin anything. She is a nice person. She just wanted to see the band. She doesn't have feelings for me anymore. You're just over thinking everything like you usually do." He grinned.

"Okay, fine! Let's grab your stuff," I said as we walked back toward the dressing room.

Kourtney was walking out of the room as I was about to walk in.

"Hey, Chloe," Kourtney said. "I didn't mean to upset you by showing up. I still think of the guys as my friends so I just like to show my support and come to some of their concerts. They went to mine last summer." She sighed. "I'm really glad that Kyle's happy, you two seem perfect together."

She wasn't so intimidating after all. I had built up an image in my head, when Kyle first mentioned her. And after I watched the interview of her online, I kept building on what I thought she would be like.

But she was nothing like I expected. If I had met her under different circumstances I would have never known she was famous. In the interview, she looked all done up and perfect, I figured that's what she always looked like. But I was wrong. She looked like a normal twenty year-old girl. And I could tell she had genuine intentions. She was here as a friend.

"Thanks. It was nice meeting you," I said.

"You too," she said before heading out the door.

Jake, Cam, Luke, Kyle, and I all walked back to the hotel together. Their bodyguard trailed behind us. It was still snowing and there was about an inch of snow already on the ground. Out of all the things I missed while living in California, snow was at the top of the list. There was something so peaceful and angelic about snow. It was like a reminder that everything would be okay.

Once we got inside and up to the tenth floor, we all parted ways. The guys were all on the same floor, but not connecting rooms, which I was grateful for at that moment.

I squeezed Kyle's hand as we walked toward his door. He got the key out of his wallet and slid it into the door. As the light turned green he slowly opened the door and had me walk in first. The room was glowing with candles and there were rose petals on the floor. I took my boots off and walked into the room.

"Baby, what did you do?" I asked as I turned to face him.

He shut the door behind him and put his guitar case on the floor as he took off his shoes and jacket.

It smelt so pretty, fruity with a bit of vanilla. But I could also smell the roses. I looked around the room and I couldn't believe what I was seeing. It was so romantic. I didn't know how he pulled it off but he did.

I stared longingly at the bed. I had never wanted a bed as much as I did in that moment. It was calling my name. I felt Kyle come up behind me. He slid off my jacket as he started kissing my neck. I turned to face him and put my hands in his hair.

"I want this to be perfect," I said as I played with his hair. "I want to just do what my body tells me to do. I don't want to have expectations because that's when disappointment appears. I don't know how far we will go. So let's just…" He started kissing me before I could finish. He picked me up and I wrapped my legs around him. He brought me over to the bed, still kissing me as he lay me down. He was over me but not on top of me, his body was on the side of mine. I reached for the bottom of his shirt and pulled it off. Seeing and feeling his abs sped my heart up faster and I didn't even think that was possible.

I rolled over on top of him as I took my shirt off. "Now, I'm not taking this off to tease you or anything I'm just hot and I..."

"Baby, stop talking," he cut me off as he grinned.

"But I just want you to know what I'm thinking," I said as I tried to unhook my bra.

"I already know what you're thinking. I know you," he said as he propped a pillow behind his head.

"Okay, so what am I thinking now?"

"You're thinking that you're hot and you want to get your bra unhooked but you can't," he said as he sat up, reached behind my back and unhooked it.

We were face to face. "You know what else I know?" He said, our lips almost touching.

"What?"

"I know that you avoid talking when something's bothering you. I know that you hate getting your picture taken for some reason I have yet to learn. I know that your hands shake when you get really nervous. I know that you're not afraid to speak your mind. And most importantly I know that your boyfriend would do anything to protect you and never let anything or anyone hurt you." His face was so sincere and his eyes were looking deep into mine.

I took off my bra as Kyle lay back down on the bed and we kissed again. But this time was so much more passionate than the others.

Chapter 20

Kissing passionately led to passionate lovemaking. It was the most incredible experience I had ever had. Ryan and I had been intimate with each other when we were dating years ago but it was nothing compared to that. You couldn't even compare that with anything.

We had just finished and we were lying under the covers. I rested my head on his chest as he stroked my back. I didn't even know what to say. What if it was good for me but not good for him? Was I worrying too much again? Probably.

He kissed my forehead. "That was *amazing*," he said. Oh, thank goodness.

"You really think so?" I asked as I looked up at him. "You're not just saying that? Because, I just want to make sure."

"When have I ever lied to you?" he said and then kissed my lips.

I slipped out of the covers and grabbed Kyle's shirt that was on the floor. I pulled it over my head and climbed back into bed. Kyle shot me a look. "What?" I said. "I didn't want to be totally naked while I slept."

"It's fine with me. Whatever makes you comfortable." He pulled me in close to him and closed his eyes.

"Oh crap!" I shot up.

"What is it, babe?" Kyle sat up, too.

"I completely forgot to call my mom and tell her I was sleeping here." I groaned, "I'll just text her. If I straight out tell her we had sex she won't ask any questions." Kyle laughed "I'm serious, Kyle. She's a weird mom."

"And she's not going to think any differently about me if you tell her this?"

"No, she will. She'll like you more. It's so sad but true." I grabbed my phone off the nightstand and texted her. Not a minute later she replied with: *K Goodnight. Tell Kyle I said hello.*

I showed him the text and we both laughed.

We both fell asleep quickly. I was woken up to my phone ringing. I checked the clock. It was nine. I picked up my phone and glanced at the caller ID. It was Sam. It was only six in California but then again she was usually an early riser.

"Hello?" I said still half asleep.

"Chloe! You're not going to believe this," she said.

"What? This couldn't have waited like two more hours?" I said as I crawled out of bed and toward the bathroom.

"No, it could not have! Do you have a computer?"

I looked around for Kyle's laptop. It was on the desk. I quickly picked it up, went into the bathroom and closed the door. "Yeah, I have one." I sat on the floor and opened the computer.

"Okay, go to Just Jared dot com, it's a gossip site, celeb stuff," she said with a more serious tone in her voice.

I did what she said and the page started loading. "OK? Now what?"

"Scroll like half way down the page."

I did. And there in front of me was what she was calling about. There were pictures of Kyle and me from yesterday. One was of us eating at the restaurant in the park. Another was both of us walking toward my mom's apartment and the last one was us kissing outside my mom's apartment. "What the hell?"

"I know! I checked it this morning. I do it every morning, just to, you know, check on everything that's going on in Hollywood and I almost screamed when I saw you two. You guys really do make a cute couple."

"Sam!" I yelled a little too loudly. "What do I do? We didn't want this to happen!"

"But, Chlo, you also didn't want to take a back seat to his life, remember? So this was bound to happen sooner or later. It's just sooner than we expected."

I was not prepared for that at all. I didn't even know what to think. It was pretty cool being on a website but I hated that my picture was plastered on there for everyone to see and I couldn't do anything about it. "But it's my picture! Pic-ture!"

"I *know* you hate having your picture taken. You're just gonna have to get used to it, superstar."

"So, that's it, everyone knows, now." I paused. "I don't even want to read this article," I said as I closed the laptop and put it on the floor.

"Kyle from Big Time Elevation heads out to lunch in Central Park, New York City on Friday with suspected girlfriend. The boys of Big Time Elevation, Kyle, Cam, Luke and Jake are in town performing two concerts this weekend. One last night and one tonight. Make sure you check them out, tickets still available for tonight's show. Exclamation point," Sam read.

"Sam, I seriously didn't want to know what it said! Why don't you ever listen to me?"

"Chlo, it is going to be fine. No kids ever go on this site and kids are like their main fan base. And Kyle will know how to handle it, don't worry." Maybe she was right. Maybe it would be okay. And this was what I wanted. Maybe it would be cool having people know who I was. Having my picture taken would be a negative, though.

After we hung up, I opened the bathroom door quietly and put Kyle's laptop back on his desk. He was still fast asleep. I was too awake now to go back to sleep so I threw on some clothes and headed out in the hallway. I walked toward the vending machine area. It was sort of a lounge. I took a seat on the couch and closed my eyes.

I exhaled loudly as I heard a door slam shut. I heard some footsteps headed toward me. It was Jake and Cam.

"Oh, hey, Glow! What are you doing up so early?" Cam asked as he took a seat next to me. Jake had a coffee in hand as he punched some buttons on the vending machine.

"Sam called me. She saw my picture on a website."

"What website?" Jake said as he pulled out a granola bar from the machine.

"Just Jared. They got pictures of Kyle and me yesterday. I didn't even know. I didn't see any paparazzi."

Jake sat down across from the couch as he opened up the granola bar. "Did they say who you were?"

I shrugged. "They just said I was his suspected girlfriend. But I can't be mad about this, right? We expected this. I decided to not go into hiding. So, we just have to tell people sooner than we expected."

"Well, you don't have to," Cam said. "I mean, the two of you could not say anything, avoid it, not talk about it."

"But they have pictures of us kissing. Uh, I was so stupid, why did I have to kiss him outside!" I put a hand over my eyes. "This just doesn't feel real."

"Did you talk to Kyle about it?" Jake asked with a mouth full of granola.

"No, he's asleep," I said still covering my eyes.

"Talk to him about it once he wakes up. You guys will figure it out. We're no help in this area. I have not had a girlfriend since we started the TV show, which is actually really sad. And Cam just kept his private and never even went out in public with Sasha, but you know all about that," Jake said. "But once you talk to Kyle it will start to make sense."

There was a long pause as we all just sat there. "So, how was last night? Did you guys…you know?" Cam asked as he started to laugh.

"Okay," I said as I stood up. "That's enough talking for now. I'll see you guys later!" I said as I headed back to Kyle's room.

After I read every magazine in the room and talked with Sam online for a little bit, Kyle finally woke up around ten.

"How long have you been up?" He asked as he got out of bed and stretched his arms.

"Sam woke me at nine. Do you want me to get you coffee or something?" I asked still sitting at the desk.

"Nah, I'm okay. Did you want to grab some breakfast though? I think they have a buffet downstairs we can see if the guys ate," he said as he walked over to me. He ruffled his hair. He was still shirtless and had some marks on his skin from the sheets.

"Maybe we could get room service instead?" I suggested as I stood from the desk chair.

"Why? What's going on?"

"The paparazzi got pictures of us yesterday. Eating, holding hands, kissing. They got it all, basically. And I'm just freaking out a little bit and kind of scared to go out in public. I don't know what to expect." I ran my fingers through my hair.

He stepped an inch closer and wrapped his arms around me. His skin was so warm and soft. "Don't worry. It's gonna be okay, I promise. We'll figure it out."

There was a bang at the door. "Wake up, Kyle! We have breakfast!" Cam yelled.

Cam, Jake, and Luke had brought food from the buffet up to us. There was French toast, waffles, pastries, eggs, bacon, sausages, pretty much anything you could want for breakfast.

"So, I told Kyle about the dilemma," I said as I finished chewing a piece of bacon. We were all sitting at the kitchen table. It was really little and barely fit us all but we made it work.

"You told them before you told me?" Kyle asked.

"Well, yeah, you were asleep and I didn't want to wake you, you needed sleep." I took a sip of orange juice.

"We weren't much help, though," Jake offered. "We don't know anything about this stuff."

"Well, neither do I. Cam knows the most," Kyle said while pouring more cereal in his bowl.

"I really don't, though. It was so simple. I just went to Sasha's house or she would come to mine, we never went out in public. She would occasionally come to rehearsal but only when there were barely any people there," Cam said. "All I know is you guys don't want to live like that. I mean, you told us that."

I took another sip of juice. "I just thought I would have more time to actually get used to us dating before everyone else got used to it."

"We don't have to talk about it. I don't have to bring it up. The guys won't bring it up. You won't talk to the press," Kyle said.

Cam nodded. "That's what I said."

"But then what do you say when they ask who you are kissing in those photos? Because they will ask in that radio interview today. I know they will. You can't say I'm just a friend."

Kyle paused. " I could just say I'm dating in general and you aren't my girlfriend?"

Well, that solved everything. I cringed when I heard him say that. Having him lie and say I wasn't his girlfriend to the whole world was more painful than having my picture taken and being in magazines and on websites.

"No. I want you to tell them I'm your girlfriend. I want your fans to know."

Chapter 21

“All right, so we are really doing this?” Kyle asked. It was about eleven thirty and he had just finished getting ready for the interview. He had his twitter open on his phone and had just finished typing a tweet. It read: *I have a big announcement for all the fans out there. Listen to 104.5 online or on the radio at noon eastern time today!*

We decided he would announce our relationship in the radio interview today. We knew the radio guy would ask him about it so we figured now was our shot.

“Yeah, we’re doing it. Tweet it!”

I took a cab back to my mom’s while the guys headed to the radio station. My mom was in the kitchen making pancakes.

“Whoa, did you and dad have a fight? Why are you making pancakes?” I asked as I tossed my keys on the counter.

“It’s celebration pancakes not disappointment pancakes!” She said happily as she flipped one.

“What are you celebrating?” I asked as I took a seat at the counter.

“We got the client! It’s the biggest client we have ever gotten and it feels amazing!”

“That’s great, Mom, congratulations. Who is it?”

“Well, I shouldn’t be discussing it with you, really. I have to sign a bunch of papers on Monday to make it official. So you don’t speak a word of it to anyone, okay? Especially your band friends.” She peeled a pancake off the pan and flipped it onto a plate with about five other ones. She turned off the stove and brought the plate over to where I was sitting.

I smirked. “Mom, why the heck would I ever talk about your work with anyone? Especially my band friends.”

She took a packet of syrup out from a drawer and placed it next to the pancakes. "I don't know. But you just have to understand how huge this is! I mean we are making big bucks with this girl. Like a fifty percent salary increase." She took a paper plate out from the cabinet and put it in front of me. She put two pancakes on my plate and handed me a fork and knife.

"Aren't you going to have some?" I asked as I picked up the syrup.

"No, I don't eat pancakes," she replied. I groaned. I should not have been surprised. "When am I going to meet this awesome boy of yours? I thought he was coming by today?" She said as she started the latte machine.

"He's coming by after the radio interview. And then he has to leave at three for the CD signing." I took a bite of the pancake. It was pretty gross. It wasn't cooked all the way through but then again I don't know what I expected from a woman who only cooked vegetables.

"Ah, well, I'm glad you guys had a good time last night. Man, do I miss those days, being young and crazy about a man." She picked up her cup and took a sip.

"Mom, it's not like you and Dad are divorced."

"I know, but it's not the same. I barely have time to see him, now, because I have been working from home on the weekends. That's another reason I'm so excited about this client. Instead of having five on rotation she will be the only one."

"Mom, you're kidding. The only client?"

"No, I'm serious! She's willing to pay all this extra money so that she will be our only client. I don't know why and I'm not going to ask." She shrugged. "But I know I'm going to have lots of free time, now."

It was getting close to twelve so I turned on the radio in the living room and sat on the couch. I had told Sam what Kyle and I decided and she said she would be listening, too, online.

The DJ was talking about the popular boy band craze before he introduced the guys. They all talked about the usual, new CD, concert tonight, and CD signing this afternoon. Then he played some music.

I was practically dying. I had to keep reminding myself how to breathe. My palms were all sweaty and my jaw kept clenching uncontrollably.

My mom came out of her office. “Are you really that excited that your boyfriend’s on the radio?”

I shook my head. “No, it’s just that he’s announcing something. So, I’m just nervous, I guess.”

She came and sat next to me on the couch. “Please, spill.”

I told her the long story about how I had been battling with whether to tell his fans or not. I told her about the pictures that were online and would probably be in next week’s magazines.

“So, we decided to just announce it. Rip the band-aid off,” I said as I pulled my knees into my chest.

“Good for you. But watch what you do because if you start being in these magazines everyone will associate you with me and I need to maintain my image.”

I rolled my eyes. It always went back to being about my Mom. She couldn’t stay happy for someone for more than a few hours.

“Hey, everyone, if you just tuned in this is Marky, here, in the studio, live, with the guys of Big Time Elevation, Kyle, Jake, Cam, and Luke!” The guy on the radio said. I turned up the volume.

“So, Kyle had something special he wanted to share with the listeners today, something you’ve never heard before!”

“Yeah, it’s actually top secret so this is pretty huge stuff you’re about to hear,” Jake said playfully.

“Well, without further delay, Kyle, take it away!” Cam said.

“Hey, guys. All the fans that are listening, we love you, guys, all so much. And I feel like it’s my obligation to always tell you guys the truth and never keep anything from you. I hate when I have to do that,” Kyle said.

“Don’t you just hate it?” Luke added with a chuckle.

“In all seriousness, though. If you have seen me around with a beautiful blonde haired girl in the last couple weeks she is, in fact, my girlfriend!”

There was a clapping noise added in for effect. I took a deep breath.

“That’s some serious stuff,” Jake said.

"We all totally love her so we want you all to love her, too!" Cam added.

"She's great and I know a lot of people have been asking about it on twitter and stuff so I just wanted to clear it up," Kyle said.

"So, you heard it here first, ladies, Kyle is off the market," Marky said. "So, now, we'll play their new hit 'Throw it up'. Enjoy!"

I turned the radio off. Well, my heart was still racing and I probably felt worse than I did before.

My mom turned to look at me. "Chlo, it's not the worst thing in the world. The man you're dating just basically shouted your name from the rooftop, most girls would kill for that."

She should have known by now that I was *not* 'most girls'.

Kyle got to my mom's a little after one. As he walked through the door, he looked as adorable as ever. His hair was all messy and his skin was glowing.

"How are you doing? Was that okay? What I said?" He said nervously.

"It was perfect." I stood on my tippy toes and pecked his lips.

"So, you didn't freak out at all?"

"Oh, she did," my mom said casually as she walked toward him. "She was a complete mess. But it's new territory for her and that always gets her nerves going."

Kyle reached out a hand to shake but my mom just engulfed him in a hug. "Kyle, you can just call me Sarah," she said as she released him. "You are so much cuter in person!"

"I forgot to warn you she's hot," I whispered to him. "Don't leave me for her."

Kyle laughed. "Um, yeah, Sarah, it's great to meet you. I really enjoy spending time with your daughter. She makes me laugh." He smiled as he fought back more laughter.

He stayed for about two hours and then left for the signing. Later that night, at the show, I decided to stay backstage. Pretty much all of his fans knew he had a girlfriend now, and if any of them had visited that website, like Sam did, they knew what I looked like.

After the show, the guys had to hop on the tour bus and start driving to Boston. I had decided earlier in the week that I would go with them and then fly from Boston to California, Tuesday morning. With the time difference, I would make it back in enough time to get to class.

The guys were all in their bunks, asleep. Kyle and I were in the back lounge area. We were going through his tweets together on his computer.

"Aw, I love her!" I said as I pointed to a tweet that said: *Kyle, you and your girlfriend are perfect for each other I'm so glad you found someone that makes you happy!*

"Tweet her back!" I said. "Oh, and what does this one say?"

"It says, 'You guys should make youtube videos together. We would all love to see it!'"

"They really like when you guys make youtube videos, huh?"

He nodded. "You could make your own twitter account if you wanted? I'm sure a lot of them would love to hear from you." He put his hands up in surrender. "Totally up to you, though. You could possibly get some negative tweets, too, but I honestly don't think it would be anything compared to how many of the fans already adore you."

I thought about it. It would be really cool to have people admire me and think it was awesome if I tweeted them. "That sounds fun. I'll do it, you just gotta teach me."

So, he made me an account and taught me the basics, like posting a tweet, replying to people, seeing the tweets that people sent me.

He tweeted on his phone for everyone to follow me and in seconds I was getting hundreds of followers. "How is this even possible?" I said as I glared at the computer. I kept refreshing the page and each time I clicked the button I had at least fifty more followers than the last time I clicked it.

"So, what should my first tweet be?" I tapped my fingers to my chin. I had no idea what to say to these people. And I had to be really careful about it, too. I would not only be representing myself but also Kyle, the band, and unfortunately my mom. It wasn't as easy as just typing how I felt.

"Just say, 'Hey everyone I'm Chloe, I look forward to sharing bits of my life with you.' Easy and simple."

I looked over at him. He was sitting to my left, laptop open but eyes on me. He was a little more than an arms length away but I wanted him closer.

He must have been able to tell because he put the laptop down next to him on the couch and slid over to me. He didn't say anything, just held me in his arms.

"What if we did the youtube thing? Is it weird for us to make videos together, just our everyday lives? And who knows, maybe we could have some answering people's questions they want to know about us," I said as he rubbed my back. It was so soothing it could have put me to sleep.

"I think you're onto something. The fans get really excited when we do stuff like that. It's like we are sharing a whole other part of our life. It makes them feel closer to us," he said. "Let's do one now."

I pulled away. "Really? Right now?" I was surprised. First off, I thought he wouldn't even want to do the videos. Secondly, he liked the idea so much he wanted to do it right now? "I thought we could wait till morning. Aren't you exhausted?"

"No! Come on, babe, let's do it. Just say a quick hello, shout out your twitter name and tell them to tweet us questions. The questions will come pouring in and we can pick some and shoot an answer video tomorrow, on our day off."

So we did. We filmed on his laptop.

"Hey, everyone, this is Kyle from Big Time Elevation and I'm here, now, with the lovely Chloe who many of you have heard about earlier today. She is my girlfriend. We wanted to make this youtube account to just give you a glimpse into our everyday lives."

"I just made a twitter account, ChloGlo, so go follow it and tweet Kyle and I any questions you have for us. We'll answer some of your questions tomorrow in another video so subscribe to this channel to be the first to see it!"

"We love you guys and we'll see you soon!"

"Bye!" We both said at the same time.

Kyle stopped the camera. I couldn't wait to see what questions they had for us. Having his fans know about us wasn't as bad as I thought it would be. It was actually really exciting. Not hiding our relationship, anymore, was so freeing and I felt like I could breathe again.

Chapter 22

Kyle and I fell asleep shortly after we uploaded the video. We arrived at their hotel in Boston around four in the morning. Their security guard woke us up and the guys quickly checked in. They had four separate rooms, again, so I went with Kyle to his.

The room was a lot bigger than the New York one was. It was more of a suite. It had a living room, mini kitchen, bedroom, and bathroom. We both instantly fell asleep the moment our heads hit the pillows.

When we both woke up around ten, we decided to go out to breakfast, together. I didn't think anyone would actually recognize me but I put on a pair of sunglasses, I packed, just incase. I slid into my best pair of jeans and a bright purple top Sam got me last Christmas. I finished my outfit off with my leather winter jacket. It was a cute outfit so that if someone did see us together they would at least think I was fashionable.

I never thought I would have to think about what I wore and what I looked like. That was one of the weirdest parts of this for me.

As we got off the elevator and started walking toward the exit doors, I could see two people with cameras. Were those paparazzi? And there was a group of girls on the outside of the doors, looking through the glass. Were they looking for the boys?

One of the girls shrilled when she saw us. I guess that answered that question.

Kyle grabbed my hand and squeezed it. He leaned into me as he said, "Don't freak out. These girls are probably fans and they might talk to us, so just be yourself. Think of them as just people who went to the same school as you but you were in different grade levels. And they know you but you don't know them."

As we walked toward the doors, I could feel my face flush. I felt sick to my stomach. I was over thinking it but I couldn't stop it. Over thinking was my thing. Even my boyfriend noticed. Would these girls notice, too? Would they think I was thinking too much and not actually just…wow. I really needed to stop.

Kyle kissed my forehead as the doorman opened the doors. The girls were on the right side, of course, the direction we were headed in. There were three of them. They looked about thirteen. A redheaded skinny one, a curly-haired brunette with braces, and a tall, muscular blonde.

"Oh my God! Hi Kyle!" The redhead squeaked. She had an iphone in one hand and a poster of the guys in another.

"Hello, ladies. How are you today?" He said as he stopped in front of them. I was squeezing his hand for dear life.

"We're good. We were waiting for you to come out for so long! Someone said you guys were staying here," the curly-haired one said as she tried to play it cool. "Can I have a hug?" She reached her arms out.

I let go of his hand. He rubbed my shoulder before hugging her. He pulled her in close like he did with my sister.

"Wow!" the girl said. "You really do give the best hugs."

"Can I have a hug, too?" The redhead said.

"Of course!" Kyle said as he released the curly-haired and went for the redhead. The blonde seemed shyer but she was taking pictures on her phone.

As he finished hugging the redhead, the blonde one said, "Where are the other guys? Do you think they will come out soon?"

"I'm not sure," Kyle said as he reached for my hand again. "We haven't seen them yet this morning."

"Wait! Hold on!" The brunette practically screamed. "That's Chloe! That's your girlfriend isn't it?"

Kyle nodded. "This is her."

I smiled. I didn't think they recognized who I was but it didn't surprise me that the curly-haired one was the first to say something about it.

"Can I hug you, too?" She asked already leaning in.

"Sure," I said as she grabbed on for dear life. She was more enthusiastic about this hug than she was about Kyle's. "Oh my

God, I can't believe I am hugging Chloe, Kyle's girlfriend, right now," she said still hugging me. "Hannah, take a picture!"

The blonde one focused her phone, so I guessed she was Hannah. We both turned to face the camera and smiled. Flash.

"I want one, too!" The redhead said. She changed places with curly and Hannah snapped a shot. Flash. I glanced back at Kyle, he was standing with his hands in his pockets flashing that adorable smile.

"Maggie, can you take one of me, Chloe, and Kyle?" Hannah asked the redhead.

So then Maggie, the redhead, changed places with Hannah and Kyle joined the picture, too. I couldn't believe Kyle probably did stuff like this at least once a day. Flash.

"We gotta go, guys, it was great meeting you," Kyle said as he took my hand, once again, and we started walking up the street. It all happened so fast I didn't even think about how I was getting my picture taken. And how these girls would probably worship those pictures.

We got to the restaurant without any other interruptions. We sat in the back where there were hardly any people.

After we finished eating, we headed back to the hotel. As we rounded the corner, we quickly stepped back. There had to have been at least fifty girls swarmed outside the hotel.

"They always do this," Kyle said with a chuckle. "They tweet that they saw one of us or all of us somewhere and then an hour later there's a swarm of them. Let me call Ronnie."

Ronnie was their security guy. He was always there in case too many fans were around. Kyle and I sat on a ledge around the corner from the hotel waiting for Ronnie to answer his phone.

"He's not answering!" Kyle said as he threw his hands up. "That's the fourth time I've tried him." Kyle walked back over to the corner and glanced toward the hotel.

"All right," he said as he walked back toward me. "There's a back exit I think I can get us through without anyone looking."

Before I knew it he had picked me up and threw me over his shoulder. "Kyle! What the hell are you doing?"

He started running to the hotel. Well, I think he was. I was upside down looking at his butt, which wasn't a bad view so I couldn't complain.

He went through the back door and once we were inside he gently placed me on the ground. "Sorry, that was the only way to go! Your shoes make noise, they would have heard us immediately."

"They aren't that loud!"

"Well, you're kind of a slow walker, too." He chuckled.

I playfully hit him. "I'd like to see you walk fast in heels."

Once we got back up to the room, I checked my twitter. When I clicked the button to see my 'mentions', or who had been tweeting me, the page was overflowing with tweets! The girls we met earlier must have posted the pictures they took with me because they kept showing up. A lot of people were saying how lucky those girls were that they got to meet me.

I gave my phone to Kyle. "Look at the craziness! I can't believe how many people like me so far and they don't even know anything about me!" I sat on the couch.

Kyle was still standing up staring at my phone. "You have like ten thousand followers already. That is *insane*. These girls really like you." He sat next to me on the couch and handed me back the phone.

I tucked my knees into my chest. "Should we figure out what questions we are going to answer for the video?"

"Yeah," Kyle said as he drew in a breath. "I'll check my twitter and pick like three questions and you pick three from yours." He walked over to his bag and pulled out his laptop.

After we both picked out our favorite three questions each, we started the video.

"So, are we gonna tell each other the questions before we answer them or should it be like a surprise thing?" Kyle asked before he pressed record.

"I think we shouldn't say them before hand because it's more real," I said as I adjusted my hair. I couldn't get over the fact that this was my life. I was dating a guy in a boy band and I was making youtube videos with him for his fans.

I had actually attempted to do my hair for this video. I put it in a high ponytail with lots of hairspray. I curled sections in the ponytail to give it more volume, a trick that Sam had once shown me. This was a really big deal for me. I hardly ever did anything with my hair. It was naturally straight and a lot of the time it was pointless to do anything with it because it would never stay how I wanted it.

"You look nice, by the way," Kyle said as he rubbed my leg. I was still wearing the same outfit as earlier, even though I had contemplated changing it, probably, ten times. "You always look nice but I like what you did with your hair. It's pretty when it's out of your eyes."

"Thanks, K." I smiled. "Okay, this is gonna be fun. Don't think too much about things and we can always edit things out." He shot me a look. "*You* could always edit things out…" He nodded. "…If we mess up or something. So just don't worry, OK?"

He pressed record. "Hello everybody! I'm Kyle."

I swallowed hard. "I'm Chloe."

Kyle continued, "And we are here to bring you the second video of this series thing. You guys sent in your questions and we are going to answer some of them right now."

While he was talking, I was trying not to think about the fact that thousands of people would be seeing this. Sometimes, I just wished my brain would shut off and stop thinking so much! Maybe it just took time to get used to, though. Kyle had become so natural at this stuff. Here I was, the girl who hated getting her picture taken, being filmed for her boyfriend's fans, and her own fans, now. It was still a lot to take in.

"Chloe!" Kyle said.

"Oh, yeah?"

"Why don't you read the first question," Kyle said.

I glanced at my twitter page. "Okay. So Dianapanda wants to know where we first met."

"Well," Kyle started saying as he looked from the camera to me. "Chloe and I actually met in a boutique in Althoridge, California. I was looking for just some cool clothes, I guess, and she was looking for…jeans! But that store stunk and there weren't any jeans her size so we basically spent half the day looking for jeans around town." He smiled as he looked at me. "She had no idea who I was. She didn't know I was in Big Time Elevation even though her roommate, Sam, is the biggest fan ever. Oh, by the way, hi Sam, I know you're watching this." He waved to the camera.

"Okay, Kyle, your turn to ask a question."

"All right, BigTimeElevators wants to know which one of the guys in the band you think is the funniest?"

"Hmm, tough question. They are all really funny guys, I have to say. If I couldn't say Kyle I would have to say Cam. Cam gave me the nickname. Glow. I don't even know if I'm supposed to share this top secret information." I laughed and it was hard to stop. Kyle started laughing, too. It was probably a whole minute later when we both stopped.

"Okay, okay, but seriously, Cam's funny. If I can't pick my boyfriend, I would pick Cam."

"What's so funny about me?" Kyle asked.

I sighed as I looked into his eyes. "You just have a way of making me laugh or smile all the time. I'm never not happy when I'm around you." I shrugged as I looked at the camera. "I think all you guys out there probably feel the same way around Kyle, if you've ever gotten a chance to meet him. And aren't his hugs to die for?"

Kyle chuckled. "Okay, next question!"

I slid my phone screen to the next question I picked out. "BTElover wants to know what the two of us do for fun." I went to play with a piece of hair but I forgot it was in a ponytail. I tried to casually scratch my forehead. I didn't know where to put my hands.

I looked over at Kyle, his hands were on his legs but he made it look so natural. Again, with the overthinking!

"Well, Chloe has been hanging out a lot at the shows and since the guys and I are on tour it's really hard to fit in date time as it is. But we went to Pacific Park one day and that was pretty fun." He turned to look at me. "Another fun time was when we hung out at Jake's house. We walked along the beach and it was just a great weekend."

He turned back to the camera and glanced at his phone. "All right, Kylelover asks 'Chloe, what made you want to date Kyle?'"

Kylelover, huh? I guessed this kid really liked Kyle. "Kyle was the persistent one. He wanted me to go to shows and on the road with him. It was a hard decision for us to make, to date. Especially me, I guess, because I'm not used to all the fame and everything." I smiled at him. "But he's pretty convincing. And it's worth taking a chance if you really like someone."

After we both finished with one last question, we finished the video and shut off the camera. We edited the video and had the guys come in to make sure everything was fine with it before uploading it.

My twitter had already gained a thousand more followers since I last checked. I was becoming more popular with every second. This could become dangerous, couldn't it? I could walk out of this hotel room and be swarmed. I felt like I was diving into the water with my eyes closed.

Kyle went to take a shower while Jake, Cam, Luke and I hung out in the living room. I was looking at the tweet mentions I was getting. A lot of them were asking about Kourtney. Had I met her, was I like her, what did I think of her?

"Okay, I have to ask," I said as I sat back into the couch.

"Ask what?" Cam said. He was sitting next to Luke on the other side of the room. Jake was sitting next to me.

"People keep bringing up Kourtney. And Jake's mom said the three of you couldn't stand her. So, I want to know why."

They all looked at each other but didn't say anything.

"I'm not judging, I promise! I just want to know what you didn't like about her. She seemed nice the other day. And if Kyle liked her there had to be something good about her, right?"

"It's not that we didn't like her," Luke started to say.

"She kinda just stole our best friend," Jake said as he adjusted his shirt. "She was on the show a year before she started dating Kyle."

"We tried to be friendly with her," Cam said as he motioned to the three of them. "But we were never friends. And once she started dating Kyle we barely ever saw him, except for work."

"During work he was normal, happy. The same guy you know now," Jake said. "But when he was with her he was so different. It was like she hypnotized him. We just didn't like what she did to him."

"He was always around her. And I guess part of the problem was that she would never hang out with the three of us. She wasn't friends with us, didn't want anything to do with us. She just wanted Kyle," Luke said as he fixed his baseball hat.

"So, we couldn't stand her. We were mad at what she was doing. She was ruining our friendship with him and she was ruining him! She was toxic basically," Jake finished.

"And you told Kyle this when they broke up?" I asked as I played with my ponytail.

"Yeah. We didn't want to say anything when they were dating because it's his life, he can do what he wants. He was in love anyway and wouldn't have listened to us," Luke said.

"What did he say when you told him?"

"He said he knew. He felt different when they were apart during tours and not different in a bad way. He felt good when she was gone," Jake said.

"Why didn't he tell me this? He just told me that they broke up because they chose their careers."

Jake shrugged. "Just talk to him about it."

The guys went back to their rooms a little while later, once Kyle got out of the shower. He was changing and I was trying to think of how I could bring Kourtney up.

He probably never brought it up for a reason, so I shouldn't be the one to bring it up, right? But now the guys knew about it and I should figure everything out. I wouldn't stop thinking about it until I did.

"So, the interview with your dad is at ten tomorrow, right?" Kyle said as he walked into the living room. He was ruffling his wet hair and he had a white tank top showing off his beautifully sculpted muscles.

"Yeah. I'm going to take a cab to his house in about an hour or so." I scanned his body with my eyes. He was looking at me with that look, that same look he had on Friday before we got intimate.

But I couldn't think about that, I could only think about Kourtney.

"Kyle, I have to ask you something."

He walked over and sat down next to me on the couch.

"Why did you and Kourtney break up? I want to know the truth."

"The truth? I told you the truth. She broke up with me right before our summer tour last June." He put his hand on my knee.

"But that can't be the truth!"

"Why not?"

I looked into his eyes as I brushed my fingers through his wet hair. "Jake's mom told me that the guys couldn't stand Kourtney and so I asked them about it. They said that you knew that she was toxic or whatever because when you two were apart during your tours you felt relief."

He took my hands out of his hair and held them. "She did break up with me. A month before she did, though, I felt so free without her, it felt so good. I think she broke up with me because she couldn't monitor and stalk me but I was ready to break up with her, too, so it worked out."

He squeezed my hand. "I was so blind when I was dating her. Things went fast, it was love, I guess, but it was stupid and I couldn't see what I was doing. I didn't see what was happening to me and I wished that one of the guys had said something while it was going on. They told me, from now on, they would tell me the truth no matter what."

"So they talk to you about me?" I asked with curiosity.

He nodded.

"Is it good?"

He nodded.

"But you're not gonna tell me anymore than that?"

He shook his head. "Some stuff has to stay between, us, guys. But you know how they feel about you. They can't get enough of you. So that says a lot."

I already knew that Cam, Jake, and Luke liked me but hearing Kyle say it felt reassuring. Jake's mom was right.

"So you haven't talked to Kourtney since you guys broke up? She doesn't know that she's clingy and toxic?"

"No, the first time I've seen her since last year was Friday. And I don't think there's really a need to tell her she's 'clingy and toxic'," He said as he held up air quotes.

"And you're positive she doesn't want you back?" How could he be so sure? She just randomly went to one of their concerts this weekend.

He pulled me close into him. Squeezing me as close to him as he could. "You worry too much, do you know that?"

"I'm sorry," I mumbled. "Let's talk about something else."

"Or," he said as he sat up and took off his shirt. "We could *do* something else."

Chapter 23

Well, Kyle sure knew how to take my mind off of things. That time seemed even better than the first.

I finished getting dressed and Kyle grabbed my suitcase. He walked me down to the elevator. I was prepared to face crazy people. My head was cleared now and everything seemed so unimportant.

The elevator dinged to the lobby and the doors opened. The lobby was scattered with people, but no one looking at us. We walked toward the front doors. There were still a lot of girls out there but nothing compared to what we saw earlier that day.

The doorman opened the door and Kyle and I quickly tried to walk to the closest cab. We ignored the teenage screams.

"So, I'll see you tomorrow at the interview. I'll head over with my sister in the morning," I said as I leaned against the cab.

Kyle kissed me, pushing me further against the car. "I'll call you tonight," he said as he released from the kiss.

The ride to my dad's house was only about fifteen minutes. I got out of the car just as the sun was starting to set. I stared at the white split-level house in front of me. Soon it would not even belong to my family at all. The place I had called home since the day I was born.

I could point out the exact crack in the driveway that I tripped over when I was three and had to get stitches on my knee. I could smell the chimney smoke from our fireplace that my dad lit every night during the month of December. I could see the broken wood where I hit my first baseball into the side of the house.

This house was a memory book of my life. And I couldn't believe I wouldn't have it in just a few short months.

"Chloe!" My sister said as the cab pulled away. She came out the front door and ran over to me as if she hadn't seen me in years.

She gave me a big hug. Her long, blonde hair smelt like her fruity conditioner that she had been using for the past five years.

"You have so much to tell me! Dad said you're dating someone. What's he like? He's here with you isn't he?" She looked around as if he would pop out of a bush.

I picked up my suitcase, but she grabbed it from me as we started walking toward the house. "Uh, yeah, but he's not here, at this moment. He's staying in the city."

Jess got excited about things like Rachel but she was really low-key about it. It was normal excitement, not crazy, enthusiastic excitement.

"What's his name?" She asked as I opened the front door. I got a whiff of steak and cupcakes?

"Did Dad tell you anything about him?" I asked.

"No, why?" She put my suitcase at the top of the landing.

My dad came out of the kitchen. "Hey, Chlo!" He said as I walked up the stairs and gave him a hug. "Jess, are you already quizzing her about her boyfriend? Let her have two minutes."

Jess rolled her eyes.

"How much was the taxi?" He pulled out his wallet. My dad always made sure to pay for everything of mine and my sisters' that he could. If he knew about it he would pay for it. Which was the complete opposite from my mom. Sometimes she even made us pay for things of hers. But my dad never knew about that, perks, for her, of them living two states away.

"Dad, it's fine it was like twenty bucks," I said, but I knew he would give it to me anyway. "What are you cooking?"

"Steak. And Jess made cupcakes earlier for the band coming into the studio tomorrow." He winked at me as he headed back into the kitchen.

"You made them cupcakes?" I said.

"Yeah! Dad won't tell me which band. He never does. But they are guys. I know that. And guys like cupcakes. Everyone likes cupcakes." She twirled a piece of hair around her finger.

"Jess," I said calmly. "We need to talk."

I sat her down in the living room and told her everything. It seemed like the millionth time I was telling the story. But I didn't mind telling it to Jess. She was like a best friend to me. We never fought much growing up. We were only four years apart and had a lot in common. So, I figured that if I just told her about Kyle she would understand.

"So you're *dating* Kyle from Big Time Elevation?"

"Yeah. And remember I said he's a totally normal guy. It's just like any other guy I would be dating. Normal."

"Normal?" She said as she tilted her head. Oh, great. Maybe she wouldn't understand.

"Jess."

"It's fine. I'm just trying to comprehend that my sister is dating a celebrity…I mean, normal guy," She said as she grabbed my hand. "But you have to think it's a little cool."

"I do. It is cool. But if you're going to come to the studio tomorrow and meet them you have to be normal."

"I'm going to meet them?" she practically screeched.

"*Not* if you act like this."

"Okay. I'm sorry. It won't happen again. I'll be cool." She played with her hair as she leaned back into the couch. "Maybe they could hook me up with a hot celebrity, too!"

After the three of us ate dinner and Jess asked every question about the guys she could think of, Kyle called. I went to my room.

"So, how did it go with your dad and sister?"

I lay back on my bed. "My sister is crazy, even crazier than Sam. We're all in trouble. She did make you guys cupcakes, though."

He laughed. "I didn't think it could get any crazier than Sam. Maybe it won't be as bad as you think when she meets us."

"I'm just hoping it doesn't get worse," I paused. "How was your day?"

"It was good. I talked to my mom earlier. My grandpa's doing fine. She wants us to come over and see him before the last show in Cali."

"Wait, she wants to see *us*? *Us*?"

"Yeah, of course I told her about you. She really wants to meet you. And she wants me to try to talk to my grandpa again." He sighed.

"It will be okay, Kyle. I'm going with you. We'll do it together. Unless…you don't survive my sister." We laughed.

Early the next morning, around six, my dad headed out to the radio station. Jess drove her and I a couple hours later. She grabbed her two-dozen cupcakes and we both headed inside.

At one point this week, I was nervous for Kyle to meet my dad, but now I was nervous for Kyle to meet Jess.

We got to my dad's studio and put the cupcakes on the counter. As we headed out, toward the lobby, Jess tapped me on the shoulder.

"When will they be arriving?"

I could tell she was sincerely trying to play it cool, and normal, and everything we had talked about yesterday.

"Kyle texted me not too long ago that they were on their way." She was biting her lip, probably to keep from squealing. "If you're such a huge groupie how did you not know that Kyle was dating me? He's sung songs about it, announced it over the radio, and has made videos, with me, about it."

"I'm not a groupie. Sam's just told me a couple times about them and how hot they are and how much she loves them. And you know me I'm all about the hot boys in boy bands. It's just because I like hot boys. It doesn't have anything to do with being obsessed with their band or whatever."

I put my hands on my hips.

"And celebrities are always hot. So that's why I couldn't believe you were dating one. I mean there's hot and then there's celebrity hot." She paused. "*Hello*, there."

I turned around. It was Jake. Followed by Ronnie, Cam, Luke, and then Kyle.

Jess leaned into me. "They are so much cuter than I imagined!"

"Jess, this is Jake, Ronnie, Cam, Luke, and Kyle. Guys this is my sister, Jessica."

She smiled courteously. “Pleasure to meet you all. There are cupcakes in there if you guys get hungry. I know it’s only ten in the morning but…”

“Heck, we eat anything, anytime, anywhere,” Cam said.

“Great!” She said. “So, you guys can just follow me this way into the studio.” She took them to the side entrance of the room.

They each shook hands with my dad and had a seat. Jess and I sat in the corner of the room, on the white couch Jess and I had gotten him for Christmas one year. The two of us liked to come into our dad’s studio a lot just to see and meet people. It wasn’t always celebrities. Sometimes it was just regular people around Boston trying to get their name out there.

There was never a place for us to sit, so we got him the couch. Well, we got it for ourselves because we were the only ones that ever really used it.

On my dad’s side of the recording table were tons of pictures of Rachel, Jess, and I, and occasional ones of just my mom and dad. The pictures with me in it did not go past age ten, except for the graduation one that was also in Rachel’s living room. I think every single person in my extended family framed that picture because it was the first one I had taken in years.

Even when it came to school pictures after fifth grade I didn’t do them. I would miss school, hide in the bathroom, basically anything that would keep me away.

“So Dad said Mom’s working on a new client. Did she tell you anything about it?” Jess asked as we both sunk into the couch.

The guys were about to go on air. They were finishing up talking to my dad.

“You know Mom, she doesn’t disclose any work information until it is allowed. Company policy.” I put my hands in the front pocket of my hoodie. I was really nervous about this. My dad was talking to my boyfriend for the first time and I wasn’t even allowed in the conversation.

“We’re on in ten!” My dad said loudly.

Kyle looked back at me and gave me a thumbs up. I guess things were going well, so far.

"Hey everybody out there, this is Robbie waking you up on this beautiful Monday morning," my dad said. "We have the guys from Big Time Elevation here this morning."

"What's up everybody!" Cam said.

"Hey!" Jake, Luke, and Kyle said in unison.

"Wait, it's Monday. Jess, why aren't you in school?" I glared at her.

"Dad said I could skip today." She pouted her lips. "And you'd only be here one day. How often does my sister come into town?"

I smiled.

"So, you guys are here in town for a show. Is that right?" My dad said.

"Yes, we have a show tonight, right in Boston, at seven. We also have an album signing at three downtown at FYE," Jake said.

"We are so excited to be here. We came around Boston last year for our summer tour and it was just crazy," Cam said.

"We seriously think Boston has the loudest fans," Luke said.

"I believe that," my dad said. "Well, everybody out there, we have two tickets and VIP passes to give away to their show tonight. So, keep listening and we'll tell you how you can win them after this commercial break."

My dad shut off the red light. "We're out!"

Jess was biting her lip, staring at the guys. They were all talking about whose section of the tour bus was the messiest with my dad.

"Jessica! Stop staring at them like they are meat. Dad said something on the phone about you hanging out with a new guy. What's he like?"

"Uh, it's nothing. It's boring." She scratched her head. "We have been hanging out for like two or three weeks. He just transferred after Christmas break. He's really sweet but…"

"But what?"

"It's boring. I look at your relationship and I look at mine and there is just no comparison."

"You shouldn't even be comparing our relationships in the first place. And if he is sweet what more do you really need?"

"I mean he's also really funny, and he is not terrible looking. I don't know. I've just never dated anyone like this before. There's no drama," she said as she sat up straighter but then sunk back down.

"You are complaining because there is no drama in your life? So you would rather have a boyfriend that steals, cheats, or talks crap about people?"

She shrugged. "I'm just not used to it."

"You should get used to it. This kid sounds nice. I want to meet him."

"Going live in five!" My dad yelled.

I looked over at Jess, she was still staring at the guys but it wasn't like she was lusting after them anymore. It was like she wanted the life they had. How sad was it that my sister had a normal functioning relationship and she wasn't happy with it? My heart broke for her.

"All right, everybody, we are back with Big Time Elevation here, live in the studio, and we have these two tickets and VIP passes for someone to win for tonight's show. So, how do you win, you might ask. We are going to ask a question, a little later, about the guys and the first person to call in and answer the question correctly will win the two tickets." He paused. "But for now we are going to play a game with the guys. We are going to put them in hypothetical situations where they can only bring one thing with them."

"Oh, man, this sounds fun," Jake said excitedly.

"All right, first situation. You have to take a shower but you can only use one thing."

"Wow," Cam said as he scratched his head. "Is there water already?"

"Yes, there is water. Something other than water." My dad laughed.

"Actually, you know there is like a shampoo body wash thing they make for guys, it's like all-in-one. So I'd go with that," Cam said.

"That sounds pretty reasonable. Okay, next one is you fly from LA to Boston in one night. If you could only bring one thing, let's say besides one pair of clothes, what would it be?"

"Hmm," Kyle said. "I think I would have to bring my phone. If we could only bring one thing."

"Aw, dude, really?" Luke said.

"Yeah! I need it to stay in touch with people. My mom needs to know I landed safely."

"But there's like payphones and hotel phones. You just totally blew that," Jake said. "I would bring my wallet because you need that. Everything else you could buy or borrow once you got there. But not your wallet." Jake smiled big.

"That's actually a good answer," Cam agreed.

"Last one is, of course, the typical stranded on a desert island. This time you can only choose between a banana, a match book, and a cell phone, but the phone has no service."

"Who thinks of these questions?" Luke laughed.

"I'm going to say a match book, because hopefully you can light a fire and someone will see you," Cam said.

"Great answer, man," Kyle said as he patted him on the shoulder.

"That was good, guys. We're gonna take a short break and play some music but stay tuned for your chance to win those tickets and meet Big Time Elevation!"

And out.

The guys stood up and stretched. My dad left the room.

"How's the big comfy couch?" Kyle asked as he walked over to me.

"It's fun." I yawned. I barely got any sleep last night, thinking about today and how it was my last day with Kyle for a while.

"You guys look so depressed!" Cam said.

I smiled. "No, it's fine. We're just tired."

Jake grabbed a cupcake and took a bite. "These are really good, Jessica."

She stood up and walked toward him. "Thanks! And you can call me Jess."

Kyle wrapped his arms around me. "Baby, what's wrong?"

"Nothing, I'm fine. I just can't believe I'm leaving tomorrow. And you're leaving. For two more weeks." I rested my head on his chest.

"It will go by fast, I promise. You have Sam's wedding to plan to add to everything else you're doing." He stroked my hair. "And you have Hawaii to look forward to."

"That's not for another two months. And then that will just be more time apart."

My dad came back in the room.

"It's going to be okay. I promise." He kissed the top of my head.

"Okay, guys, let's get back to position. We're on in ten."

I released from the hug and sat back down on the couch. Jess plopped next to me.

"Back again, with Luke, Cam, Kyle, and Jake of Big Time Elevation. And we are about to give out tickets to tonight's show as well as VIP passes to meet the guys before the show. The first person to call in and answer this question correctly will win." My dad paused. "What is the name of Big Time Elevation's most recent album that came out in November? Call us now for your chance to win!"

Not a minute later, the phone was off the hook. The first call was being put through to my dad's line. "Hello, who's calling?"

"Hey, this is Trevor."

"Hi, Trevor, do you know the answer to our Big Time Elevation question?"

"I do!"

"Oh, God," Jess said

My dad started reading the question off again.

"What is it, Jess?" I asked.

"Trevor. That's totally him. That is *him*."

"Who?"

"The kid that I have been dating!"

"Why is he calling here?"

"I have no clue!"

"The CD is called Rush," Trevor said.

"That's right!" My dad said. "You just won two tickets and VIP passes to meet Big Time Elevation tonight at the Comu Center in Boston!" My dad clicked the red button off and started playing a song. "Trevor, I'm going to transfer your call to the receptionist and she'll take care of everything. Congrats, kid!"

Jess' jaw was open.

“Are you sure that was him?”

“Yes!”

“Maybe he was getting the tickets for you,” I added.

“Maybe. I mean I played him the CD once. Sam gave it to me for Christmas.” She turned and looked at me. “You really think he got them for me? No, he probably got them for his sister, I bet. She’s like twelve, really adorable.”

“I still think he got them for you.” I smiled.

A half hour later the guys, Jess, and I were all getting ready to leave.

“It was so great to meet you guys. Come back anytime,” My dad said as he shook their hands goodbye. “And Kyle I hope to see more of you soon.”

“It was great to meet you, too, sir. We will definitely be coming back,” Kyle said.

“Call me Robbie.” Oh, Dad, he was getting all sappy. He hated goodbyes.

“Dad, they have to go now and you have to get back to your show. See you later tonight.”

Chapter 24

Jess and I headed home. As we walked in the front door, Jess' phone buzzed. She pulled it out of her purse and glanced at it as she shut the door. The corners of her lips showed a faint smile.

She rapidly texted something and shoved the phone in her pocket.

"What was that about?" I asked her as we headed up the stairs.

"Trevor. Said he has a surprise for me tonight and he'll pick me up at six," she said as she casually put her purse on the kitchen counter and headed toward her room.

"So he *did* get you the tickets," I smiled gleefully.

She shrugged as she walked down the hall.

I knew she wasn't used to guys treating her with respect and actually caring about her, but I really hoped she was going to give this guy a chance.

Later that afternoon, after my dad came back from work, Jess and I were helping each other get ready.

I was trying to find a top that actually fit me in my closet when I heard Jess scream.

"What?" I frantically ran to our bathroom that joined our two rooms. She was running her finger under cold water, her hair half curled.

"That's the third time I've burned myself! Curling your hair isn't even worth it!" She turned off the faucet and dried her hand on a purple towel that matched the shower curtain and rugs on the floor. The bathroom used to be blue when I was in high school but once I moved out, Jess redecorated. I think redecorating was her way of keeping her mind off of all the boy trouble she was consistently having.

"Your hair looks nice," I said as I leaned into the room. She huffed. "I, on the other hand, can't find a shirt that doesn't swallow me."

"Try something in my closet," she suggested as she carefully picked up the curling iron and wrapped a piece of hair around it.

I hadn't been able to fit into Jess' clothes since I was in high school. All of my clothes at my dad's house were from early sophomore year of college, when I had reached my peak. Now that I was twenty pounds lighter it was worth a try to fit into her clothes again.

I walked behind her and into her room. The walls were a light shade of coral and covered with black and white photographs. It was amazing how opposite our views of pictures were. Almost every picture in her room had her in it.

I opened up her closet and scanned through the tops before I picked out a white one that fit perfectly.

"What time is it?" She asked as I headed back toward the bathroom.

I glanced at her alarm clock. "Five thirty." My eyes shifted to the picture on her nightstand. It was none other than that graduation picture. I couldn't help but laugh. That picture obviously had serious value to my family.

But there was a picture next to it that I didn't recognize at first. "Oh my God!" I screeched. I took the picture and brought it to Jess. "You have my *PB and gross* picture on your nightstand?"

She shifted as she unrolled a piece of hair.

"How could I have not noticed this?" It almost burned, holding it in my hand.

"You were adorable and I'm kind of in love with that picture."

"What is *wrong* with you?" She stared at me quizzically. "This picture ruined me. It started my phobia of picture-taking."

"You were ten," she said as she flashed me her ten fingers. "How can you still feel that way about pictures? Not every picture is going to come out terrible, and you can look at them later and remember the stories that go with it."

I stared at her.

"Come here." She grabbed my wrist and pulled me into her room.

"See this," she pointed to one of the pictures hanging on the wall. It was Jess and Rachel, two summers ago. I remembered it because Sam had come to visit the week that picture was taken. We were having a barbeque in the backyard. Mom wasn't able to be there but it almost felt complete.

"Yeah, I remember it." I smiled. "Look, you can actually see my ankle in the corner. That counts!"

She rolled her eyes as she pointed to the next one. It was a picture of Mom and Dad from this past Christmas. Mom had been able to get a few extra days off and stayed from Christmas until the day before New Years. I remembered that she had to head back because one of her clients was performing at the New Years Eve show in New York City.

The picture was taken outside the house with the lights all lit up, and I could see the chimney smoke from the fireplace. They wanted to take a picture with Rachel, Jess, and me too but I didn't want to. I felt sort of guilty now. It would have been nice to have a picture of all of us at Christmas since the past couple of years my mom couldn't even make it.

Maybe I was being overdramatic about the whole picture thing. And I had ruined other people's memories because of my stupid fourth grade picture.

"You're right. It is dumb of me to not want to take a picture because of what happened when I was ten."

She smiled, flashing her perfectly white teeth. "Well, then let's take some pictures tonight at the show, to make up for lost time!"

I took a cab to the show a little before six. I texted Kyle and met him at the back entrance. A half-hour later Jess called me. I met her at the back door with Ronnie.

"Hi!" I said as Jess and Trevor came inside. Trevor was tall, probably a little over six feet. He towered over my five-foot-five sister. But they looked cute together. He had dirty blonde, short, kind of curly hair.

He was holding my sister's hand and reached out his other hand to shake mine.

"I'm Trevor. It's nice to meet you."

"I'm Jess' sister, Chloe," I said as I released his hand. He slid it into his pocket.

"I know. I've heard a lot of great things about you. I have an older brother so I can relate."

He had a little bit of a southern accent.

"Where are you from?"

"West Virginia, originally. When I was eight we moved to Virginia, and then in December we moved to Boston."

This guy seemed so genuine. I knew I had been fooled in the past with Jess' boyfriends but this one was different.

"Glow!" I heard Cam call out.

I looked over Trevor's shoulder. Cam's head was sticking out of the dressing room.

"You guys can come in!"

After I introduced Trevor to all the guys and Jess had taken as many pictures as I would allow, they both headed out to their seats.

I watched from backstage again. I could see Jess and Trevor sitting in the front row. I couldn't help but smile every time I glanced at them. She was laughing and having fun, something I hadn't seen her do in a while.

But I couldn't help but think about what she had said earlier. How her relationship was boring compared to mine. Would things have been different with Kyle and me if he wasn't in a world famous band? Would our relationship have been boring?

I had to admit it was really exciting being a part of his crazy life. I could understand what Jess was talking about. Maybe that's why she had chosen those men in her life before. Not the fact that they were destructive but because they were exciting. You could never guess what they were about to do.

I was just glad she found Trevor when she did. I mean how could you not give a chance to a guy who won you tickets to an amazing concert? He obviously cared about her and I thought she was starting to see it too.

Once the show was over, I said goodbye to Trevor and told Jess I'd see her back at the house. I walked down the hall to the dressing room. I slowly knocked on the door.

Jake opened it. "Oh, hey, Kyle's just packing up his stuff. Come on in."

I walked in the room and sat down on one of the couches. There were three more doors in this room and I could hear Cam singing from one of them and Luke telling him to be quiet. Jake took a bite of a cookie as he threw his bag over his shoulder.

"Be right there!" Kyle said from another room.

Cam and Luke came out of one door. They were both carrying huge, Santa-like bags.

"It's from the fans. Usually Ronnie takes it out to the bus but today he complained his back was hurting," Cam said as he dragged his bag. His hat was falling off, covering his eyes.

"Ronnie's lying. He only said that because this load is twice as heavy as it usually is," Luke added.

"Why is it twice as heavy?" I asked as they dropped the bags in the middle of the room.

Cam adjusted his hat as he said, "Half of it is yours."

Chapter 25

I laughed. "You're joking right? There is no way you're being serious."

Luke shrugged. "It's the truth. Ask Kyle. They all told him about it. And then Cam and I were putting them into the bags when we realized it."

Jake walked over, cookie still in hand, and looked into one of the bags. "They're not kidding."

"So, you're telling me that after three days of your fans knowing that I exist half of the ones that had VIP got me presents?" I was in shock. I didn't even think about it before.

"We can try to sort it out now," Luke said.

"Or we can wait until the end of the tour because we know you'll get more," Cam added.

I just couldn't believe it. Would I end up with my own bags of presents once the tour was done? And what would I do with it all?

"What do you guys do with all of this stuff?"

"Depends. If it's something we will never use or need we donate it. But if it's like a t-shirt or bracelet we usually keep it," Jake said.

"I have a whole room in my house where I just keep stuff from fans. A lot of the stuff is actually useful," Cam said. "I always get a lot of hats so I wear one everyday, a lot of the time they are from fans."

"I'm just overwhelmed, I guess. But I'm curious as to what they got me!"

"Take a look inside." Luke opened up the bag he was carrying.

I could see clothes, candy, personalized CDs, movies, books, hats, and letters. That was insane. How did they ever know what belonged to who?

"Everything is usually easy to determine who it belongs to. A lot of the time the fans will tell us what they got us and stuff so out of memory I think Kyle knows what's yours," Cam said.

"Van's loaded guys, time to go," someone yelled from around the corner.

But where was Kyle?

"We'll sort these all out on the bus and try to keep your presents separate. And when the tour's done we will give it all to you," Jake said as Cam and Luke picked up the bags.

"Where's Kyle?" I asked.

"I think he's in that room," Jake pointed to the door on the right wall. The three of them headed into the hallway.

"Kyle?" I said as I knocked on the door.

"Yeah?"

"It's Chloe. Can I come in?"

"Yeah."

I opened the door. It was a pretty big room, empty though except for the blanket on the floor and the candles and rose petals all over. There was also a bouquet of roses in the corner.

"What did you do?" I asked as I shut the door behind me. "What is this?"

He was standing on the blanket. "This is the last time we will see each other for a couple weeks. I wanted it to be special."

I moved in closer. He smelt clean, like he had just taken a shower.

"But they are waiting for you on the bus."

He shook his head. "That was just a diversion. Ronnie and the guys know I wanted time to say goodbye. We aren't scheduled to leave for another hour."

I leaned in close so our lips were touching. "This is very clever of you."

"I'm just gonna miss you. I wanted to show you how much."

"Shh, no talking."

Thirty minutes later we were blowing out the candles and picking up the rose petals.

"Is it just me or does that keep getting better every time we do it?" He said as he picked the blanket up off the floor.

"It's not just you," I smiled.

He handed me the flowers as I opened the door. We headed out into the dressing room and into the hallway.

"Thanks," I said. "For doing all this. And for the flowers. I'm gonna miss you, too."

Once we reached the tour bus, we said our goodbyes and I hopped into a cab to head home.

Four o'clock the next morning, my alarm went off. I put together the last of my stuff and headed into the kitchen. My dad was up, making coffee. He was going to take me to the airport before he headed to work.

"What kind of pancakes do you want?" My dad asked as I sat down at the counter. What was with my parents and pancakes?

"You don't need to make me anything, Dad, I'm fine. I'll have something at the airport."

I was still on West Coast time so I wasn't all that hungry anyway.

"I talked to your mom last night," he said as he leaned against the counter. "She signed all the paperwork for the new client. So it is official."

"That's great."

He nodded. "It is great. There's just one thing that comes with the job." He paused. "She has to move."

"Mom has to move out of New York?" I asked, shocked. "Where is she moving?"

"California."

"Mom's moving to California? Does this mean you and Jess are moving there, too?"

He nodded.

That actually could be a good thing. All of us living in the same state again! I wouldn't have to travel across the country to see them. Except Rachel.

"Does Rachel know?"

"Not yet. Mom's telling her today, and I'm telling you now. I'll tell Jess later today." He poured the coffee into a mug and twisted the lid shut.

“Did you know Mom was going to have to move?”

“Yeah. She told me when she got offered the job a couple of weeks ago. We both thought long and hard about it. We figured it was well worth it with the salary increase your Mom’s getting. Jess and I would be moving in June anyway so it’s just a different location.”

“And you’ll live closer to me! Your favorite daughter.” I grinned.

“Speaking of my favorite daughter, we better go before she misses her plane.”

He dropped me off at the airport and I headed to the gate. I put on a baseball cap incase anyone recognized me. It’s not that I considered myself famous, by any means. But my rapidly growing twitter followers and the amount of attention I was starting to get was in the back of my mind. I knew how famous Kyle was and if people knew of Kyle they probably knew of me.

Thankfully, no one recognized me, no one that I saw anyway. I arrived at LAX hours later. Sam was picking me up.

Once I entered the baggage claim, I saw her waiting at the door. I picked up my bag and walked over to her.

“How was the journey?” She asked as she took my carry on bag.

“Long. I slept, though, for most of it,” I said as we headed out the doors to the parking lot.

“Miss!” I heard someone yell.

I turned around. It was a paparazzi guy, I was pretty sure. He had on one of those vests you always see them wearing and he had a camera in hand.

“Do you need something?” Sam snapped at him.

“Are you Chloe? The one dating Kyle from Big Time Elevation?”

Sam and I kept walking. “She’s not commenting,” Sam said.

We started walking faster as he snapped a couple pictures.

Finally we made it to Sam’s car and got in.

“I cannot believe you. You go away for a few days and you come back, all famous, bringing the paps with you!” Sam said as she turned the engine on.

"It's weird," I said as Sam backed out of the parking space. I looked out the window. The guy was gone. "It's really weird."

"Then, I don't know how you'll feel about this," Sam said as she reached behind my seat and pulled out a magazine. She handed it to me. "Page fifty-seven."

It was a teenybopper magazine. I opened it up and flipped to page fifty-seven.

KYLE IS TAKEN, the caption read at the top of the page. There was a big picture of him on the left side of the page.

On the right side were pictures of him and I in New York. There was one picture of me, Kyle, and Hannah, that blonde-haired girl we met outside the hotel in Boston. The magazine must have gotten that picture from twitter.

Then, on the far right side there was a box and it was a mini article about our youtube videos. It had a screen shot of the video where Kyle and I asked each other fan questions.

"Did you read all of this?" I asked Sam.

"Every word." She flipped on her turn signal as she turned out of the lot. "Basically it says how Kyle started off the tour by dedicating a song to a girl none of us knew yet. Then as the tour progressed so did his relationship with this 'mysterious girl'. And then viola you finally come out of hiding."

I flipped to the next page and it was still the same article.

"Her name is Chloe, she's super friendly. Some fans have even had the chance to meet her. Her and Kyle started a youtube channel where they answer your fan questions. If you want to get to know her she's all ears. Pretty much sums it all up."

She pushed a silky smooth strand of hair behind her ear. "I still can't believe my best friend is famous. I know it must be really hard to adjust to but you got to admit it's super cool."

I pressed my lips together as I closed the magazine.

"I'm sorry," Sam said as she flashed an apologetic smile. "I know you don't like talking about it. Let's talk about something else."

I threw the magazine in the backseat without looking.

"I know!" She chirped. "Tyler's mom has been bugging us about the wedding. We told her it was in July and she completely freaked out. She was like 'How can you say the wedding's in less than six months and you don't know anything about it?' So we gotta start planning!"

So, for the next two weeks, in between classes, homework, and everything else, Sam and I started planning the wedding. She didn't want it too big, but not too small either. She wanted it on the beach, in her hometown.

She picked a location, a minister, the black and white theme, and she was starting to work on the guest list.

I hadn't noticed any paparazzi since the encounter at the airport, but I assumed it was only a matter of time. And I had spent so much time focused on the wedding and worrying about the paparazzi that I almost forgot Kyle would be coming back to town.

He called me on a Friday, the day before his last show. I was in the middle of making Sam and I dinner when my phone rang.

"Hey! How is the tour going?" I asked as I flipped a burger. Sam was on the couch watching reruns of the guy's show.

"It's amazing. More than amazing. I have some great news to tell you when I see you Sunday."

Sam burst out laughing, completely unaware that I was on the phone.

"That's great," I said as I added cheese to the two burgers.

"Yeah. So anyway, how's it going with Sam's wedding?"

I had been talking to Kyle at least once a day on the phone or Skype, sometimes, because the guys wanted to say hi, too. So, he knew pretty much all about the progress Sam and I were making on her wedding.

"It's going well. Progress is being made. She's been working on the guest list with Tyler. I think they have about one hundred people so far."

I looked back over at Sam. She looked like a little kid watching her favorite cartoon on a Saturday morning. I couldn't believe she would be hitched in just a few months. To me she looked so young and carefree, not wife material. Not yet, anyway.

"It's fun to be the planner, though. And help her through it all."

"It's what you know best."

"What, the planning or Sam?"

"Both."

After we hung up, and I tore Sam away from the TV show, we sat down to eat.

"I'm gonna miss your cooking," Sam said with a mouthful.

I smiled. "I know you will. But before you get married I'll teach you some easy recipes."

"I'm just bad. I've accepted it. Tyler said it doesn't matter and he likes to cook anyway. I'm not gonna keep trying something that doesn't work."

She took a sip of her favorite red wine. I personally couldn't stand red wine and with my mom constantly down my throat, I figured I better not drink my calories, anyway.

"What time does Jess' flight get in tomorrow?"

"Two forty two." I had this number engrained in my memory because for the past week my mom had sent me a text once a day, as a reminder.

"What are you guys gonna do?"

I hadn't thought about it much, really. My mom wanted everything to be planned but I knew Jess and she wouldn't care what we did. As long as she got a tour of the school, the rest didn't matter.

"Tomorrow we will probably just come back here. She'll be all messed up with the time difference." I finished the last bite of my burger. "And then Sunday, Kyle's coming here. He said he's gonna take Jess and I out. I think he's bringing Cam along so Jess doesn't feel like a third wheel."

"Where are you guys going?"

I shrugged. "I have no idea."

I honestly didn't. Once again, he pulled the surprise card and wouldn't tell me where we were going. I knew it was more of a surprise for my sister than anyone, but he still wouldn't tell me.

"Well, can Tyler and I come? We don't have anything better to do." She grinned.

"Of course."

The next day, I picked Jess up at the airport, right on time. My mother, of course, called to make sure of it.

“She is way too protective of me,” Jess said. She changed her focus to the lady outside the door, holding a camera. “What is she doing?”

“It’s just paparazzi. They like to hang out at the airport. They’re harmless.”

We stepped through the door and walked to my car. Surprisingly, this lady didn’t say anything to me. Just flashed a few shots and walked away. Maybe the picture taking was dying down.

We hopped in the car, drove to campus, and spent the rest of the day hanging out in the house. Sam had attempted to make us all dinner. Erica and Lindsey were there for once. It had been a while since the four of us actually sat down and had a meal together.

After Sam successfully cooked five pieces of chicken, we all sat down to eat.

“It’s good to finally have time to talk to you guys again,” Lindsey said as she took a bite of the chicken. “Things have been so hectic for me. I have like two projects due next week and of course my partners are serious slackers.”

Lindsey was an overachiever, no doubt about it. She had high honors since she was nine. She rarely spent any time doing leisure activities during the school year. Even during the summer she spent time with internships and outside school projects. She was working her way into law school next year so she had a good reason to crack down.

“Not to mention you’ve been seeing a total cutie!” Erica added as she started cutting her chicken.

Lindsey blushed. “We practically never see each other. It’s no big deal. We spend time about once or twice a week together.” She shrugged as I took a sip of water. “But he understands school comes first, so it’s working out.”

I almost choked. “You only see each other at the most twice a week? And you both are okay with that?”

“I can’t spend any more time with him than I do. He isn’t my first priority. But it’s a relationship so we are making it work.”

I could barely handle the schedule with Kyle and that was unavoidable, couldn’t be changed. But Lindsey was setting these rules herself. I couldn’t imagine purposely not seeing Kyle.

Sunday morning, Cam and Kyle picked up Sam, Tyler, Jess, and me at the townhouse. I gave Kyle a huge hug when he came to the door. My body couldn't physically let go until Sam pulled us apart. "We don't want to be late now, to wherever you are taking us," she stated.

The surprise destination turned out to be downtown LA. Kyle had planned a whole day of sightseeing. We went on a bus tour, we walked by foot, and then another bus tour. It was a lot of fun. Kyle never disappointed with the surprise dates.

Jess enjoyed it a lot, too. I wondered if she could picture herself living there like I did. I knew after the first trip I took that this was my home.

We had dinner at a restaurant overlooking the beach. All six of us sat at a round table, next to a large window. The windows were shut but I could still hear the ocean waves crashing. I was sitting next to Kyle. The whole day, I had been very restrained, even though all I wanted to do was jump on him.

I didn't even kiss him, out of respect for my sister. I felt if our lips touched I wouldn't be able to pull them away.

I wanted nothing more than to leave this dinner and head to Kyle's house in Burbank, I was dying to see it. And then we could fool around as much as we wanted. I seriously contemplated it about five times during the day, just coming up with a reason to have to go with him and leave my sister with Sam.

But that would be horrible, wouldn't it? Leaving my sister, the second day she was here, to go hang out with my boyfriend. No. I had finally convinced myself it was selfish of me to think like that. And Jess would be gone at the end of the week. Kyle wasn't going anywhere for a while. And he didn't start filming the show for another month.

I felt his hand brush against mine, which tore me away from my thoughts.

"There's something I want to talk to you about," he whispered in my ear as he opened his napkin and took out the silverware.

Sam was telling my sister the story of how Tyler proposed. And Tyler was asking Cam for dance lessons for the wedding.

My sister threw her head back in laughter.

"Oh yeah?" I asked, hesitantly.

"It's nothing bad," he paused. "We just confirmed this week that we are going to be going on a summer tour. It's going to be ten times bigger than this one was."

I swallowed hard.

"They did this winter tour really to see if we could pull off a bigger one. And this one was such a success. So it's going to happen."

He looked into my eyes. Looking for a reaction. I was surprised. I didn't even consider that they would be having another tour this year. I thought that after this one was over that would be it. But I was going to have to do this all over again, and for an even longer period of time.

"What month does it start?" I managed to say.

"July, the fifth, until October. I wanted to tell you as soon as I could, but I wanted to tell you in person." He reached for my hand but I scratched my head. He looked hurt. "Chlo, don't get upset. You and I don't even know where we will be in July."

"Well, I'll be here."

"No, I meant where we will be in our relationship. It could stay the way it is, or more serious, less serious. We don't know where we will be. That's almost half a year away."

The waiter came over and took our drink orders.

When the waiter left Sam looked over, as if about to say something to me. But she quickly changed her mind when she looked at Kyle.

"But what if it does get more serious?" I asked him. I was looking down at the table. I couldn't look him in the eye. I felt hurt. Not by him, but just hurt, in general. This was a big deal, why did he not see it that way?

"Then we will figure it out when the time comes. All I'm saying is we should just focus on today, take things one day at a time."

He was right. We should be just focusing one day at a time. That's how this relationship started anyway.

I stared out the window. I could barely see the ocean now that it was getting so dark outside. I remembered the first time we almost kissed in the ocean at Pacific Park, the rush of the cold. I shivered.

"Please, baby, just don't worry about it now." He rubbed my shoulder as I turned back to face the table, and then him.

I nodded.

I had lost my romantic desire to go home with Kyle. It wasn't his fault. I knew that. And I wasn't about to get mad at his job because I signed up for that. But I just couldn't get the thought out of my head. He would be gone for months. And why were they promoting it as a summer tour if it went from July to October? That was just dumb.

But my boyfriend, well, if he still would be my boyfriend six months from now, would be gone for sixteen weeks. I didn't know what dates he would have off and what dates he would be home. I didn't even want to ask.

On the way home, I didn't say a word to anyone, and when saying goodbye to Kyle I just squeezed his hand. I was probably over reacting but I could tell in his eyes he understood.

The next couple of days dragged by. Jess had school tours and she made some friends that she went with to a school hockey game one night. I was still pretty down. Sam had dragged it out of me and gave me her advice, which was to go on the tour with them. Not surprising.

Before I knew it, it was Friday and Jess was heading home. I hadn't talked to Kyle all week.

After I dropped Jess off at the airport I texted Kyle.

What's your address?

Less than thirty seconds later he responded.

I took a deep breath and hit the gas.

Chapter 26

After thirty minutes, I pulled onto his street. It was full of fences and shrubbery and beautiful houses. I saw his car in the driveway and I pulled in next to it. I walked up to the front door and knocked.

I heard some dogs barking on the inside, along with some footsteps. Kyle opened the door, a serious look on his face, not his typical smile. He had a dog in his arms. She barked once at me then was silent.

"Can I come in?" I asked putting my hands in the pockets of my jeans. I was wearing an oversized sweater. Oversized, as in, used to fit me before I lost weight, but now it looked oversized on purpose.

Kyle opened the door wider as if to say yes.

I stepped inside as he closed the door behind me. He put the dog on the floor and she scurried further into the house.

"Is anyone home?"

He shook his head as he walked toward the back of the house.

I followed him. We walked past the living room, dining room, and stairs.

The house was beautiful. When we walked down the hall, the kitchen was on the left and another sitting room was off to the right. Kyle took a right and sat down on a couch.

He placed his head in his hands as he let out a sigh.

"I'm really sorry. I didn't mean to do this to you. I don't want you mad at me," I said as I stepped into the room.

"Don't be sorry," he said with his head still in his hands. "I'm not mad at you. I'm mad at me."

I stepped further into the room. There was a fireplace with a flat screen TV above it. On the mantel were pictures of three different young boys. I assumed it was Kyle and his two brothers.

There was a desk in the corner with an open laptop on it. It looked like Kyle was on his twitter page.

Kyle saw me looking at the computer. "We are announcing the tour tomorrow, on the radio, so I just tweeted about it," he said sitting up straight.

"Oh," I said almost forgetting what he had previously said. "But, why are you mad at yourself? That's just ridiculous."

I sat down on the couch next to him. I sunk into it like it was a cloud.

He took my hand, as he looked me in the eyes. "You trusted me and you told me that we could take it slow. But it's my fault, really. I pushed you into this."

He fell back into the couch, still holding my hand, looking at the ceiling.

"Kyle, I just needed some time to think about everything. But I'm not mad about it. I'm certainly not mad at you and you shouldn't be either." I leaned back against him, laying my head on his shoulder. His heart was beating fast and his skin was hot.

"This is your job. And you were right, we don't know where we will be in six months, so let's just take it a day at a time like we have been."

He turned his head to me and cracked a smile. "Thanks," he said gently.

I nodded my head. Just as I did, Kyle's cell started to ring.

He reached in his back pocket and looked at the caller ID before answering.

"Hey Mom, what's up?" He paused. "No, I wasn't planning on it. Okay. See you soon. Bye."

He hung up and shoved the phone back in his pocket. "How would you like to meet my mom?"

"You mean, right now?" I asked, breaking my hand from his and fidgeting with my sweater.

"Mhm. My aunt is watching my grandpa for the day so my mom wanted to come over and see me. If you hang around, she'll be here within the hour," he said as he stood up from the couch and headed over to the laptop. He typed something and then closed it.

"I…guess," I stuttered. There was no way I was prepared to meet his mom. If I knew, I would have put on nicer clothes. My jeans had holes in them, my boots were pretty scuffed up, and my hair was in a really messy bun, I hadn't had time to wash it. What would she think of me? Would she like me the way Jake's mom did? Or would she hate me and think that no one was good enough for her son?

"I know what you're thinking," Kyle cut off my thoughts. He looked in the mirror, in the hallway, and played with his hair, trying to flatten it. "You are scared to meet my mom, you weren't prepared, a million things are running through your mind but I promise there's nothing to be afraid of."

He stopped fixing his hair and walked over to the kitchen, I followed. He opened up the fridge and looked inside.

"So, who lives here with you?"

"It was my mom, dad, and one of my brothers. Now, it's just my dad, since my mom has been staying with my grandpa and my brother moved in with his girlfriend."

I sat down on a stool at the island in the middle of the kitchen. "So your mom and dad don't see each other that much anymore?"

He closed the fridge door and opened up a drawer. "She's only been staying with my grandpa since Christmas. And she moves back home next week, the doctors say he's fine now." He paused. "Actually, they said he was fine two weeks ago but my mom's extra cautious about everything."

He pulled out a take-out menu and placed it on the counter. "I'm going to pick up food. We don't have like anything here and it's lunchtime. So pick something out and I'll call."

I pointed to a sandwich on the menu as Kyle pulled out a pencil and post it and wrote it down.

"My mom's moving here," I said.

"Here?"

"California. The new client she got needs her here. So she's moving in July, with my dad and Jess." I crossed my legs.

"Wow," he said as he finished writing. "Are you excited?"

"I don't know. I haven't had much time to process the idea. It will be weird not going back to New York and Massachusetts."

I could always go back and visit but it would never be the same. I wouldn't have a house to go to. I was barely prepared for my dad to move to New York, now I had to deal with my mom and dad moving to California.

"It might be nice to be able to visit them whenever you want. My parents may live in the same house with me but I'm barely ever home. So I don't get to see them as much as I want. Look at this as a good thing."

He was right. It was going to be different but it was going to be better, not living so far from them.

After Kyle called the restaurant, he headed out. He promised me he would be back before his mom got there.

I wondered what his bedroom looked like. It wouldn't be bad to go in it alone, would it? He'd been in my bedroom.

So I walked upstairs and slowly through the hall. The first door on the right was shut. I opened it. It was just a bathroom. The first door on the left was wide open. I peaked inside. It was the master bedroom. I kept walking. I opened the next door on the right. It was a bedroom but it looked more like a guest bedroom, or possibly one of his brother's bedrooms. I shut the door and kept walking.

There was another door on the left. The door was open so I glanced inside. This had to be Kyle's room. The walls were covered with posters and pictures. He had a guitar tucked into the corner next to the bed. There was a card on the dresser. I walked over to it. The card was outside the envelope, which was addressed to me. What was the card for?

I opened the card. *Happy Valentine's Day!* It said.

Oh my gosh. I had completely forgotten about Valentine's Day. Did I miss it? What day was today? I glanced at my phone. It was the tenth. So I still had a few days. I couldn't believe I almost missed it. If I didn't see the card I probably would have never remembered.

I closed the card and walked toward his nightstand. There was a bottle of water, a phone charger, and what looked like a schedule.

It was a piece of paper with boxes for the dates. It looked like he was trying to plan a vacation with the guys. He had highlighted days they each had free. A few days overlapped in April. Actually, it was around the same dates that Sam and I were going to Hawaii.

Wait.

What if the guys went to Hawaii with us? Kyle didn't know exactly when Sam and I were going. He just knew that we were. And then if the guys could come Tyler should, too. That way, Sam and I could have time to ourselves and then time with the guys! That would be a perfect vacation. And that could be a perfect Valentine's gift.

Twenty minutes later, Kyle was back with the food. Not long after, his mom arrived. Kyle opened the front door as I finished off the last bite of my sandwich.

"Hello!" I heard her say.

"Good to see you, Mom."

"Give me a hug! I haven't seen you since Christmas!"

I walked around the corner toward the front door. She was a head shorter than Kyle with dirty blonde hair, pulled into a messy bun. She didn't see me until she pulled away from Kyle's hug.

She looked at me, then Kyle. She didn't know I would be here, Kyle never said anything on the phone.

He smiled. "Mom, *this* is Chloe."

She looked back over at me with the most genuine smile. "So nice to meet you." She came over and hugged me. It was just like Kyle's hugs, warm and snuggly.

"Kyle told me about you on the phone a couple times. I didn't know you would be here, though. This is a nice surprise."

"Well, come on in, we bought you a sandwich," Kyle added as we all headed into the kitchen.

Kyle, his mother, and I spent the next two hours talking about almost everything. She was so easy to talk to and I didn't feel nervous even for a second. I wasn't worried about her judging me. She was so laid back it put me at ease. It was even easier than talking to my own mother. This was a different kind of mother, one that I had never experienced before, more nurturing and positive than I was used to.

Before she left, Kyle told her that we would both stop by sometime soon to visit with his grandpa. She hugged us both, said goodbye, and was on her way.

I left shortly after.

Tuesday was Valentine's Day. Kyle invited me over his house for dinner. His dad would be spending the night with Kyle's mom at his grandpa's house. He bought me flowers and chocolate. He made steak and even a heart shaped cake, too.

After dessert he handed me the card that I had seen on his dresser a couple of days before.

"Thank you," I said after I read it.

"Wait, that's not all." He handed me a little box wrapped with hearts.

I ripped off the paper and opened the box. It was a white gold necklace with a pendent on it. It was outlined in what I assumed were real diamonds and said *Glow* in the middle.

My mouth dropped opened. "I can't believe you did that!" I took it out of the box and clasped it around my neck. "You didn't have to buy me anything. This is so thoughtful, thank you." I kissed him.

"I know I didn't have to, but I wanted to."

"Okay, I have something for you," I said as I sat up straighter. I pulled a card out of my purse and handed it to him. I had stuck a brochure about Maui in the card earlier.

He opened the card and pulled out the pamphlet. "What's this?"

"Well, you know Sam and I are going to Hawaii for spring break and I thought it would be fun if you and the guys came with us, like a group trip. Tyler's coming, too, Sam talked to him earlier today."

"When are you guys going?" He opened the flyer and started looking through it.

"The second week of April. I think you all have off that week." I was really hoping he would say yes, already. The anticipation was killing me.

"Wow. That's a really great idea." He smiled at me. "Good work, babe. I'm sure the guys are gonna be stoked."

I slept over his house that night, feeling the best I had in a long time. I was in an amazing relationship that was getting better day by day. I had nothing to complain about. Yet.

Chapter 27

February and March flew by. I spent equal time with Kyle, homework, and planning Sam and Tyler's wedding. Everything was set for the wedding except half of the reception. It was almost starting to drain me.

Kyle started filming the television show again, in the beginning of March. I got to stop by a couple of times and watch. It was pretty funny and their characters were so much like themselves, but pushed to the extreme.

Kyle and I were constantly making movies to upload for the fans. I was up to 120,000 followers on twitter and still managing to get hundreds more every day. More paparazzi were starting to follow me and I had actually been in a couple magazines. Crazy, right?

The guys had finally given me the bag full of goodies that the fans had got for me. There were letters, clothes, stuffed animals, make-up, pictures, books, pretty much anything you could think of. I was starting to understand how the guys felt.

My sister officially accepted my school's offer and would be starting school in the fall. My mom and dad had come over in the middle of March to look for houses. They decided on a location, Anaheim. And would come back in June, for my graduation, and actually pick a house then.

Everything was falling into place. I was more than halfway done with the semester and already ready to graduate.

It was now the middle of April and Sam and I were on our way to Maui, Hawaii. All of the guys would be flying out the next day.

We landed at about one in the afternoon. Sam had already taken her tank top off and was just wearing her bikini with a pair of short shorts.

Sam and I had planned to stay at a *Four Seasons* hotel near the beach. When Kyle and the guys decided to come along, they upgraded us.

As we got out of the car, I couldn't believe my eyes. The Villa was incredible, looked to be worth ten million dollars. It was filled with open archways that led outside and you could see the pool from the front of the house.

"Good afternoon, ladies." We were greeted by a short, dark-skinned woman. She looked to be about my mom's age. She held a tray in her hand with two pink cocktails sporting blue umbrellas, whip cream, and a cherry. "My name is Apona, welcome to Kapalua. How was your trip?" She held the drinks out to us motioning for us to take them. We did.

We both took a sip. It was the most delicious drink I had ever tasted. Like a pina colada but with a strawberry-marshmallow taste to it as well.

A man came around the corner, introduced himself as Kayl and took our bags inside.

"The trip was great," Sam added as she ate the cherry.

Apona put the tray behind her back and smiled. "Let me show you around."

We walked through the front door and my mouth dropped to the floor. I glanced at Sam. She almost dropped her drink.

"The luxurious two acre villa was built twenty five years ago. It is located on the eighteenth green at the Kapalua Resort's world-renowned Plantation Estate Golf Course," Apona said.

"Two acres?" Sam asked stunned before taking another sip of her drink.

Apona nodded. "This six thousand, five hundred square foot, four bedroom, four full-bath and two half-bath villa features a fully equipped gourmet kitchen, top-of-the-line appliances, and designer furnishings."

The walls were sky high and the view from outside looked unreal. The living room featured a flat screen television, which I couldn't imagine anyone even using while on vacation *here*.

To the left was the kitchen. Which was probably the size of my whole apartment at school. There was a massive island in the middle, with a stove, and I almost had mistaken the refrigerator for two giant cabinets.

"The kitchen comes with a juicer, blender, microwave, toaster, toaster oven, food processor, coffee maker, coffee grinder and dish washer." Apona showed us where everything was. "And there are some waters in the fridge as requested by Mr. Schmore." Kyle.

"Let me show you to the bedrooms."

There were four bedrooms. Four! Three with king sized beds and one with two twin beds. I took the master bedroom. It was a lot bigger than any of the others but Sam said I could. "I'll be in a big bed in a couple months on my honeymoon, anyway," she had said.

We figured the other three guys could argue over who got the last king bed.

After Apona left, I changed into my bathing suit as Sam lay on my bed.

"I say we have a sleepover tonight. In your room, since it's so amazing!" Sam cooed as she lay on her stomach gazing out at the ocean.

"Sounds good to me!" I added as I slipped on my bikini bottoms. Sam and I went bikini shopping a couple of weeks earlier since I didn't fit in last summer's suits anymore. Sam convinced me to get this gorgeous push-up suit. Since I kept losing weight my boobs kept shrinking. This suit made my chest look even bigger than before I lost weight.

"Let's go swim!"

Sam and I spent the rest of the day swimming in the pool that looked out onto the ocean. I had to say it was really weird being on vacation at a house instead of a hotel. Having the whole place to ourselves was pretty amazing. I knew once the guys got here we would have no peace or quiet.

I was enjoying every minute. The sun was starting to set and the sky was turning a deep shade of pink.

"Mmm. I'm so glad we waited until senior year to do this," Sam said as she got out of the pool and lay down on a recliner and closed her eyes. "I can't imagine a better place to go."

"This *is* pretty perfect," I added, leaning back in my chair. It was just another thing added into my newly surreal life. I glanced at my phone, Kyle had texted me asking how our day was.

Perfect. Can't wait for you to get here, I responded.

"So how's Kyle?" Sam asked, almost on queue, her eyes still closed.

"Good. I didn't see him at all last week, though. He was just so busy with work and I was busy with school." I adjusted my bathing suit top. When I lay down my boobs went flat, again. "I just can't wait for school to be done."

"Uh, me too. I'm so over it. And I just can't wait to get married. I've been ready for like a year."

There was a moment of silence.

"Is it too late to have my wedding here?" Sam opened her eyes and flashed me a shy grin.

I burst out laughing. "Samantha!"

"What? It's just a thought. If it's not possible, okay. But if at any way it is possible, you should make it happen." She shrugged, like it was the most casual thing in the world.

"Sam," I said as I sat up. "We just spent three months planning your wedding that is *happening* in three months. And now you are seriously telling me you want to move the wedding from Laguna to here?"

"Don't be mad, Chlo. It's just a thought. And if you went somewhere and knew that was the right place for you wouldn't you do anything to make it happen?"

I groaned, "But can't we just plan your honeymoon here? I mean you'd be asking people to fly five hours to go to your wedding. That's a lot of money. We'd have to shrink your guest list."

"I'm okay with that. Chloe, this place feels right. And we can still have our honeymoon here. I'm gonna talk to Tyler about it when he gets here."

"So, everything we planned will just go to waste?" I was so mad, but I knew I shouldn't have been. This was her wedding and part of the event planner's job was to expect things like this to happen. But if this did happen with a client they would probably pay me to make up for it.

"I'm so sorry. I know. This is a terrible thing to do to you."

I exhaled loudly. "It's fine, Sam. I'll deal with it when we get back home, okay?"

She nodded. "Let's not think about it. It's *party* time!"

"Dinner first, party later."

We both got ready for dinner and walked to the restaurant down the street. Apona said it would take about three minutes. After the first thirty seconds, I could see it.

It was called the *Pineapple Grille*. Inside smelt like coconuts and citrus. We sat outside on the patio. It was just breathtaking.

Okay, so I couldn't blame Sam for wanting to get married here. I over reacted. Yes, it sucked that we had to cancel everything, from the location to the florist, but none of the reservations we made had a cancelation fee up until the last month, I made sure of it.

And if Sam had her wedding in Hawaii it would give us another reason to come back. I couldn't complain about that. It was only Friday and we weren't leaving until the following Sunday. That would give me plenty of time to plan some things for the wedding but also have time to relax and have fun.

The next morning, when I woke up, Sam was still curled up, fast asleep. I headed out to the living room and turned on the laptop on the desk.

I searched local places that hosted weddings but I was coming up with nothing. Apona came into the room and offered me a mimosa.

"Thanks," I said as I took a flute. She started to walk away when I had an idea. "Apona!" I called after her.

"Yes, Miss?"

"Do people have weddings here?"

"All the time. There are many different rentals to choose from depending on how many people you have. You can have no more than forty though." She shifted her weight. "Were you thinking of having a wedding here?"

"She was." I pointed to the bedroom. "Not until July, though."

"You better move fast. July is the busy season."

I nodded. "Do you know of any event planners?"

She gave me an address and went back to work.

I glanced at the clock. It was just about ten. The guys would be here in an hour. I peeked into the bedroom. Sam was still asleep. I wrote her a note and headed toward town.

Apona said the best event planner was just a ten-minute walk from here. She planned the best weddings on the island. I figured I had enough time to meet with her and get back before the guys got there. And Sam wouldn't wake up unless someone woke her.

The place was right on the water. I opened the front door and headed toward the receptionist.

"I don't have an appointment or anything but I was hoping I could just talk to someone about planning a wedding here."

"Have a seat," she said in a pleasant voice. "Tamra will be with you in one moment."

I sat down and picked up a portfolio on the coffee table. There were hundreds of pictures inside of flowers, cakes, churches, pools, brides, grooms, everything wedding.

The thought of picking everything out again was making my head spin. As I set down the portfolio, a skinny blonde came out of the room behind the receptionist.

She came over to me. "I'm Tamra, would you step into my office?"

Her office was filled with bright colors, aquas, pinks, and sea greens. The room had gigantic windows that, of course, looked out into the clear ocean. The walls were decorated with pictures of brides, smiling and looking ultra glamorous.

"What can I help you with today?" She asked as she shut the door. She headed over to her desk and sat down.

I sat down on the sofa. "Well, long story short, I was planning my friend's wedding in California and she just recently decided she wants to have it here instead. I don't have it in me to plan a whole other wedding so I need help."

She smiled gracefully. "Well, let me tell you a bit about what we do here." She handed me a pamphlet and explained everything in detail.

"How long are you and your friend here for?"

"Just until next Sunday."

She waved a hand. “That’s plenty of time! I can meet with her later today at…” She looked down at her calendar. “Four.”

“Okay, sounds good. I’ll let her know.”

“Will you be back with her?”

I was pretty much done with the whole wedding planning thing. It was okay the first time, but thinking about doing it again made my brain want to explode. Maybe Sam changing her wedding was a wake up call for me. Wedding planning was not my calling.

“No,” I responded. “It will just be her.”

Chapter 28

When I headed back, it was just about eleven. Sam was still asleep when the guys pulled up in a huge hummer jeep.

"Woohoo!" I heard Cam call as I opened the front door. "We're here!"

I leaned against the doorpost as they parked the car and started taking out their things.

All five of them had sunglasses on. Jake was shirtless, not surprising.

"Woo!" Jake called as he made his way up the front walk. "Hey Glow, how's it going?"

"Great." I nodded. "Oh, you guys should know there's only one king-size bed left, the last two get stuck in twin beds." I shrugged playfully.

Jake whizzed past me "She will be mine!"

"No way, man!" Luke said as he ran after him. Cam followed.

Tyler trudged up the walk. "Is Sam still asleep?"

"Yeah."

"I was here first!" Luke screamed.

"Okay, she probably isn't anymore." I chuckled.

As Tyler made his way past me, I headed toward the jeep. Kyle was searching the car.

"Missing something?" I asked.

His eyes shot up and a grin crossed his lips. "Baby," he said as he made his way over to me. He picked me up and straddled my legs around him. I kissed him.

"Missed you, babe," he added, still holding me in his arms.

His face was freshly shaved and his skin felt hot. His hair looked shorter than the last time I saw it. Not as fluffy and touchable.

He noticed I was looking at it. “I know. I don’t like it either, but the producer wanted it shorter for the show.”

I messed it up before he put me down.

“How was your flight?” I asked as he picked out two suitcases and put them on the ground. I took one and started wheeling it to the house.

“Good. How’s it been with Sam?” He wheeled the other suitcase with one hand and grabbed my hand with the other.

“Perfect. It’s been so nice here.” I paused. “Sam wants to get married here.”

He smiled. “Who wouldn’t?”

“No, she really wants to get married here. I have to call and cancel everything.”

He looked shocked. “She’s making you do this all over again?”

“No. And I’m not. Once was enough for me.”

Once we finally reached the front door, the guys were in full-blown mayhem. Apona seemed utterly terrified, in the corner of the kitchen.

“Guys, what the hell?” Kyle said as he put the suitcase down.

“I get the king bed, I was there first,” Luke said while on top of Cam.

“I’m the one who needs it. You both snore.” Cam said while on top of Jake.

“That’s ridiculous. I’m the tallest, so I should get it,” Jake said as he wiggled to get free. “Get off me, man!”

This was the first time I had actually seen any of them have an argument. Well, except for two weeks ago when Luke and Cam were fighting over a girl, but that ended quickly when they found out she had a seven-foot tall boyfriend.

The first few months I had hung out with them they were always so calm, polite, and gracious. I was starting to see their true colors. That probably meant they were getting more comfortable with me.

Kyle let go of my hand and walked over to them. “Get up, all of you.”

“Why don’t you pick a straw or something?” I suggested. “The one who gets the shortest straw gets the king bed.”

So they did. Jake ended up winning. Cam was a sore loser but Luke got over it fast.

Once Sam was awake, we all hung out at the pool. It was about eighty degrees outside, even warmer than the day before.

Tyler was starting to get to know the guys and I think they were all starting to become friends. Tyler had a similar sense of humor to the rest of the guys. They even gave him a nickname, Ty-Rod.

"Why don't I get a nickname?" Sam had said.

"Uhm…" Cam stumbled for words.

"We haven't hung out with you enough," Kyle said.

"But you just met Tyler," Sam pointed out.

"But he's a guy, that's different. We hardly ever give girls nicknames," Cam said.

Sam huffed.

"Sparkle?" I suggested.

She smiled, accepting the name. It wasn't really the same as everyone else's because I had been the one to come up with it but I didn't think any of the guys were going to reach for one and Sam didn't seem to mind.

At four, Sam and Tyler headed to the wedding planner's and I finished making all of the calls to cancel everything.

I sighed of relief. Now I had nothing to worry about, at least until I started school again.

Cam, Jake, and Luke were playing some sort of touch football on the other side of the yard. Kyle was standing in the hot tub.

I put my phone away as Kyle beckoned me to come in. I took my drink and made my way into the tub.

I took a sip. The drink was blue and it tasted like peaches and mangos. So good.

Kyle kissed my neck, tickling me a little bit.

I giggled as I pulled away.

"I missed you so much this week, babe," he said as he sat down. He pulled me onto his lap and kissed my neck again. This time it didn't tickle.

I put my drink down, grabbed the back of his head and kissed him. I straddled my legs over him.

"Have you ever done it in a hot tub?" He asked me with a grin.

"No," I laughed. "And we're not."

He put his hands up in surrender. "Okay."

"Save it for later." I kissed him once and got out of the tub.

"What? You can't do that!" He said playfully. "Babe!"

"Later." I grinned.

Once Tyler and Sam came back, we all went out to dinner at a bar downtown. There were tons of people out. Girls in short skirts and guys with pants so low you could see their underwear. I hated that look, ack. Thankfully, Kyle didn't wear his pants like that and neither did any of the other guys, including Tyler.

Sam was wearing a bright purple strapless dress with five-inch heels to go with it. I was wearing a white off-the-shoulder top, black dress shorts, and a cute pair of wedges my mom got me for Christmas. Probably the only sensible gift my mom had given me this year.

I put on my new perfume that smelt very tropical. It was perfect for this vacation. The smell of it wafted through the air as we finally made it to the bar.

We were seated quickly and after ordering, our food came just as fast. Sam and I were having margaritas by the pitcher while the guys stuck to beer.

I was on my fourth glass when Kyle cut me off.

"But, baby, I only had four," I slurred. Okay, he was probably right to cut me off.

He laughed as he ran his hands through my hair. The waiter dropped the check off at the table.

"I think you and I should head back." He motioned something to Cam and grabbed my hand.

"But I wanted to go out dancing tonight!" I practically screamed.

Sam had only had two or three glasses and she was fine. But she could hold her liquor better than I could.

"We can go dancing tomorrow night, Chlo. You go back with Kyle. We won't be out too late." She rubbed my back.

I was starting to feel dizzy. I wobbled and almost fell to the ground. Kyle caught me.

"*Okay*, that's my queue. Will you guys stay here with her? I'll go up to the house and grab the car."

They must have said yes because Kyle transferred me to someone, either Jake or Cam.

"Glow's totally trashed!" Cam said.

"I'm okay!" I said, trying to keep my eyes open. "I didn't even do anything."

They all laughed. I couldn't control what was coming out of my mouth. I knew it made no sense but I couldn't form normal sentences.

After what felt like forever, Kyle pulled up and they all put me in the car.

"Take it easy, Glow!" Jake called as he shut the door.

I slid down into the seat but tried to hold myself up.

"We'll be back in a minute, babe, hang tight."

Not a minute later he came to a stop and helped me out of the car.

"Let's go swim!" I said as I threw my hands in the air.

He chuckled. "No swimming for you. Let's go to bed." He opened up the front door and walked me to the bedroom.

The bed looked so tempting I dove right into it. I closed my eyes and felt him rub my head. "You're so good to me."

"I didn't think you would drink so much." I could hear a smile behind his voice.

"Let's go to bed," I said, already falling asleep.

"I wanted to tell you something tonight," he whispered as he continued rubbing my head.

"Tell me tomorrow. When you get up, just tell me what it is. I don't want you to tell me now and then I'll forget."

He kissed my forehead. "Goodnight, babe."

I woke up to the sunlight shining on my face. I felt around me. I was tucked into bed. How did I get there? I remembered passing out but I definitely didn't tuck myself in.

I sat up. Kyle wasn't there. His side of the bed was made neatly like he never even slept in it. I turned over to my clock. Whoa, it was already two. No wonder why he wasn't in bed.

I slipped out of the covers and went to change out of my outfit. But I wasn't in my outfit. I was in my pajamas. Kyle must have changed me before he tucked me in.

I changed into a bathing suit and some shorts and headed toward the living room.

No one was there. Not the living room, not the kitchen, not even the pool.

"What the hell?" I yelled.

"Miss?" I heard Apona say. She came from outside.

"Oh, sorry. I was just wondering where everyone went."

She nodded. "They went into town, didn't want to wake you because of what happened last night."

I tilted my head confused.

"But, Sam wanted me to tell you to call her when you woke up. She was going to pick up some stuff for your hangover, she said."

Hangover? I didn't have…oh wait, there it was.

"Thanks, Apona." I smiled. I turned to go outside but felt Apona still looking at me like she had something else to say. When I turned back to face her she hesitated and walked away.

I stepped outside. It was chillier than it was yesterday, more wind. I slipped into the hot tub without a second thought.

I didn't even know where my phone was to call Sam. The last time I remembered having it was before we left for dinner, in my room. But when I woke up I didn't see it. It didn't matter much, anyway. They would be home sooner or later.

I loved being alone, especially at this resort. It was the perfect place to escape from everything and just think. I hadn't had a lot of time to think since January, when Kyle and I had first started dating. Actually, a week from today would be three months. Sometimes it felt longer, sometimes shorter.

But I thought I was truly starting to fall in love with him. Neither of us had said it to each other, yet. And up until this trip things between us didn't even feel that serious. Last night was one of the first times when I really felt connected to him in a way I couldn't even describe.

When he had told me in February about the tour in July, I had been so shocked but I had gotten over it because we agreed to take things one day at a time. But now that July was only three months away it felt scary. If my feelings were becoming this deep I knew they would only grow stronger.

When I was dating Ryan, it was about four months before we both said *I love you*. But I didn't have any worries. I didn't think that the stronger the feelings the worse it could become. If I started having really strong feelings toward Kyle I would just be more hurt each time he went away. I would be in more pain than happiness. Back to square one.

I just had to think about this moment. This trip. No matter where things would be in July I needed to tell him, now, while we were here together, that I loved him.

"What the hell, Chlo?" I turned around to see Sam bust through the front door.

"I literally just woke up." My voice was raspy and I could still feel my eyes drooping, barely staying open.

"Oh. Well, I brought you some stuff to make you feel better." She walked over to me and handed me a greasy burger, water, and Tylenol. Greasy food always seemed to make the two of us feel better when we had hangovers.

"Where are the guys?" I asked as I hopped out of the tub and sat on a recliner. Sam unloaded some things into the fridge.

"They left for the beach at like twelve, after we all ate lunch downtown. I'm sorry to have left you out of it but I didn't want to wake you up. You needed sleep."

I took a bite of the burger. It tasted better than it looked. "What did you guys end up doing last night?"

"Well, after you and Kyle left, we went to this club that was right around the corner from the bar. We were there until like two, I think. When we came back, you and Kyle were knocked out." She finished putting away groceries and came outside.

"And Jake brought home a girl last night," she said as she sat next to me on my chair.

"What?" I said with a mouthful of food.

I could not picture Jake hooking up with someone just like that. But if any of the guys were to do it, it would make sense that it was him.

I finished chewing and swallowed. "Did she sleep over?"

Sam shook her head as she put her hair into a ponytail. "No. She stayed for like an hour or two. It was a pitch and ditch."

"I'm sorry, a what?"

"Pitch and ditch. He pitched it to her and then she ditched."

We both laughed hysterically. It was things like that that made me love Sam.

After I finished my burger, Sam and I talked outside for another hour or so before the guys came back.

Everyone discussed what was happening tonight before any of them took a shower. Jake was going to meet up with that girl for dinner. Cam and Luke were going to grab something to eat and then go jet skiing. Sam and Tyler were having a picnic on the beach.

"I'm staying here," I said as I curled into a ball on the chair. "I'm still recovering."

"I'm gonna stay here, too," Kyle added.

"Babe, no. Go out. You don't have to stay here with me. You can go jet skiing with Cam and Luke." I waved my arm in a shooing motion.

"No way," he said as he took my hands in his. "I'm staying with you."

"Gross!" Cam said jokingly as they all dispersed.

I raised my eyebrows at Kyle. "You should not let me hold you back."

"You're not holding me back. I'll go out with the guys tomorrow, I promise. But tonight, I'm all yours."

After everyone left, I headed into the shower. The shower was huge. It was basically a room itself. The water came out like rain, beading down my back.

The door opened and Kyle walked in.

"Showering over here," I said as I put on body wash.

"I know," he said as he stripped down. Damn. I couldn't get enough. He knew what he was doing, too.

I was still soapy when he stepped inside.

"Why do you do this to me?" I asked as I pressed against the window. Yes, there were huge windows everywhere. The shower was no exception. They were shielded with plants outside, though, so privacy wasn't a concern.

"Because." He kissed my neck, not in the ticklish spot. This time he kissed it in the right place, first. Again and again. He worked his way up to my mouth. I kissed him passionately, the most intense kiss I had ever given or gotten. I could feel the suds on me wash away.

"What are you doing?" I interrupted. I didn't have to ask. I knew, technically, what he was doing. But things had become so much more passionate with us in this area, too. I knew he felt it as well. I just wanted him to admit it. I didn't want to be the first to say the *L word.*

"I'm just kissing you," he said so close to my lips my heart started to beat faster.

"You *know* what I mean."

He didn't move an inch. "You feel it?"

I nodded.

"Everything feels so much deeper, stronger, more passionate with us. I didn't want to be the only one that felt it."

"You're not," I whispered.

"I wanted to make it special. I was going to do it last night but then you got so drunk," he chuckled. "And then, I had a whole breakfast thing planned for us but Sam said not to wake you, so after eleven I decided to hold off again."

He kissed me again. "I love you, Chloe." He looked into my eyes and I could see his vulnerability. He wasn't some untouchable superstar. He was a normal man who was in love. With me.

I could feel the smile curl onto my mouth. I couldn't control it. And at the same time, I felt like I was going to cry. The tears were burning behind my eyes.

"I love you, too," I said as one rolled down my cheek. "And I've been wanting to tell you, too. Things just have felt different with us lately. It's not so casual anymore. I'm in love with you."

He started kissing me again, and this time when we made love we really made love.

Chapter 29

The rest of the trip was filled with walks on the beach, paddle boarding, surfing, snorkeling, cliff diving, exploring, partying at night, and everything in between.

Sam and Tyler finished planning the wedding. It was going to be July fifteenth. Now, the only planning I had to do was for Sam's bridal shower, since I was the maid of honor. I was thinking of having it in June after graduation, in Laguna, where the wedding was supposed to take place.

Before we left, everyone was piling into the jeep when Apona stopped me. She had the same look on her face as the day I woke up with a hangover.

"Miss," she said.

"Yes?"

She looked nervous, not the way she looked at the beginning of the trip when she would look us right in the eye when speaking.

"There's something I must ask." She paused. "Is that Big Time Elevation?"

I smiled. "Yes, it is."

She smiled, too. "I thought so. And you're Chloe, Kyle's girlfriend. I didn't recognize you at first but once the gentleman got here I put it all together."

She looked relieved.

"Could I get your autograph? My daughter is such a huge fan of yours and the band." She pulled out a pen from her pocket and took a pad of paper off the kitchen counter.

I signed it. "I can get the boys to sign it, too, just give me a minute."

I ran out to the car and got the guys to sign it before heading back inside.

"Apona, I'll be back here in July. If I could get your card I could call you and maybe go out to eat with your daughter. I'd love to meet her." I handed her back the paper.

"That would be lovely, thank you so much, Chloe." She bowed her head and handed me her card.

It was astonishing that on such a small island they still knew who the guys were, and even me. I didn't really know Apona but after this trip it felt like I did. And to hear her say her daughter looked up to me was a lot different than just some random stranger saying it.

"What was that about?" Kyle asked as I hopped into the car.

"Do you ever get tired of people looking up to you?"

He shook his head. "Never."

We got back to LA early in the morning. Sam and I headed back to campus and the guys headed their separate ways. They would be back to filming early the next morning and it would be that way for the next four weeks. They had, like, three days off in that time. But they had to finish filming before they started tour rehearsal in June.

Tour. I shuddered at the thought. I tried to keep busy those four weeks. It wasn't too hard. I had a lot of final presentations and I had to write a twenty-page paper on what I had learned and how I was taking that into the real world.

Well, I had learned I didn't want to plan weddings. I was one step closer to figuring out what I did want.

Sam was pretty busy, too. Her and Tyler didn't see much of each other these days, either. We were three weeks from graduation when I finally got to see Kyle again. We stayed in touch via Skype and phone but nothing compared to the real thing.

He took me out to dinner at this semi-fancy Italian restaurant. I had been there a couple times with Sam. We loved their garlic bread.

Kyle looked exhausted when he greeted me at the front door. His hair was matted down and it looked even shorter than it did in Hawaii. His face looked gaunt and his eyes were droopy.

"Are you okay?" I asked as he grabbed my hand and we started walking toward his car.

"I'm fine. Just tired. We finished shooting last night, or this morning, at three."

"We could have rescheduled. You need sleep! Did you even sleep at all today?"

"No, I couldn't sleep thinking about seeing you." He squeezed my hand but I could barely feel it.

He helped me into the car and we drove away.

He took a deep breath. "I'm so happy to see you. It's been like two weeks."

I had seen him two weeks ago, when I stopped by the studio one day. They were trying to finish up an episode. I think they were running behind. I only saw him for an hour on his lunch break but it was better than nothing.

"Yeah. We've both been really busy."

He nodded. "I'm glad I have a week break before tour rehearsals start."

"I've been meaning to ask you something. I know you are probably exhausted and this is probably a bad time, but my sister wanted to invite you to her graduation. I'm leaving on Thursday for it. Just until Sunday. I completely understand if it's too much. I just wanted to extend the offer."

It was really bad timing. Especially seeing the way he looked. I had contemplated not even asking him but Jess told me I had to. And both my parents wanted to see him again anyway.

He pressed his lips together. "I would, babe. But we're having a big cast and crew party on Friday. We won't see any of them for a while, if we even get picked up for another season."

He looked at me sincerely as if to say, *I'm the worst boyfriend ever but I'll make it up to you.*

"Oh. That's okay." I was a little bit surprised that he hadn't told me sooner. He was usually the one to make sure I knew everything that was going on. But it was my fault, too, for not asking him sooner. Even though I, myself, had just found out the date a week ago. Oh well, it didn't matter. It was just one bump in the road.

"Have you talked to your mom about visiting your grandpa?"

He nodded. "I was hoping you could come with me next week while I had time off. Oh, and then the following Saturday we start tour rehearsal if you want to come watch."

"Yeah!" That was the one day I didn't have a group project to work on. And then the following Tuesday and Wednesday, all my final work was due. I was glad at least one thing was working out for us.

Once we got to the restaurant and ordered, I felt someone watching us.

"I should have known there would be paparazzi here," I said as I looked over my shoulder. There was one standing outside the window, looking in. "How is it even possible to take a good picture through glass?"

Kyle walked over and pulled the shade down. "Hey," he called to one of the waitresses. "Do you mind taking care of that?"

She nodded and walked toward the front door. She closed the front door and started putting all the window shades down.

"Thanks," Kyle called out to her as he sat back down.

She winked at him. Ugh. I hated her. She was gorgeous, thin, big-boobed, and hitting on my boyfriend.

Kyle smiled at me. Oblivious.

I rolled my eyes. It was dumb to get jealous, especially about stuff like that, girls mindlessly flirting with him. But could you blame me? He was sexy and popular. And then he was with me, someone who was becoming famous for just being with him.

After dinner, he walked me to the front door, kissed me goodnight and took off. When I got up to the room Sam was up there alone. She was reading a Nicholas Sparks' book on her bed.

"Do girls ever hit on Tyler in front of you?" I asked as I took off my boots and sat down next to her.

She closed the book and put it aside. "All the time. He's sexy and I know it. He knows it, too. He didn't before. He was so nonchalant about it, completely oblivious. But after like a year of us dating, people were constantly looking at us and girls would be all over him. One day he was just like, 'Why do girls do that?' So I told him it wasn't just me that thought he was hot. He really was hot."

"Okay?" I shook my head. "But, our waitress tonight kept flirting with him and he didn't even realize it."

"That's a good thing, right? If he noticed it and acted on it then you should be worried. But if he doesn't even know, it's harmless." She picked the book back up and shoved it in my face. "Take this book for example. The main character is hot, and there's this girl that's all over him. She's like the same popularity status as him, too. But he falls in love with a girl who is lower status than him. He gets crap for it all the time. But he loves her so he doesn't care. And he ignores everyone else."

I started at Sam. "Hmm, I might have to read that book."

She made a good point, for once. I shouldn't have even thought about all the attention he was getting. And I knew this would come along, anyway. He was in the public eye. But I should have only been worried about the way *he* felt. Not how anyone else felt.

"Is he going to Jess' graduation with you?"

"No. He has a party to go to."

"I'll go with you," she suggested.

So she did. We left Thursday and got to Boston by dinnertime. My mom was flying in the next day with Rachel and Todd.

"Sam!" My sister cried as soon as we got to the baggage claim. "Chloe!" She ran over to us and gave us a joint hug.

"Jess! How are ya?" Sam asked as she adjusted her purse strap.

"Good. Missed you guys."

Jess' hair was more blonde than the last time I saw her. And she had on make-up, which she rarely wore, at least since the last time I saw her.

"You did something different, didn't you?" Sam pointed out as she skimmed Jess.

"My hair," she said as she ran her fingers through it. "And make-up," she whispered to us as if it were a secret.

"Where's Dad?" I asked as I looked around.

"He's at home. Cooking dinner," Jess said as Sam analyzed her.

"So, you came here by yourself?" Just as I said it I saw Trevor outside, next to his pick up.

"Ah." I waved to him. He grinned.

"Well, hurry up we don't want to be late for dinner," Jess called as she headed toward the exit.

It was strange to come home and see the 'For Sale' sign out front. The lawn was perfectly manicured, the flowers were in full bloom, and it looked as if there was a fresh coat of paint on the front door.

Dad greeted Sam and I with Mudslides, which were the best, never had one better than his. Trevor stayed for dinner and we quickly learned that him and Jess were an official couple now. He was going to a school out in LA, as well, so they conveniently wouldn't have a distance problem.

I was happy for them. For everything that happened with Ryan, I wouldn't wish it on anyone. I was actually surprised I hadn't heard from Ryan since the last time he contacted me. He said he would leave me alone but I hadn't believed him at the time. I guess I was wrong.

The next afternoon, everyone had arrived. We were having a cookout in the backyard. Mom and Dad were all over each other, which they usually were, since they rarely saw each other. None of us could blame them.

Rachel was talking to Sam. They hadn't seen each other since last summer. Sam was filling her in on the wedding and pretty much everything about it.

Trevor and Todd were talking about New York and Jess and I were swimming in the pool together.

"I'm really glad you gave Trevor a chance," I said as I adjusted my sunglasses.

"Me too. He's a really good guy and I'm starting to really like him a lot."

I could tell she was really happy. Especially since she was putting time and effort into her hair and make-up, and even her outfits. It was the exact same way I was when I started seeing Kyle. I wanted to make an effort to look good because I had a reason to.

"How are things with Kyle? We were all crushed when you told us he couldn't come."

"I know. I'm so sorry. I wanted him to come as much as everyone else. He's just been so busy. He just finished season three of the show. They were having a rap party today. And then in two weeks he starts rehearsal for the tour that starts in July and goes until October."

Her eyes grew big. "That's a *really* long time. Are you okay with it?" I could hear the concern in her voice.

I still wasn't sure if I was okay with it. But what could I say to Kyle about it; *No, I don't want you going*? There was nothing I could say. It was his job. This was a part of his life. I almost couldn't breathe thinking about it.

"No. I'm not okay with it. I don't know how anyone could be okay with it. But there's nothing I can do. That's just the way things are right now."

"Have you told him you feel this way?" She glided across the water closer to me, her body resting on a noodle. I could see my reflection in her sunglasses.

I shook my head. "We haven't talked about it since February." I shrugged. "But, I don't know what to say. I have *no* clue."

"From what I've seen," she said as she pushed her sunglasses to the top of her head. "He seems to really care about you and your opinions. So, I think no matter how you put it he's going to listen and do what he can to make it better. Just say something."

"Everyone!" Rachel called as she stood out of her chair. "Todd and I have an announcement." She grabbed his hand and squeezed it tight. Her smile was glowing. It was probably the biggest smile I had ever seen on her before, and that was saying something.

"We're pregnant!" She exclaimed.

"Oh my gosh!" Jess said. "How far along?"

"About fifteen weeks. The only person we told was Mom. I even told her before Todd. But we didn't want to tell anyone else until we were supposed to." She touched her belly gently.

"So this means," Mom started to say. "She is moving to California, too!"

What?

"So that Dad and I can help her with the baby. And we don't want them on the other side of the country. Todd is going to work on finding a job. We'll all be in California by August!"

Well, I was in shock. I figured Rachel and Todd would have kids sooner or later but I definitely thought it would be later. And I still couldn't wrap my brain around the thought of my mom and dad moving to California. Now it would be Rachel and Todd, too. Everything was changing. There was not one thing in my life that would be the same come July. I didn't know if I was ready for it all.

Chapter 30

On Saturday, Jessica graduated from high school. We made sure to take lots of pictures, since I was allowing them now. My baby sister was all grown up. And in just a few months, there would be a baby in the family. I was glad I would live close enough to them that I could watch the baby grow up. That was one thing I was looking forward to.

Sam and I headed back to school the next day. I was supposed to meet Kyle on Friday to go visit his grandpa with him but Kyle started not feeling well.

"So, we're not going?" I asked Thursday night on the phone. I was sprawled across my bed. I had just gotten back from a three-hour group project meeting. I was exhausted and at my wits end.

"I can't. I've been sick all day. I'm really sorry, babe."

I groaned. "It's because you've been working nonstop. Even this week, which you were supposed to have off, you've spent everyday doing something. You've either been in the music studio or coming up with music video ideas. This week you were supposed to rest." I sounded on edge.

"I can't sit still. Especially after everything's been nonstop, I can't just stop."

I stared at the new poster Sam hung on the wall, promoting the guys' *Summer Tour*. I saw advertisements for it everywhere. If it wasn't a poster it was an ad online, if it wasn't that it was a commercial on TV. I was starting to resent that tour.

"Can I tell you something?" I asked hesitantly.

"Of course."

"Are you worried about us? Like what's going to happen to us when you go on tour?" I bit my lip. I didn't want to be the one to bring it up but he hadn't said anything about it. He didn't seem the slightest bit worried.

"I'm not worried about us. I think we can make it work. I'll visit you when I'm around. You can visit me when you're around. It's going to be really hard, though, and I'm going to miss you like crazy." I cracked a smile, thankful we weren't having this conversation in person. I wouldn't want him to know that the thought of him missing me gave me joy.

"Are you worried?" He asked.

"Honestly, yeah. I haven't been able to stop thinking about it. It hurts me to think about it." I didn't know what else to say. I didn't want to tell him that I'd probably cry the whole first month that he was gone. I'd feel numb the second month. I'd probably drink myself to sleep the third month. And by the fourth month, when he finally came back, I would probably break.

It didn't seem like it was hurting him as much as me. But then again, he would be on a fun tour and I would be sitting around by myself counting the days until I wasn't alone again. It wasn't like I'd be able to turn to Sam. She would be in her first months of wedded bliss. And my family would be going crazy trying to move their lives across the country.

"Baby. We are going to get through it. I'll be thinking about you the whole time I'm away. I will make sure to see you as much as I can. Trust me, we will work it out."

That made me feel a little better.

"Ah, I wish I wasn't sick. I really want to see you. The guys miss you, too," he said with a cough.

"You sure you're not faking so you can get out of seeing your grandpa?"

"I'm positive. I haven't gotten out of bed all day."

When we hung up, I got an idea. I could go visit his grandpa by myself. The whole point of the visit was to convince him that Kyle's job wasn't the worst thing in the world.

I called Kyle's mom the next morning to let her know I would be coming over. She gave me the address and I took off.

What was I going to say? What could I do to convince this man Kyle was having the time of his life? Obviously, words meant nothing to him. Kyle said he tried convincing him before the stroke and nothing worked. He said his mom tried, too. What made me think he would listen to me?

I knocked on the front door and Kyle's mom answered. She hugged me and showed me into the living room. His grandpa was sitting on a recliner watching *The Price is Right* with a wool blanket over him. He looked to be about eighty or so with barely any hair on top of his head. He had glasses on that seemed to be too big for his tiny face.

"Dad, this is Chloe," Kyle's mom said as she tapped him on the shoulder. I stepped into the room, but not too far. I felt like this was his territory and I didn't want him to get angry with me.

"She's Kyle's girlfriend. She came to say hello." She sat down on the couch next to him and motioned for me to sit in the chair next to the couch.

He looked up at me for the first time but didn't say anything.

I sat down. "Hello, Sir." I smiled, trying not to show the fear I felt. It wasn't like I had Kyle here to hide behind.

"Hello. How do you do?" He said stiffly.

"Fine, how about yourself?"

He had a coughing fit for what seemed like five minutes. "I've been better," he said as Kyle's mom handed him a glass of orange juice. He took a sip.

"Where's Kyle? I thought he was dropping by," he said as he put the juice down on the coffee table.

"He really wanted to come but he started feeling sick yesterday. He needed to rest before…" I chose my words carefully. He already didn't like Kyle's job so if I brought it up he might have freaked out. "Uh, before he goes back to work."

"Oh." He paused. "Well, in that case. Tell me about yourself, Chloe."

For the next two hours, I told this man almost everything about me. Childhood, parents, sisters, school, Sam, the whole works. The two of us seemed to get along really great. He had Kyle's sense of humor and also his sereneness. After talking to him, I almost forgot how nervous I was when I first got there.

The time was now. I had to bring up Kyle. This man seemed to like me and I thought if I slid in the nasty stuff now it wouldn't be so nasty.

"There's one more thing I wanted to talk to you about."

He nodded for me to continue.

"I know that you really don't like Kyle's career choice. But I just want to understand. Please, explain it to me?"

He sighed. "It's complicated. But if you really want to hear it." I nodded. "Okay. When Kyle was three his grandmother, God rest her soul, ran every last penny we had into the ground. She had a lot of money from working on Broadway. She started when she was just seventeen. She had mixed feelings about it but in the end it was her time to leave the business and she did. So when the paychecks stopped coming she kept spending."

He lifted a hand to his forehead. I could tell this wasn't easy for him to talk about.

"We had nothing left after just one year of her not working. We were in serious debt. Our children thankfully helped us get outta that hole we were in. But it was never the same. She would talk about the 'good ole days' and how life was terrible now that she wasn't working. That's why she was spending the money in the first place, to fill the void. When Kyle was just five years old she took her life."

I gasped.

"Shocking I know. She hated everything, didn't want to live, became sick in the head." He paused. "That's why I got so angry when Kyle said he wanted to go into the show business. I kept picturing him doing exactly what she did. Quitting, spending all the money, and then not wanting to live."

I didn't expect the story to end like that. I honestly didn't know what to say. There was no way I could say Kyle wouldn't end up like his wife because I never knew his wife. How would I know how Kyle would end up? Oh, this was bad.

"Dad," Kyle's mom said. She touched his arm but he pulled away. He was upset now.

"Dad, listen to me. Mom didn't have anyone to turn to. Both Nana and Papa were gone, she had no friends left, they all moved to Vegas, and you were never home! You were out working almost all day trying to make back the money she was spending. Mom was alone, that's why she spiraled out of control. I know you hate hearing it, Dad, but it's true." She touched his arm again but he didn't pull away this time. "There was nothing any of us could do. Mom was sick. It was her time to go."

I tear rolled down his cheek. "I just don't want Kyle to be unhappy." He gently started crying. Kyle's mom tried to comfort him.

"He's not unhappy. I promise you. He loves what he does, he wouldn't change a thing." I flashed him a smile.

Another idea. "Why don't you come to rehearsal tomorrow? The guys start rehearsal for their tour and that would be the perfect place to see how happy he is!"

"I guess it couldn't hurt to go," he agreed.

Perfect! This could be what changed everything.

Early the next morning I dragged myself out of bed and over to the dance studio where the guys were having rehearsal. Kyle's mom and grandpa were going to meet me over there. I really hoped Kyle wouldn't get mad that I did this behind his back. But I never second-guessed it. I figured I couldn't hurt his relationship with his grandpa. This could only, possibly, make it better.

The guys started at seven and I got there at eight. Kyle called me late last night to tell me that he was feeling better and couldn't wait to see me today. *Oh if you only knew*, I thought to myself. His grandpa and mom were already waiting in their car when I arrived.

We all headed inside together and watched the guys from the viewing window. The guys couldn't see us but we could see them.

The choreographer was getting into one of their songs. "We'll start out with the most difficult song first," she said to them.

The guys all looked at each other.

"What does that even mean?" Luke said.

"Love me," the instructor said.

"Aw, man!" Cam said as he threw his hood over his head.

"Shouldn't we start from the easiest and work our way out?" Jake suggested.

The instructor replied with an abrupt, "No."

After they choreographed half the dance, Kyle's grandpa was already shaking and dancing to the music. Kyle's mom shot me a thumbs up. So far so good.

When the first dance was finished there were shouts of joy.

"It gets easier from here?" Cam asked, hopeful.

"No," the instructor answered flatly as she grabbed a towel and wiped the beads of sweat off her face. "But take a fifteen minute break, you guys did good."

I peeked my head around the corner so Kyle knew I was there.

"Glow!" Cam called. "You made it!" I walked over toward him and he gave me a sweaty hug.

"I'm gross and polite so I won't hug you," Jake said as he shot Cam a look. Cam rolled his eyes.

"Sup, Glow?" Luke said as he took a sip of water.

Kyle was finishing a bite of a sandwich. "Hey, babe." He swallowed and kissed me.

"I have a surprise for you," I said to him as I lightly touched his hand. I turned around as Kyle's mom walked his grandpa slowly into the room. I stepped back and watched Kyle's facial expression change. It was utter shock mixed with delight and disbelief, like a kid meeting Santa for the first time.

"What are you doing here?" Kyle asked as he lifted up his hat to ruffle his hair.

"Chloe came to talk to me yesterday. And she really wanted me to see for myself how happy you are." Kyle glanced at me, speechless.

"I can't believe how wrong I was. I can see now, you were meant to do this," his grandpa said as he leaned into Kyle for a hug.

Aw. I couldn't help but smile. Not only were Kyle and his grandpa on good terms again but it was because of me. It felt really good.

Chapter 31

"You amaze me, everyday," Kyle said. We were sitting on his living room couch. He had finished rehearsal about an hour ago and invited me to sleep over. How could I refuse? We only had about a month before he took off on his big US tour. I wanted to spend as much of it as I could with him.

"I'm not that amazing."

"I beg to differ. I have to be the luckiest guy in the world."

I blushed. It was nice having someone compliment me like that. I still hadn't gotten used to it.

"Then, I must be the luckiest girl."

His eyes lit up. "That reminds me! Your birthday is in less than three weeks. What are you doing for it?"

It hadn't even crossed my mind. Sam and I were graduating in two weeks and my birthday was the day after.

"My family would be up for my graduation so I figured I would just go out to eat with them or something."

He grabbed my knee. "No! We've got to do something special. Like, go to Mexico."

"Mexico?"

"Yeah!"

"Kyle, that's really sweet but I don't want a big thing. I just want something simple. My family and you. Nothing fancy."

He cocked his head, looking for more of an explanation.

"What? I'm serious. I'm turning twenty-two it's not even a big number."

"Baby."

"Kyle, seriously. I don't want anything big. Don't worry about it." I played with my pant string.

"Have you ever had a birthday party?"

"What? Of course I have. Who's never had a birthday party? That's like…what?"

"You've never had one, have you?" He was grinning at me like he guessed the right answer on a test.

"What are you talking about?" I said coyly.

"You've never had a birthday party!"

"Okay!" I shouted. "You're right. The only party I've ever had was for my high school graduation and that was combined with Jess' middle school graduation. So no, I've never technically had a party just for me." I stopped playing with the string and looked up at him. "Is that what you wanted?"

He nodded.

"What's the big deal? I never needed one." It was true. Up until the time my mom moved, she was always busy anyway. And my friends would come over and hang out but it was just too much work for my mom, she said. The only parties we were allowed to have was sixteen and eighteen. Rachel got both of hers but since my mom was gone when I was nine I didn't see a point in having a party. Why bother when my whole family wouldn't even be there? It just never seemed to work out.

"Everyone needs at least one birthday party. Let me throw you one, please? You don't have to worry about anything," he practically begged.

"Why?"

"Because I love you and I want to do something for you, just like you did something for me." He kissed my forehead. "Let's get some sleep, though. I have a meeting tomorrow with the tour production company and everybody. They want to discuss some stuff. I'll let you sleep in, though. I couldn't wake your perfect angelic face."

I laughed.

We both fell asleep right away and when I woke up Kyle was already gone. It was late afternoon when he came back.

I had spent the day on twitter, responding to as many people as I could. Kyle and I hadn't made a youtube video since Hawaii and the fans were starting to get upset. I posted that we would do one soon, maybe even today. But in the meantime, I would just answer their questions online.

A couple of them asked if I would be going on tour with the guys. I didn't answer that one, yet, because I still didn't know. Tour was fun but there was nothing there for me. I felt like I was just a drag-along doll. I loved being with Kyle but I felt like wasted space, like I could have been doing something great but I wasn't.

I had thought about what it would be like to be a tour manager. I was leaning toward it more everyday. If I went on tour with them it would probably make up my mind.

"Hey," Kyle said as he came into the kitchen. I had just finished eating a sandwich.

"How'd the meeting go?" I smiled at him but stopped. His face was serious like something bad had happened. His eyes were cold and there was no smile in sight.

"What's wrong?" I asked, not sure if I was ready for the answer.

He took my hand and sat me down on the kitchen stool. He sat on the one next to me, holding both my hands.

"Oh God, what happened?" I asked. I was completely freaked out, now. What could have happened at this stupid meeting?

"All right. What I'm about to tell you is a little bump in the road for us, but we can get through it. It's a small bump, very small." He squeezed my hands. I said nothing. My heart rate was dropping. I felt like I was about to pass out and I didn't even know the news yet. I wished he would just say it, rip it off like a band-aid.

"Well, the good news is the guys and I are going to Europe!" He said with a little bit of enthusiasm as if to tell a little kid school was out for the summer.

"Oh, that's great!" I said relieved. Europe's far but I was sure it wouldn't be for too long and he was right, we could handle it. "What's so bad about that?"

He pressed his lips together. "Babe. The guys and I are going to Europe in two weeks." He cringed as if he was expecting me to punch him.

"After my graduation and birthday?" I asked hoping the answer wasn't what I thought it was.

He shook his head. "We're supposed to fly out the day before your graduation." He looked like he was about to cry. I *felt* like I was about to cry. This was like my worst nightmare come true. First, he wouldn't be there for Sam's wedding because of the tour. Then, he couldn't come to my sister's graduation. Now, he wouldn't be there for *my* graduation or my birthday.

But I didn't want him to feel badly about it. It wasn't his fault and this was an incredible opportunity for him.

"Don't be upset. This is incredible, it's great news!" I could feel the tears welling up but I didn't know what more to say. This wasn't the first time he would be missing something important to me and it definitely wouldn't be the last. My heart couldn't keep going through that. It was breaking.

"I need you. I don't want to be selfish, but this isn't fair, for either of us." A tear fell down my cheek. "I can't be without you, it hurts too much, especially when there are special things I want to share with you. I don't want to break up and it's going to kill me to not have you in my life. But knowing you can't be with me when I need you is more painful."

He had an aching look in his eyes and I had to look away. "I love you so much but I can't do this anymore. And I can't ask you to choose me over your career."

He pulled me close into a tight hug and as much as I wanted to pull away and run away my body couldn't. I kept trying to fight back tears.

"I love you," I continued. "And I hope we can be friends one day. I know you'll continue to be successful in your career but I really do wish you the best."

I let go of him and headed out the front door before he could say anything. I started walking faster as tears poured down my face.

Chapter 32

I moped around the rest of the week. Finally, on Wednesday, Sam told me I should go take time away and be by myself. So, I hoped on a plane on Thursday, after class, and flew to my dad's. I told him and Jess what had happened.

My heart had never hurt so much. I lay on my bed and stared at the ceiling. I didn't want to eat. I couldn't sleep. I was glad the semester was over and all my work was complete and handed in. I wouldn't have been able to concentrate on anything if I tried.

It was Saturday, and I was flying back on Tuesday. I had two finals to take and then I would be done. Graduation was a week from today but the thought of graduating brought my eyes to tears. Kyle would be leaving the country on Friday. And I couldn't get him out of my head no matter how hard I tried.

I had cried nonstop up until this morning. I think I ran out of tears. When I woke up, they just stopped. I was still in pain, still felt the same, nothing had changed inside me, but I had no more tears to give.

Jess came in early that morning to check on me but I just told her I wanted to be alone. My dad had just gotten back from work when Jess left to go out with Trevor.

"Call me if you need me," she had said.

But I didn't have anything to say to anyone. No words could describe the hurt I felt. I wanted to be mad at someone. But there was no one to be mad at. This wasn't my fault. It wasn't Kyle's fault. There was nothing that could have been done to change the outcome. No matter what happened, Big Time Elevation had to be on a plane on Friday. That's just the way it was.

But I couldn't stop myself from saying *I told you so*. I had a gut feeling, since the beginning, that I couldn't handle a relationship like that, and I was right. Why did I have to listen to my heart?

I think my dad, at some point, called my mom and told her about the break up, because she texted me just saying she was thinking about me. And that never happens.

Rachel found out, somehow, too, because she asked if I needed anything. But what I needed could not be given to me.

I was going onto the fifth hour of staring at the ceiling when the doorbell rang.

I heard some muffled voices and then my dad coming toward my room.

He opened the door. “Ryan’s here to see you.”

I groaned as I buried my face in a pillow. Why was I not surprised? He basically told me that if Kyle and I ever broke up he would pop up again.

“Want me to tell him to leave?” My dad asked.

“No, cause he’ll find another way to get in.”

My dad turned around to get Ryan but he was already there. He walked into my room as my dad left.

“What do *you* want?” I asked as I threw the pillow off my face and sat up.

He walked toward me. “I thought you could use a shoulder to cry on. I heard about you and that guy. I’m sorry.”

I’m sure he was really sorry. Not. And how did he even find out about it?

“My sister found out from Jess. I don’t want to bother you. I’m serious. I’m just here if you need me.” He looked around my room as if he was nervous. He looked so out of place. Even though he had been in this room so many other times before.

“That’s nice, really, but I’m okay. I just want to be alone.” I fixed the ponytail that was on top of my head and pulled it tighter.

“You are not okay. We dated for three years, I know you better than you think.” He grinned at me.

I sighed. “Well, what do you suggest?”

He took me to an arcade that had indoor go-carts and batting cages. At first, he had to drag me into the car and the building but once I got inside I forgot all about why I was upset in the first place.

We raced a bunch of times and then I whooped his butt in the arcade. I was having so much fun. I wasn't thinking about all the bad stuff that had happened between Ryan and me. At that point, I think I was so broken and defenseless that I didn't even care who tried to cheer me up. I just wanted to feel happy. I was sick of hurting. That was the whole reason I broke it off with Kyle, anyway.

We headed back to his car when the arcade was closing. It was dark, almost black outside. I slipped into the car and sank into the seat. Ryan had won me a stuffed panda.

He had won me one before, in high school. It was on our second date. He was trying to impress me the whole time but he played it cool. I could see right through him, even then. His hair was shorter and so was he. We were so young. It was a shame we couldn't stay that young forever.

"I had a good time," he said as he got into the car and started the engine. "I think you did, too."

"Yeah. I had fun. Thanks for making me do this." I exhaled loudly as I closed my eyes. I wondered what Kyle was doing. He was probably at another dance rehearsal. It was only seven in California.

"Why'd you come back?" Ryan asked.

I kept my eyes closed. "I don't know. It felt like the right thing to do."

"I think it's because this is your home and you know it."

"Ryan," I said. "This is *not* my home. How many times do I have to tell you that?" I opened my eyes.

"Easy there!" He put his hands up in defense. "We're just having a conversation. No need to get upset."

"I'm not upset," I said as I straightened out my shirt. It was riding up my back from slouching.

"Chloe."

"If you want to be friends with me, don't keep saying that. I love California that's where I want to live. Whether I'm dating Kyle or not."

"There's nothing you miss in Boston?"

I squeezed the panda. "Of course there are *things* I miss in Boston. But that doesn't mean I want to move back." I wanted to emphasize the things I missed were in fact things and not him.

"I still love you," he said casually.

"I know. You already told me that." I rested my arm on the door and covered my hand over my face. "Is that what this is? Is that why you brought me here tonight? You're trying to get me back? If that's the case then that's pathetic because I just got my heart ripped out, smashed up, broken into a million pieces, and I can't believe you are doing this to me." I started to cry.

I curled my body over my legs and cried as hard as I could.

Ryan rubbed my back but didn't say anything.

"I don't need this. Not from you." I mumbled into my legs. "I'm in so much pain and I don't know how I'm going to make it through ever again, but I just try to do it one day at a time but then that makes me think of Kyle because he taught me to do that."

He kept rubbing my back. "Shh, it's okay, Chloe."

"It's not okay."

"It will be though. Not now, but it will be. You're right, you should just take it one day at a time. You're one of the strongest girls I know. You just tend to overthink everything."

I let out a breath and a sniffle, still hunched over my legs.

"No matter what happened with this Kyle guy, I know that he meant a lot to you and it might take a while until everything feels better again. It may not ever be the same but it will get easier."

He was now running his fingers through my hair. It felt so good I wanted to fall asleep.

"It took me a year and a half to feel better after we broke up. They say it takes half the time of the relationship. But even after a year and a half I still felt like something was missing." He paused. "But none of it matters because all I care about is you. I just want you to be happy."

I sat up and looked at him. He looked so sincere and defenseless. This wasn't the same Ryan that broke my heart freshman year. This was a totally different man.

"What about you and Nadine?" I wiped a tear from my eye.

"We went out for like two weeks. It took me two minutes to get over it."

I smiled.

"Yes! I love seeing you smile." He held my chin. "I hate to see you cry."

"I know. And I, too, wish things worked out differently with us. I was upset with you for how you broke up with me and the way you looked at me killed me, even to this day it does."

"What do you mean?"

"I was sweating really bad because I was so nervous and you were all like, 'It's not hot in here.' And then you looked at me like you thought I was the most pathetic person you had seen in your life." At one point in my life pigs would fly the day I would tell Ryan that. But everything in my life was different and I didn't feel the need to hide anything anymore.

"Wait, what? I would have never done that."

"But you did."

He looked so beyond confused. "Are you sure I wasn't looking at Sam?"

I rolled my eyes. "Sam wasn't even in the room."

"Yes she was. Just after you told me you were hot she walked in the room like half naked, picked up her shower caddy and left. You must have not noticed, you were too nervous."

"That's the biggest load of bull I've ever heard!" I hit him off the head with my panda.

"I'm totally serious, you can even call Sam and ask. When she came in she looked at me quick and then ran off. She'll tell you."

He was totally serious. I could see it in his eyes. He wasn't making this up. So, all of these years I had that look stuck in my face, he wasn't even looking at me. He was looking at Sam. What else had I misinterpreted?

I brushed it off. "Well, in any event. *You* dumped *me*. So."

"And *you* dumped *him*. It's in the past. We both have to move on. Deal?" He gave me his hand to shake.

"Deal." I shook it and he drove me home.

When I got back, my dad was sitting on the living room couch, reading a book.

"Hey, Dad," I said as I walked through the front door. I walked up to the living room and sat down next to him.

"Hey," he said as he put his book down. "How'd it go with Ryan? Haven't seen him around in years."

"It was actually pretty fun. We had a good time."

My dad raised an eyebrow. "You're not getting back together with him, are you?"

"Ew, Dad, no. Even if I wanted to date someone again, I'm not ready and it would *never* be him." I shuddered at the thought of dating him again.

"I just remember how crushed you were when he broke up with you. You didn't even come home until the summer because you were afraid of seeing him."

"I know. But it's in the past. We're okay now. We're not really friends but I don't hate him so much anymore." I crossed my legs and leaned back into the couch. I loved this couch. It had so many memories behind it and on top of that it was super comfortable.

My mom had bought it a year before she moved. She just came home with it one day, out of the blue, said she didn't like the one we had in there. Not that she ever even sat in there.

After she moved, Dad would sit on this couch everyday. I'd get home from school to find him reading on it, watching television, or doing a crossword puzzle. I think he just liked it because my mom did.

"Dad, how hard has it been for you to not live with Mom?"

He ran his fingers over his buzzed hair. "It was really hard at first. I would always come back from work expecting it to smell like her or find a note from her. It took a while for it to sink in that she wasn't here anymore."

I remembered those first few months. Mom didn't come back for three weeks, then after that it was every weekend. At least we saw her twice a week. It could have been worse.

"Distance is hard. And it's not for everybody. But your mom and I made it work. We trust each other and we love each other very much. And we knew that one day we would all be together again. I think that's what got us through it."

"And your thirtieth anniversary is coming up!"

He nodded. "October twenty third. Cannot believe it's been that long."

"I'm really glad I had you guys as parents. Not everyone can do long distance but you both showed me that it *is* possible. I probably wouldn't have even tried to date Kyle if I had never seen a long distance relationship work. So, thanks."

"I'm glad to have helped you. Your mom and I love you, all three of you. And we just want you girls happy. No matter what that means, as long as it's legal." He smiled.

My dad was always the mushy one. It was good, though, because it made up for my mom's lack of noticeable affection. I knew she loved us, she just had a hard time showing it.

"Love you, Dad. Thanks for everything." He may not have said much but he said everything I needed to hear.

Chapter 33

It was finally graduation day. I was dreading it because I kept thinking of Kyle. But I knew once it was over, I could move forward. But then I would have my birthday and their summer tour. Okay, so, October I could move forward. But then I'd probably be hearing about him all the time, online, in magazines, and on TV. So, maybe it would never be over.

But I had friends and family who would do anything to help me through it and that was all I could ask for.

I didn't have the nerve to go on my twitter account. Sam had offered to delete it for me but I declined. I didn't want it to be gone. I felt like if I deleted it then I was deleting the past five months and I didn't want to do that. Even though the relationship had ended, it was still the best five months of my life. And my twitter was the last thing I had left to remember it by. Well, that and the stuffed giraffe.

I had been avoiding all gossip sites and magazines. I didn't want to know what the press was saying about Kyle and me. I had hoped that once people noticed I wasn't around him anymore they would put it together.

Now, Sam and I stood next to each other in line. We walked to our seats and sat down. The Dean started speaking. I looked behind me and saw my family. Dad, Mom, Jess, Todd, and Rachel, who still looked the same size. Sam's family sat next to them.

The thought of Kyle in Europe just sent my mind wandering. What were they doing? What time was it there? Which country were they going to first? I didn't want to care about those questions but I did, and I couldn't get them out of my mind.

How much longer would the ache last? Would it be two and a half months since we dated for five? I couldn't last two and a half months with that pain. And I still had to figure out who I was going to live with. I didn't want to go back to living with my parents. I was so used to living with someone else.

And I still had to figure out what kind of event planning I would be doing. In my twenty-page paper, that was due last week, I wrote about how I could do any number of types of event planning and I would soon find out which one would call my name. I still had time to think. I wasn't in a hurry to get a job, especially since my mom would be getting a pay increase starting in just a couple of months.

The Dean called us up, we got our diplomas, and we dispersed. I headed toward my dad and he gave me a hug. It was a good hug but not as good as Kyle's. Dang it, I was doing it again.

"We're so proud of you!" Rachel said ecstatically.

"So proud," my dad said as he kissed my head.

My mom was checking her cell phone, surprise. My dad whacked her arm. "Ow," she said as she looked up, noticing me for the first time. "Oh, good job. We're so proud. Honors, woo!"

"Where to now?" I asked. "Do you guys want to go eat somewhere?"

Sam brushed up next to me. "Oh, they are gonna follow us. We're going to a good place for food. You guys are going to meet us there. It's all been planned." She glided off towards the parking lot.

"Okay," I said as we all followed.

We drove to an upscale restaurant and went toward the side entrance.

"So," Sam said as she grabbed my hand and pulled me toward her. "On a scale of one to ten how much do you love surprises?"

She opened the side door. "Well I guess they…"

Oh my God.

"Surprise!" A roomful of people jumped out at me. Lindsey, Erica, Tyler, and a bunch of people I didn't even think I knew.

"What the hell is this?" I asked completely stunned.

"Someone wanted to plan you a surprise party. For your graduation and birthday," Sam said as she backed away.

I felt someone touch my back. I turned around.

"Kyle?" He was standing there in a casual suit with his hair blowing in his face. He reached out to hug me. I couldn't even move. What the hell was he doing here?

"Hey, Glow!" I heard someone say.

"Oh my God, that's Cam. Where is he?"

Kyle pointed to the dance floor. Cam, Jake, and Luke were all in the middle of it, doing the Macarena.

I stepped out of the doorway and into the room.

"I'm so confused. Tell me what's going on."

"Don't be mad. Just promise you'll listen first."

I took a deep breath. I had heard that before.

"I was devastated when you walked out. I couldn't think, eat, sleep. I couldn't even breathe. I didn't know what to do. Chloe, you're the best thing that's ever happened to me. And I can't let you go. At least not without a fight."

He grinned as he ran his fingers through my hair. I had curled it earlier in the day and it miraculously stayed in tact. I had a feeling that he messed it up though, but I didn't care, not one bit.

"And you did so much for me. I mean you went on tour with me, you made the twitter, the youtube videos, you even told the public who you were, changed your whole life. And on top of that you even managed to get my grandpa to talk to me."

I blushed.

"And I had done nothing for you."

"That's not true." I quickly opposed. "You wrote that song for me, you made me feel loved in ways that I never had felt before, you gave me a family."

"But those aren't good enough. Not if I can't be around for the moments that matter. So, I knew I had to be here. No doubt about it."

"Did you come to the graduation?" I wanted to kiss him so bad I was staring at his lips. But I tried to control myself. There was still a lot we had to talk about.

"Yep. I was there. I sat next to Todd. He's a nice guy. The guys stayed here, I knew they would blow cover and I needed someone here to set up anyway." Now, he grabbed my head with both hands.

"Baby, there's no way I wasn't giving you a birthday party."

He kissed me.

I pulled back. "But how did you do this? You're supposed to be in Europe."

"I told them we couldn't leave until tomorrow because I needed to be here. I didn't care what they did. They could do it without me. But I'm not about to lose the woman I want to spend the rest of my life with."

He looked deep into my eyes. The rest of his life? He wanted me?

"You want to spend the rest of your life with me?"

He nodded. "I can't see it without you. There is no life without you."

He put his hands into my hands and laced our fingers.

"But just because you changed some dates doesn't mean you'll be able to be around when I need you."

"I know." He looked sad now as he looked at the ground. The music in the background changed from the Macarena to an up-tempo hip-hop song. "There's no way I can ever promise you that I'll be around when you need me. It kills me. But I'm going to try everything I can to be there for you and make this work if you give me the chance."

I was at a loss for words. I was just coping with losing him forever, now I was trying to wrap my brain around the fact that he was here, in front of me, begging for me back. He had risked his job to be here for me. That said something. But then, what about huge events in the future? Sam's wedding? The birth of my niece or nephew? My parent's thirtieth anniversary party?

There were so many events in the future that I wanted him around for. I didn't know if I could handle it. It was promising, though, to know that he would try everything he could to be around for the really important ones.

Sam spun over to us. "How's it going, you two?"

"Still discussing things," I said as I curled a finger around a loop of hair.

"Oh, that reminds me, Sam's wedding," Kyle began to say.

"Yeah, you guys are doing your US tour then, I know. You can't make that one." But I had known that since he told me about the tour in the first place.

"No." Sam shook her head. "The guys will be there."

Kyle nodded in agreement. “We’re the wedding singers. No way we could miss it.”

Wedding singers? When did they plan that? It must have been in Hawaii. But why didn’t they tell me?

“You didn’t think I would have anyone else perform, did you?” Sam nudged me as she made her way back to the dance floor.

My jaw dropped.

“See. We *can* make this work. Together, you and I can do anything,” Kyle said.

His attitude was reassuring. But then again it always was, always so confident, like he could conquer anything. Maybe, together, we really could do it. He was trying his hardest, how could I say no? I, too, thought he really could have been the person I spent the rest of my life with.

“Okay,” I said, smiling. “Let’s try it again. One day at a time.”

Chapter 34

I looked at myself in the mirror. My hair was curled up into a fancy updo and my dress was a peachy-coral color. The lipstick stained across my lips matched the dress. I had tan eye shadow swept across my lids with a touch of eyeliner and mascara.

My skin was a glistening bronze shade and it sparkled with the powder Sam had just put on. My nails were freshly painted a nude pink color and the necklace on my collarbone reflected in the sunlight.

It was Sam's wedding day. We had spent all morning getting ready. Sam's mom and two cousins were in the other room. Sam and I were in the bathroom. She was just finishing up her own makeup.

She was in an undershirt and underwear but she looked as glamorous as ever. It took me a while but I was finally starting to accept that my best friend was getting married. She was ready for it. I was too, finally.

As she finished applying her red lipstick, I turned to her. "Sam. Can I tell you something?"

"Of course," she said as she took a tissue and blotted the lipstick.

"It was really hard for me at first when I found out you were getting married. I couldn't picture not living with you, or near you for that matter." I felt like I was going to cry but I tried to hold it back. I didn't want to ruin my make-up.

"You're my best friend. I don't want to lose you."

She grabbed me and pulled me into a tight hug. "You're not losing me! I'll always be around."

I felt a single tear roll down my cheek. "But you guys are moving to Colorado."

We released from the hug. "Actually, we're not. Tyler told me he doesn't want to live in Colorado, anymore. His life's here. So both of our parents went ahead and bought us a house in Laguna! It's only like an hour and a half drive from LA. We won't be that far away, after all."

I hugged her again. Was this really happening? Everything negative that had been happening was all starting to be canceled out by something good.

After my graduation, my mom and dad went to search for a house in Anaheim. They found a *gorgeous* five-bedroom house in the Anaheim Hills that was surprisingly in their price range.

Rachel and Todd found a place in Althoridge that was just about twenty minutes from my parents. It was the perfect house for them, with three bedrooms. The people they bought it from had already made two of the rooms into nurseries so Rachel and Todd didn't even need to do any work.

They also had a small guesthouse out back complete with a mini kitchen, small living space, bathroom, and bedroom. They invited me to move into it and I gladly accepted. It was perfect. Sam would live about forty minutes south and Kyle lived twenty minutes north.

While my dad had been searching for a new job, Jake came across a tweet from a fan saying the Orange County radio guy, Nick, from 101.7 quit because he was fed up with the kids that kept calling in. He was the one who kept saying rude things every time the microphone went off, when the guys were on the show. Some DJ he was.

So, my dad ended up applying for the job and got the position.

My mom would be working in LA, my dad would be in Orange County, Rachel got a job in Althoridge and Todd ended up getting one a little west of LA. Now, I was the only one left.

Sam adjusted my necklace, breaking me out of my thoughts. It was the *Glow* necklace. I never went anywhere without it.

"Well, let's do this! I'm getting married!" Sam said as she exited the room.

The ceremony was beautiful. Sam kept the black and white theme. All the men were in different colored tuxes and the girls wore bright, colorful gowns. There were just about forty people.

Sam and Tyler's families and a couple of their close friends. My family had been invited, too, since they were close with Sam's.

Apona and her daughter were there. They were both thrilled to watch the guys perform, and her daughter was so happy when she got to meet me. I didn't think that feeling would ever get old.

I looked over into the ocean as the reception started. Sam had chosen one of the villas to have the reception in. The band was set up outside and everyone was already dancing to the beat. The guys were on stage singing a fast song as Tyler and Sam came out onto the dance floor.

"Give it up for Mr. and Mrs. Hayes!" Jake said as everyone started clapping.

Sam had never looked more beautiful. Her tan skin glowed and her chocolate locks of hair spilled down her back. She wore a veil with a crown earlier, but took the veil off for the party.

She looked like a princess in her mermaid dress. It fit her flawlessly and hugged every curve. We had spent many a day searching but she finally found that one about a month ago.

After Sam and Tyler's first dance, the band took a break. I was at the bar getting a drink when Kyle brushed up against me and kissed my neck.

"That tickles!" I said as I cringed.

"Man, and I thought I was getting better."

His hair was swept to the side and his silver tux fit his body just right.

He touched my necklace.

"Haven't taken it off since you got it for me," I said as the bartender handed me a Bay Breeze. I nodded toward a straw behind the counter and he placed it into the drink. I thanked him.

"I'm glad. I have something like it." He was looking away now, into the crowd as I took a sip of my drink. Delicious.

"You have something like my necklace that says *Glow*?"

He waved to Cam who was dancing with one of Sam's cousins.

"Well," he said as he took off his watch and handed it to me.

"What's this?" I asked confused.

"Check the back." He was still looking out onto the dance floor.

I flipped over the watch. On the back was engraved a simple *K*. I gasped.

"You did this? When?"

He looked down at me and put the watch back on. "I think it was the day after we broke up. I didn't know what I was gonna do then. But I knew I needed a piece of you with me all the time. So I thought that was the most healthy way to go about it."

I pouted my lips. That was one of the sweetest things anyone had ever done for me. It was a simple gesture but it meant a lot.

"This party is great!" My mom said as she and my dad came over toward us. Sam was making her way over, too.

"Yeah, she planned one hell of a wedding!" Sam added.

"Me? Not me. I didn't do anything."

"Sure you did. We did everything the same except for the location and the services. But the food's the same, the flowers, the outfits. We just relocated. But it was all you." Sam patted my shoulder and then asked the bartender for a Cosmopolitan.

"So, how's that new client of yours, Mom?" I asked as I took another sip of my drink. Kyle slid his arm around my waist and pulled me in closer. Oh, how I had missed that.

"Well, I guess now that everything's final I can tell you all who it is." I was dying with anticipation.

"Drum roll," my dad said as he started drumming the bar.

"Tasha Edwards." She grinned happily.

"Holy crap! You don't mean Tasha Edwards the country singer? Six Grammys, eleven AMAs, seven CMAs, six ACMA's thirteen BMI's, multi-platinum recording artist!" Sam exclaimed. The bartender handed her the drink but she could barely hold it.

My mom nodded. "That's the one! We have been working on her since last summer. It's incredible that she picked me. I get to be an independent agent because of her. It's incredible. I've been dying to share."

"Don't tell Tyler!" Sam said. "He loves her. And if he knows that you know her he will try to get her. Oh my gosh." She turned to me. "Chloe, remember what I told you about the pact the two of us have?"

"You mean, about how you can go bananas over any celebrity you want because it's not like you have a chance with them?" I flashed her a knowing smile.

She looked panicked.

"Sam, you need to relax. It's going to be fine. You're married now, you basically have him on a leash."

She ran to the dance floor, spilling her drink everywhere. Now she had another thing to worry about. I wouldn't hear the end of it.

My mom shrugged and walked over to her table, my dad following.

"Hey, Glow," Cam said as him Luke and Jake walked up to Kyle and me.

"What's up, guys?" I said as I finished my drink and placed it on the bar.

"We have something we need to discuss," Luke said seriously.

"All of us need to discuss?" I asked questionably. What did they have up their sleeves this time?

"Well," Cam began. "The four of us would like to offer you a job. As our tour manager."

Jake cut in, "Yeah, it's a totally awesome job because you get to plan all our tour dates, book venues, and get everything ready for it."

"And you wouldn't be alone," Luke added. "There's a ton of people that would work under you, to help with everything.

Cam looked giddy. "And you get to see us all the time, what job lets you do that?"

"Are you guys serious?" I asked. "You want *me* to be your tour manager?" I had to admit I was caught off guard, especially since I had just met the other tour manager a couple months ago. "What happened to the other one?"

Kyle said, "Well, it's Luke's uncle actually and he says he wants to pass the torch. He's been our tour manager since we started, not to mention a handful of other bands in the past." Kyle rubbed my shoulder as if to soothe me. He knew me and knew my brain was probably about to explode.

"And the fact that he's having his first baby in November, he wants more family time," Luke added.

"So me?"

"We knew you'd be hesitant," Jake said as he took a deep breath. "That's why we're having you come on tour with us this whole summer. You can see what Luke's uncle does and see *everything*. Then you can make your decision."

The three of them scurried off as if nothing had happened. I looked up at Kyle. He had a smirk on his face.

"You knew they were going to ambush me like that and you didn't warn me!" I playfully hit his chest.

"Hey! That was not an ambush. That was a job offer." He kissed my forehead. "Don't over think it, babe, like you usually do. Just go with the flow. You're coming on tour with us this summer and that's all. We are taking it one day at a time."

One day at a time. That's all I could do at this point since I had no plans for the future, anyway. I didn't want to think about it, though. So I didn't.

"Okay, everyone! Group picture," I called out.

This was a day I would want to remember for the rest of my life. I didn't care what I looked like, that didn't matter. What mattered was how I felt, and that was something I wanted to make a memory of.